I0576037

The Blade of Milan

Warren R. Basla

Copyright © 2025 by Warren R. Basla

All rights reserved.

No part of this publication may be reproduced, distributed, or transmitted in any form
or by any means, including photocopying, recording, or other electronic or mechanical
methods, without the prior written permission of the publisher, except as permitted by
U.S. copyright law.

For permission requests, contact Warren R. Basla at warrenrbasla.com.

The story, all names, characters, and incidents portrayed in this production are ficti-
tious. No identification with actual persons (living or deceased), places, buildings, and
products is intended or should be inferred. No generative A.I., or Artificial Intelligence
software of any kind, was used in the creation of this novel.

Book Cover & Illustrations by Jonathan Sainsbury

First edition 2025

CONTENTS

To the strong women in my life

Holy Roman Empire

Late 13th Century

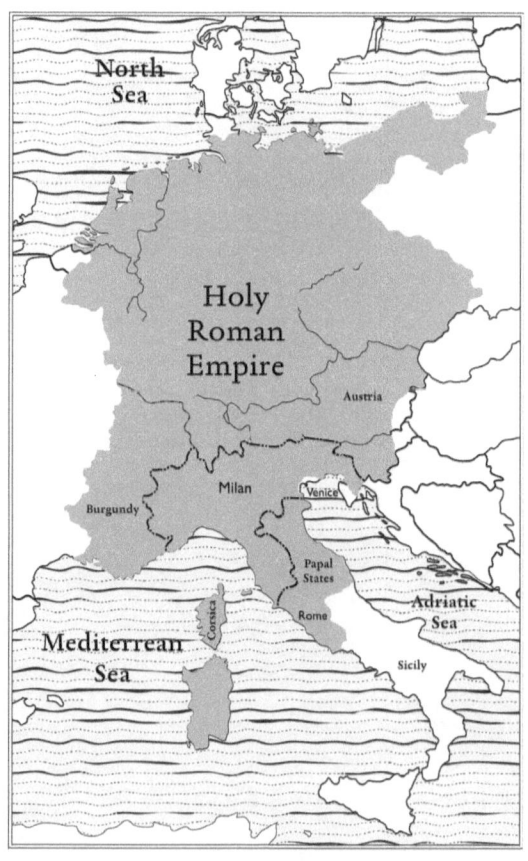

REGION AROUND THE REPUBLIC OF MILAN

LATE 13TH CENTURY

HISTORICAL CHRONOLOGY

1096　First Christian Crusade waging war in the Holy Lands

1190　Teutonic Order of Knights founded in Acre

1191　Richard the Lionheart captures Acre from Saladin

1202　Arabic numerals including zero introduced in Europe

1210　Hermann von Salza ascends to Grand Master of the Teutonic Order of Knights

1215　King John of England signs the Magna Carta

1225　Cotton cloth is first manufactured in Spain

1231　Pope Gregory IX begins European Inquisition

1236　The Great Mongol invasion of Poland begins

1241　The Battle of Mohi between the Mongol Empire and Kingdom of Hungary

1242　Genoese and Venetian merchants begin slave trade with Mongols; Alexander Nevsky prevents the Teutonic Knights from conquering Russia in Estonia

1256   The War of Saint Sabas in Acre and Tyre between Venice, Pisa, and Genoa

1260   Mamluk Egyptian army forces an invading Mongol army to a halt in modern day Palestine

1262   Rebecca Guarna is born; Pope Urban IV appoints Ottone Visconti Archbishop of the Kingdom of Milan

1264   Brothers and merchants Niccolò and Maffeo Polo travel east along the Silk Road to trade with Kublai Khan

1266   The Polo brothers enter Kublai Khan's service

1268   Charles of Anjou conquers Naples and Sicily

1269   The Polo brothers return to Venice

1271   Teutonic Order castle-fortress of Montfort in Galilee is lost to Mamluk forces

1273   Count Rudolf the "Mediocre" of Germany crowned Emperor by Federation of Princes

1275   Marco Polo, Niccolò's son, enters Kublai Khan's service as an emissary, tax collector, and translator

1277   The Visconti family seize economic and political power of Milan and Pavia

1282   Albert, son of Emperor Rudolf I, named Duchy of Austria and Styria

1284   The Kingdom of Genoa absorbs a tract of Corsica; Salvino D'Amante invents eyeglasses

—•—

DRAMATIS PERSONAE

Rebecca Guarna. Stewhouse courtesan searching for something more to life.

Martina. Rebecca's mother and madam of a stewhouse brothel in Milan.

Leonardo Salvagno. Doctor and trusted advisor to the judges of Milan. Salvagno is one of Rebecca's repeat patrons.

Rustichello da Pisa. Also known as the "Fixer." He is the head of the Sons of Saint George.

Azzo. A fellow Sons of Saint George trainee.

Lorenzo di Costa. Vicar of Santa Maria Maggiore in Pavia.

Behemoth. Fraternal member of the Sons of Saint George.

Carlo. Fraternal member of the Sons of Saint George.

Franco. Fraternal member of the Sons of Saint George.

Marchetto. Captain of *The Corsican.*

Tommaso. First mate of *The Corsican* and fraternal member of the Sons of Saint George.

Alessandro Boccanegra. Captain of the people of Genoa.

The Austrian. A member of the Nightshade Brotherhood.

Lady Coraline di Parma. Noble heiress of Parma.

Corrado della Torre. Head of the wealthy della Torre family.

Matteo Visconti I. Governor of Milan.

Emilio Paoli. Famed shipbuilder of Genoa.

Philippe Legrande. A Burgundian vintner.

Jacopo Mosca. Bishop of Milan.

— • —

The Blade of Milan

1

THE STEWHOUSE KILLER

The steam and perfume and carnal musk in the brothel clung to skin like vine tendrils to a tree. No bout between pokes in the night air could obstruct the seepage of aromas claiming the fabric of patrons and entertainers alike. Sour in the back of the throat. Bed frames ground wooden floorboards, staccato moans permeated the senses. The orchestra of nocturnal activities were an old friend of Rebecca's as both observer and active participant.

She tossed a bundle of aromatic herbs and spice sticks into the hot bath as the kettle came to a boil. When the copper jug hissed, she tipped it over the coals. The heat forced a sharp inhale from her patron. Sumptuous oils coated their skin. Rebecca pocketed a smudge stick to wash at home later. The blade strapped to her thigh would make a mess.

Kneeling behind the learned clergy of the Church in the tub, Rebecca scrubbed his back. Working the water to a lather, she admired his fine cotton smock and deep red chaperon hat by the door. The belt-rope, coiled on the floor, was flung from his waist quicker than Rebecca anticipated his wire-frame capable of moving. His earnestness to be rubbed and seduced in spite of his profession repulsed her.

But he was not unique. Rebecca encountered all sorts in the brothels for the better part of her twenty and three years. Tanners and smiths, clergy and night watchmen. She knew them. Their contrary behavior fascinated her.

They bought wares and traded livestock at the central market. They kissed wives, tossed children into the air, and prayed in the Basilica of Saint Ambrose. At night, Rebecca poured their wine, drew their baths, and endured their rancid breath. Stubbled cheeks rubbed her bosom raw and sweat beads dripped onto her throat. For their measly coin, she spread her legs.

Blessed by the Lord above and deemed indispensable by the noble, earthly lords, the stewhouses served their purpose. The hot-blooded sons of the republic required release from their desires and Milan required a tax base. The logic was sound yet the patrons were swine. This clergy, a hypocrite. Rebecca hated them.

"Nasty business these killings," he said. "And in the stewhouses. Has decency been surrendered? Must be a Jew."

Rebecca *tsk*ed in assent and massaged his narrow collarbones.

"You suspect multiple killers, father?"

"Ha! I should hope not. I pray this work of a godless devil is not the doing of more than one man. The affront to the sanctity of life appalls me."

Rebecca relaxed her grip. A heat rose to her cheeks; he did not consider a female killer. Few would. A specter marred the onset of Lent, punctuating the observation of Jesus Christ's resurrection with literal Death. No amount of fasting or prayerful devotions could drive the fear of three vicious murders from the minds of the patrons. The clergyman shrugged, encouraging her fingers to continue.

"The archbishop is joining our special procession tomorrow through the city. This criminal must heed our plea for peace."

Rebecca drove a thumb into the meat under his scapula. An involuntary utterance escaped his lips as he flinched.

"Take heed, slattern!"

Rebecca stood too fast, blood rushing to her head. The insult, an all-too-common curse to her ears, felt enough of a signal to get on with her deed. Her other assaults gathered in her mind. Growing from tepid to assertive—a hidden jab in the back alleys, a swift stab between pokes—and a quick escape. The fear of being discovered, ever-present, bobbed in her throat now.

Drunken hollers competed with the lutenists downstairs by the bar. Peals of laughter from unfamiliar whores danced atop the guffaws of regulars.

"My apologies, father. Talk of murder has me anxious." She scratched his neck with a loving caress.

"These are trying times, dear. Remember to trust in the Lord. His heart has eternal love even for you."

Even for me.

The same Lord who ignored her childhood prayers would not answer their pleas. The clergy did not care for the worries of the people, but required peace of mind to enjoy the pleasure houses without fear of slaughter. The vanity and bald condescension turned her stomach. Whether patrons indulged here or in Rebecca's home—Mama's stewhouse—she would forever be an object of derision. Until she decided to take matters into her own hands.

"Of course, father."

"Join me, will you?"

Rebecca walked around to face tonight's victim. He patted the water's surface, not noticing the grimace of rage on her otherwise slender jaw. She rearranged her expression and caressed her abdomen and hips, and drew her hands back towards her groin. The patron and his member stood at attention. His tumescence served no compliment. She knew her worth.

At average height, Rebecca's striking features included lustrous black curls that danced between her shoulders and lips framed underneath almond-shaped eyes. Eyes that held an eternal blaze appraising all they held in lurid scrutiny. In her own estimation, the only flaw to her face was a Roman nose that must have belonged to her truant father.

A leather sheath clung to her inner right thigh, buried beneath folds of ragged dress. She learned during her last foray that if she split her undergarment from crotch to knee against her leg, it allowed the blade smoother egress.

Rebecca shrugged out of the shoulder straps as the patron reached for her hips like a suckling babe for its mother. The clergyman's gaze trained on her hosiery. She felt her muscles tauten, the strength of youth masquerading under the calorie deficiency of poverty in her glistening curves. The art of seduction crescendoed with her hand clutching the black-pommeled blade from between her thighs.

The patron's eyes seized on the naked iron dagger. A knock at the private steam bath door. Another courtesan sought to entertain a guest. The patron twisted in the tub.

"Help!"

Rebecca launched into the tub and clasped his gaping mouth. She lodged the blade into his throat. Her full weight pressed behind the thrust. Pink water splashed onto the floor. Staring into the patron's wide eyes, Rebecca watched as fear blossomed to terror and faded to black.

Breathing hard, she prayed her fellow courtesan would get the hint they had unfinished business. *Knock. Knock.*

Blood rushed to her eardrums. Then another. Add it to her unanswered prayers. Rebecca admired her only and most prized possession in this world—the pommel jutting from his neck. She tugged the blade from his flesh.

A gurgle escaped the wound. She pressed on the hole, futile and panicked, to conceal the aspiration. A fresh tune from the lutenist struck a lively dance, yet the courtesan, or patron, tugged at the locked door.

Rebecca jumped from the tub and threw open the window. The steam flumed outside. The glow of the embers threw shadows onto his surcoat. Why she bothered to visit the stewhouse in the first place came to mind. She dug into his pockets until she found a coin purse.

After redressing, she tangled her hair ahead of her ears to drape her face. Pulling on her hood, she draped his coat over her forearm. In the hallway, a drunken pair, arms in a tangled mess, leaned against the far wall. Lechery could not wait. Rebecca slunk to the stairs, where a patron grabbed her backside. She threw the dead clergyman's coat over his shoulders and straightened it with a smile.

4

Taking his arm, she led him back downstairs. Luck shone through his drifting gaze. As they reached the landing, three Signori di Notte, the city's night watchmen, entered. They could not yet know. The armed guards must have stopped for a free meal and flagon of wine. A shriek pierced the revelry. All eyes turned to the second story except Rebecca's. A black-clad figure stood across the crowd staring directly at her. He offered a slight nod and wink from behind a curtain of greasy hair.

"He's dead!" A half-nude patron leaned over the rail, pointing into the stew room Rebecca vacated.

The night watchmen drew swords. A thick punch slammed into Rebecca's shoulder blade. The drunken stooge dressed in the clergyman's surcoat would not be distracted from a small issue such as murder. He demanded the false hope of a courtesan's attention. Rebecca would give it to him. She screamed. The night watchmen paused on the stairs. "He's wearing the dead man's coat." Rebecca pointed in the patron's face. "He did it!"

With the night watchmen descending on the innocent patron, and the crush of the crowd pressing towards front and back exits to scatter, Rebecca elbowed through the harried bar. The man with the greasy hair aimed to follow. She knocked into the lutenist and kicked his instrument amid cries of protest. Without another glance, she burst into the night.

She couldn't go straight home—to the last brothel on the road in the pleasure quarters—so she took the left turn. A voice floated over the cacophony demanding to question the courtesan with the patron in the surcoat. Rebecca hugged the city's outer defense wall. She found herself near the livestock pens.

Stopping to assess her trail from behind the sheep pen's corner post, she heard watchmen calling to note their lack of progress. Fortunes favored her. The Signori di Notte would report no quarry to their masters tonight, save a bewildered drunkard in a dead clergyman's coat.

Rebecca decided to round the pens and backtrack to the pleasure quarters by way of the central market. She paused behind a stable to examine the coin purse. She had not expected a hefty sum, but was underwhelmed by the yield. Three silver grossi and two Ambrogino d'Oro. The Venetian coins could be traded for florin, but the newly minted Milanese gold held value only within the republic. She'd need to find a local merchant willing to part with florins or guilders. She didn't wish to depart Milan as a pauper.

Her dreams of the means to escape distracted her from her feet's effort. A whimper rendered her thoughts inert. She had reached the backside of the Breaking Wheel. Clouds shifted. Moonlight lanced the macabre scene. A gentle pitter-patter of rain drummed her hood and the dirt road.

The Wheel—the final destination for condemned men and women—consisted of a single wooden post in the center of a raised wooden platform. The wagon wheel was nailed into the post, and tonight was decorated with the mangled form of a victim.

"Is there someone there?"

She froze. Grit and gravel aggravated the voice, parched from naught a drop of water and cries of agony from a protracted torture. Twisted and mangled limbs, broken and weaved through wheel spokes at unnatural angles, greeted her. Once condemned to the Wheel, an executioner bludgeoned arms and legs with a maul, the flat stone hammer, until they cracked. Unable to stand, the broken limbs were weaved into the spokes until the Condemned died of suffocation or the elements.

"I don't want to be alone."

Neither would she. Rebecca struggled to recall his crime. It mattered not, because if Milan's noble judges sentenced a man to this fate, how would they punish a woman who killed individuals contributing to the public health and economy of the republic? Rebecca's breath drowned his whimpers. She whispered. "I'm here."

The prisoner's jagged breaths eased as she squatted behind him, maintaining a silent vigil. Rebecca waited to depart. No one should have to go out of this world alone. Resentment tasted bitter in her mouth at the thought. She began this life alone. The criminal's head fell limp, and she wondered if the crows would eat his eyes in the morn.

Her actions in the stewhouses were bound to catch up to her—consequences she was not yet prepared to pay. Curtains of frigid rain battered the streets. Mud splattered her ankles and hem as she stalked a wide berth past the livestock stables. Back to Mama's brothel.

She corrected herself. Back home.

2

— • —

AN OFFER

R ebecca peeled her tunic from her skin, the folds of fabric
sopping wet. A draft from the depths of the modest wine
cellar prickled her bare skin. She plucked her thumb through a
hole in the base of an empty barrel, one of two hiding spots from
childhood, and deposited the coin purse and dagger in exchange
for a dry ankle-length tunic and overdress.

"Where were you tonight, Rebecca?"

Mama's voice made her jump. Rebecca shifted to hide the open
barrel storage door. Comporting her face from shock to defiance
was never an easy task with her mother; the severe madam's threat
hadn't eased with the passing of years.

"Am I no longer allowed to step outside for a respite from the
heat?"

Mama's harsh demand brought Rebecca right back to her
youth. She cowered in this cellar, the stairwell, in the coat closet,
and among the stew rooms innumerable times as Mama berated,
beat, or threatened her.

"I own you, and every minute you aren't offering our guests
accommodation costs me."

Frustration choked her lungs. Rebecca's hand twitched to her
right thigh, but the deposited blade was under the barrel. Although, she couldn't rightly kill the most profitable stewhouse's
madam outright should she want to. Nor could she afford it—yet.

"Rebecca, are you listening? Get upstairs. That tanner who fan-
cies you is here tonight."

Mother and daughter shared almond-shaped eyes and a slender jaw, yet Mama aged without grace. Hard lines gouged her cheeks, whereas Rebecca—radiant, olive-skinned, and onyx black brows—put her matriarch to shame. No pinch, slap, or shove followed Mama's reprimand. Rebecca tensed at the lurking suspicion behind Mama's gaze.

Rebecca sighed as Mama ascended the stairs. The madam paused on the stone landing.

"Earn your keep tonight, Rebecca."

Rebecca lodged the barrel slat back into place and hurried to the bar. Zita, a buxom, matronly sort, was serving guests tonight. She produced a glass of opaque swill, the vino blanco reserved for Mama's girls, at Rebecca's request. She downed it, grateful for the non-diluted sting, and signaled for a refill. Her friend obliged.

"Peaky tonight, Rebecca?"

Rebecca's eyes softened on the aging courtesan. Zita often supplanted the tenderness Mama should have shown over the years. A soft consolation or matronly cooing—remedies for the body and soul. Rebecca would miss the kindness when she escaped.

"Just tired."

"The fleas weren't so bad last night, were they? Could always be worse, remember that. The tanner is there."

Zita nodded toward the cluster of dancing patrons and girls. Sure enough, Aldo the tanner sat at the gambling table behind the group. Guild members would gamble pay or barter services at a discounted rate among one another. A windfall at dice games could make or break an empty stomach or resourcing the finest materials. Rebecca gambled on Aldo, who customized her blade's sheath. For the price of secrecy, he desired extra attention.

She put on a false smile. Smiths and merchants grabbed at her arm, cloying for her attention. She enjoyed a successful career in Mama's brothel by playing hard to get. She would tease a patron who couldn't afford her or suggest they needed to allow someone else the pleasure of her entertainment before another visit. Mama reappeared at her elbow and guided her through the crowd with a sharp pinch to the back of her arm.

She jerked her arm free and sauntered to Aldo. She dropped into his lap, resisting the urge to retch, and glared at Mama. Aldo's fat belly, peeking from his breeches and coated in a film of sweat beneath the wiry hairs, rolled in delight at her attention. He patted a pile of silver grossi on the table, fortune favoring his luck tonight. He called over Rebecca to Mama, speech slurred.

"Shall I pay you for the night now, madam?"

Like a fly to shit at the mention of coin, Mama's hand jutted below Rebecca's face. The graying madam simpered gratitude as she accepted the payment. That suspicious glance from before was replaced by a smug smirk.

Mama pressed a hand on Rebecca's shoulder. Audible to her daughter alone, she said, "To go with the rest."

Rebecca couldn't discern the meaning of her comment or why it was reserved for her, but drunken Aldo didn't notice. Mama slipped through the crowd and out of sight. Rebecca distrusted everything about the woman. No profit from Aldo tonight, but she forced the memory of her new coin purse in the cellar to the forefront of her mind to ease the nerves. Her bounty would join her larger, hidden coffer tonight. A sweaty palm caressed her bare neck.

"Excuse me while I prepare the stew, Aldo."

Too drunk to argue, Aldo couldn't restrain Rebecca as she stood. Grateful to avert her distant gaze, the veil between her forced profession and bid at freedom eroded to tatters.

"Don't be long!"

A whiff of dank, damp earth like the space beneath the wine barrels caught her nostrils. A patron sat on a stool beneath the staircase, appraising Rebecca as she reached the landing. He wore a black surcoat, upturned collar, black breeches, and black leather riding boots—his attire reminiscent of someone. A wide-brimmed hat sat on his knee, and he examined a flagon of red wine.

"The madam's daughter," he said.

"Pleasure." Rebecca nodded and smiled. "Signore?"

He sucked the vintage through crooked incisors.

"Can't a man have a poke in the comfort of the stews these days? Or must he concern himself with the point of a blade, Rebecca Guarna?"

Rebecca's insides squirmed, the smile faded to a grimace. She prayed he failed to notice the sweat at her temples.

"Murders do tend to frighten—"

"Four," he interjected, leveling his piercing gray eyes with Rebecca's gaze. His beard and hair were flecked with saltpeter. Rebecca gauged they would be of similar height when standing.

"There have been four murders in four stewhouses. Do you know how many brothels are in Milan's pleasure quarters?"

Five, Rebecca thought. She straddled a stool and pivoted her hips towards the Man in Black. Spreading her knees, Rebecca hiked her frock to mid-thigh. How he knew about the fourth murder raised her heart rate, so she helped herself to his wine and tossed the remnants back.

"Are you suggesting we are in danger, here, signore?"

"I'd say—a skilled killer is stalking influential patrons. A vintner, a textile merchant, captain of the night watchmen, and now a servant of the cloth."

The man with the greasy hair! She remembered his roguish wink from the other brothel. He wore a black surcoat of the same cut. They were in collaboration. But who were they? She lingered too long.

Taking his hand, she said, "May I interest you in entertainment in the baths? Maria may be available. The steam will wash away such dreadful talk."

The Man in Black examined her hand and laughed. "There's blood caked beneath your nails."

Rebecca jerked it from his grasp. He dropped the empty flagon to the stone floor and stood. She was correct about his height and build.

"Someone with such prodigious skills need not toil in a place like this. Sure, there's, ah, charm here," he said, appraising the barroom. "Where the clientele have limitless resources to pay those in your standing."

The chitarra lutenist struck a new tune, the quickened pace melded to the beat of Rebecca's heart. The rage she felt in the moments before driving her blade into the clergyman's throat earlier in the night returned, and the man must have caught the glint in her eye.

"With the right training and guidance, they could profit handsomely from such skill, say, in Genoa. Even decide how to live one's life. Chart a path to your own desires. The rewards are endless for those in my line of work."

He reached inside his surcoat and Rebecca flinched. The second time tonight her hand plunged for a blade that did not sit against her thigh. His brows raised at her instinct and smiled. The Man in Black produced a slip of parchment and dropped it in her lap.

"Your line of work?"

With a pat on her forearm, the dank scent emanating from his pores enveloped her as he whispered in her ear.

"You have twelve hours to decide."

Rebecca felt winded. "Or else?"

"I'm not certain you'd like to find out. The city judges need not receive my anonymous tip. Consider my proposal. The world is a bigger place than the stews. It would be a shame to die here."

The cracked bones and contorted limbs on the Breaking Wheel came to mind. The Man in Black departed the brothel. Rebecca secreted the parchment into her sleeve. She scanned the room. No one noticed their interaction over the music and gambling and drinking. This stranger and his accomplice must have been keeping tabs on her for longer than she was aware. Goose pimples dappled her skin.

Then again. An offer at training. Endless rewards. The freedom to decide where to go, what to do. Did he sell falsities or was his offer true? The snake's tongue felt pleasant to the ear, she reminded herself.

Another consideration though. Nothing kept her in Milan. She had enough funds to start fresh. Where she would go was unclear, but now was the time to run. This man knew she killed those men; how, she didn't care, but his warning foretold danger. Mama was nowhere to be seen. Most likely hiding the pittance silver away in her quarters. She'd gather her stash and flee, making a respectable distance before dawn.

Rebecca took the stairs two at a time and beelined to her quarters, shared with Maria, Paula, and Zita. She slammed to her knees harder than intended, hovering above her rags for a bed. She tossed them aside and pried the loose floorboard open. The cavity should have contained three heaping felt bags of earnings, coin gathered in secret from patrons including *him*—mostly from him—but found nothing save the worn, folded sheaf of parchment. Her stomach dropped. Gone. Ten years of secret and stolen payments for her innocence, her funds to buy her way out of the republic—to where—nowhere of consequence now. She snatched the parchment and stuffed it into her dress.

To go with the rest.

Mama stole it. She found her hidden silver and gold and absconded with her means to escape. The hollow dread pierced behind her ears, ringing numb by her temple. Crushed. Mama, once again, humiliated her. Demeaned her pitiful existence. She gathered the rag pile and shoved them into her mouth. A guttural, rasped scream emitted from the depths of her soul.

Rebecca rocked back and forth, clamping onto the rags between her teeth until the taste of sweat and perfumed notes from smudge saturated the back of her throat. She tossed them aside and marched for the stairs. She made it halfway to the landing, intent on gathering her dagger and fleeing, when *he* arrived. Entertaining patrons and courtesans alike, the typically gregarious Doctor Leonardo Salvagno held a somber court in the raucous bar.

Zita, Maria, and Paula clustered around his striking figure in the crimson surcoat. The newcomer, gray at the temples, accepted a glass of wine. Zita refilled it the moment he emptied it.

"Thank you, dear. Rough night."

Maria took his coat. "Doctor Salvagno, you look strained. Please, sit."

He complied. Rebecca kept him in view, but hung behind the musicians. She rather hoped not to be delayed by her first romantic partner, but the complication seemed inevitable. As long as she departed before Mama resurfaced.

"Well, doctor!" a smith said. "What news?"

Leo Salvagno placed both palms on the gambling table and rolled his tongue around his mouth. Rebecca's breath caught in her throat at the sight of blood on his sleeve, unsure if the sight prompted the smith's question. With certainty, the same blood she drew from the priest naught hours prior.

"Another murder."

Gasps and grunts rumbled through the bar. Several patrons headed to the door, eager to be in the safety of their homes.

"Who this time?" Aldo asked.

"Can't tell you who yet, Aldo, but offer a prayer to the Lord and His Son's most sacred heart." He blessed himself. "It was a priest."

Aldo mimicked Leonardo and Zita hung her head. Maria piped up, hand on a generous hip.

"Shameful!"

"Bad for business," Paula said, underneath her breath.

"Shut it, Paula," Zita said.

The smith joined Doctor Leonardo Salvagno at the table and waved in dismissal.

"Eh, the priest should have kept his cock holstered under the robe, especially with the other murders."

"You believe it was his fault?" Leonardo snapped. "No one deserves to suffer. Not the way he died."

"And during the Lenten season!" Maria said. "Is it true if you die during Easter, your sins are commuted, doctor?"

Leo placed a hand on Maria's shoulder in comfort.

"Yes, the only time our souls bypass purgatory for the grace of heaven. Shame the clergyman . . . well."

Rebecca wiped damp palms on her knees. She bit skin from the inside of her cheek to stymie the retort she wished to shout. The priest deserved every inch of her blade.

Each victim chose their profession, were cherished by loved ones or the church. They were free and she was bound to their desires. Like ore from the crucible, anger bubbled from every fiber of her being. She decided she couldn't avoid Leo any longer and she certainly couldn't tarry all night.

"How have the city judges taken the news?"

Leo's brows raised and his shoulders relaxed at Rebecca's sight. He rotated his glass like a guilty child caught stealing fresh bread from the table.

"They're my next stop. But first, if I may have a private word with you, Rebecca."

The crowd eased back into chatter and debate about the doctor's ill tidings. Quite a few more guests funneled for the door. A killer prowled the stews and most had mouths to feed. The inconvenience of having your throat slit became too real. Lingering patrons finished their deeds in the baths and Zita traded brooms with the musicians for their instruments.

Forced into an unavoidable confrontation with Leo, Rebecca grabbed him by the elbow and guided him to the wine cellar. Each coin he traded for her company, a subtle investment in stripping her dignity, lost to Mama. She needed to keep moving. Meeting his eye took effort, but since this may be their final meeting, she complied.

"Rebecca, where are you taking me?"

She shoved him out of sight of her secret barrel and told him to stay put. Gathering her dagger and the paltry coin bag, she returned to her first lover.

"I'm leaving Milan." She patted his cheek. "Tonight."

His body heat pressed through his tunic. She stared into his wide-set, chestnut eyes. Was it pain staring back? Had he ever felt true concern for her safety?

"Leaving? What do you mean?"

"You're no closer to catching this killer and I cannot work for Mama another day."

"Mama." He shook his head. "The city judges were foolhardy to hire me, but I promise you I will catch him, and when I do, I'll have the time for us to be together." He placed his hands on her belly. "We can try again, Rebecca."

"Leo, no! Stop." She removed his hands, delicate but firm, and shook her head. Whatever despair she felt at the sight of her lost treasure, Leo knew how to inflict pain. He didn't mean it, but Rebecca would rather not remember the scare he referred to, not when she did not love him or wished to carry his child. "No. I must go."

He grasped her upper arms and drew her in close. She inhaled him. Leather and shaving putty. Not quite uncommon scents. They brought no comfort. They were his scent.

"Then ride to Salerno. The medical team will offer refuge. Wait for me till I catch this villain and then we will go anywhere you desire. A fresh start!"

"Salerno?" Rebecca unlatched from his grip. "You wish for me to enter a convent? To become a nun?"

Leo took a tentative step forward at her mocking laugh. He held his hands aloft at a loss. He paid for companionship and fell in love. Siphoning his coin for profit, futile now, would pale in comparison if his investigation into the murders proved a success. There was no way around it. Any false comfort derived from him was an illusion. She tarried too long.

"I'll give my report on the priest and come gather you in the morning. I'll deliver you to Salerno myself, then return to finish my employers' request."

Rebecca shook her head, but the doctor could not, or would not, hear her.

"Leo. Hear reason. Men are being killed. Not women. I'm in no danger, but I am leaving, now, tonight, and I will not wait for you."

It was the physician's turn to dismiss her comment. He shook his head.

"Be ready to ride south at the terce hour. I'll collect you. We'll travel light."

He kissed her forehead and left her alone in the cellar. Her legs felt heavy climbing each stone step. One guest remained, snoring drunkenly on the floor. Zita stacked chairs. She gave the bar one final turn, her home for ten and seven years. Mama dragged her out of the cold, a bedraggled, skin bag of bones, and into the church of lust. Grateful for the shelter, Rebecca resented what occurred here. It was time.

Leo's proclamation ringing cheap in her mind against the context of their relationship. She would not miss home, as she would not miss the carnal compliance, the risk of repeating a failed pregnancy. A man with the funds to do whatever he wished. She withdrew the scrap of paper from the Man in Black. In looping curled scrawl, it read:

Palazzo San Giorgio.

She wiped a tear from her eye. To Genoa? To the lake country in the north? It did not matter. With nothing but her thin surcoat, Rebecca checked her inner pocket out of a needless abundance of caution for the light coin purse and weathered parchment.

Rebecca halted in her stride as the front door of the most profitable stewhouse in Milan banged open, emitting four Signori di Notte, pikes in hand, with Mama directing them from the rear. She pointed a finger in Rebecca's face and ordered her sole daughter to be arrested.

She tarried too long.

3

—·—

THE BREAKING WHEEL

S hackles cut into Rebecca's wrists as the night watchmen paraded her through the waking city. They marched past the guild quarters, Rebecca focusing on the heraldic wooden signs for a distraction from their terminal destination—a presentation in front of the city judges.

The smith's anvils. The metalworkers were heating the furnace bellies with nettle and black locust firewood. Her blade, paid for by her siphoned earnings, not favors, was forged by an apprentice, eager to practice his craft. The prized possession, ripped from her thigh sheath, was being unceremoniously carried by a guard. Rebecca cringed. Once examined by an expert—one Doctor Leonardo Salvagno—it would provide all the proof of her guilt. Would Leo be present for her sentencing? The judges may condemn the doctor for failing to recognize her as his quarry. He couldn't have known. Rebecca's last words might even be to refute such a claim. The depository receipt from Mama and dead patrons' felt purses on her possession would corroborate the truth.

Mama.

Their final parting held no surprise yet stung no less. Mama left Rebecca in Aldo's lap and deposited her daughter's hidden coin to her account. Mama couldn't be bothered to pay the watchmen for their troubles. Rebecca's stomach turned at the sight of Martina licking her lips to buffer an excuse.

"The money was nominal," she told the guards. "You patrolmen may enjoy the services of the stews at half price through Easter."

Rebecca scoffed at Mama's offer. Condemning Maria, Zita, and Paula to diminished wages was low for the madam. She slapped Rebecca as the watchmen gathered the parchment, sheath, dagger, and the dead clergyman's coin purse from her coat. Rebecca would never forget the disdain on Mama's face or her parting sentiments, the final words Rebecca hoped they exchanged in this lifetime.

I never loved you.

Rebecca spit in Martina's eye. The Signori di Notte dragged her from the brothel.

"I hate you, Martina!"

Love left when Papa abandoned them and Mama allowed patrons to grope her daughter's august physique. She prayed the stewhouse and its vile stench of body odor, sweat, and stale wine burned to the ground. The clang of hammer to iron set the metronome of their pace.

They rounded the northwestern corner of the central market as the sky brightened. Merchants, in their fanciful wool breeches and draped chaperon hats, sounded from the square, unpacking wares for the morning rush. Rebecca could picture them tossing the folds of the headwear over a shoulder to greet customers emerging from the adjacent inns. The patrolmen prodded her beyond the piazza towards the wooden signs of the textile and tanner quarters. Rebecca inhaled, and not from the brisk morn, but in the direction the patrolmen chose. Away from the judges' quarters.

She kicked her heels into the ground. Two Signori laughed and hoisted her forward. On the northeast side of the market lay the pens, caging countless sheep owned by Milan's elite. The beasts bleated in protest for being confined near the stench of the butchery houses and tanner dyes, or because they were sheep and that's what they did. Rebecca pitied the beasts who stood guard as wool was sheared, throats were slit, and the tanners scraped skin from bone.

"No," Rebecca said, as they turned past the pens to face the Breaking Wheel. "No!"

The dead man hung on the wheel, eyes not yet pecked from the sockets. She bit her quivering lip. To utter a prayer for mercy to the Lord was to shout into the Void. A yawning silence. No mercy would be offered by man or God. No sentencing for a woman. Straight to her inevitable end. A watchman smacked her in the back with his pike. Another leered in disgust.

"You killed our captain. Giovanni was a good man."

Rebecca recalled her victim. She hadn't regretted it because he died dragging a courtesan into the alley behind a stewhouse. She was quite proud of besting a trained soldier. They threw her against the platform wall, two guards leveling their pikes. Another climbed the ladder and began untangling the limp corpse from the spokes to make room for her.

"He died a coward, whining for his useless life! God damn his soul." Rebecca spit at the watchmen.

Let the Void hear her final prayer, a defiant war cry in spite of a stifled existence. Why she had been dealt such poor odds in His game of dice was beyond her knowing.

Whack.

A pike to her gut knocked the breath from her lungs.

"The governor ordered us to bring the killer to the judges," the head watchman said. "But since you're resisting—" He swatted her with the pike handle again.

The patrolmen's hatred cut through their laughter. Rebecca wondered if she would survive their beating to be delivered to the judges or simply hung on the Wheel as a message. Fate determined either outcome would draw a crowd chomping on hunks of cold bread or dried pork to admire the woman who met her fate—punished for existing, for desiring what was given to men without question. At least in the hands of the Signori she would avoid the executioner's maul mutilating her limbs, weaving them through spoke, bone cracking and contorting through skin.

"Giovanni died in the gutter among the scat and urine."

A mirthless laugh escaped her lips, rang out cold and true. The guards pummeled her with foot and fist. She dropped to her knees, vision blurring from the pain.

"This bitch's brain is filled with worm-rot," another patrolman said. "To laugh at your own death."

They propped her against the platform. Mustering her final strength, Rebecca landed a kick to a patrolman's crotch and the buffoon fell to the ground moaning. Oblique sunshine warbled over the outer defense wall. The light bore no heat, but Rebecca loved the cold. It was a good day to die. Alone. She refused to beg or scream for aid, although no one in the market would hear her over the bleating of the sheep. A personal joke from the silent Void? There could have been worse ways to go.

Shadows obscured the guard in front of her. A wet, warm spray splattered her face. He dropped to his knees, eye to eye with Rebecca. Shock plastered his ugly face, a blade lodged in his neck.

The dank earth scent met her unclogged nostril. Black boots thudded to the ground, and the flash of steel blinded her in its swinging arc. The other Signori swung pikes as the Man in Black danced between their futile defenses. He launched another dagger, where it squelched into a watchman's eye socket. He produced two more daggers, twisting a pike thrust to loosen the guard's grip. Jab. Sweep of the feet. Slice.

With a side step, he gutted one guard, entrails spilling into the dirt. One coward scrabbled away. Rebecca blinked through the blood and light. A second black-clad figure emerged—the man with the greasy curtain of hair. He kicked the crawling watchman back towards her savior's feet. He retrieved Rebecca's blade. The newcomer gathered the keys to her manacles and unbound her.

"You may call me the Fixer." The Man in Black offered Rebecca the pommel of her blade.

She accepted. The long-haired companion propped the guard onto his knees and caressed his neck with steel.

"Please . . ."

The Fixer rolled his eyes. She didn't know what miserable existence the night watchman clung to, but his whimpering offended her.

"I offered you a path in your mother's brothel and a deadline. I'm not a patient man, Rebecca Guarna."

Rebecca envied his skill with the blade. She couldn't stay in Milan and did not intend to ride to Salerno with Leo.

"To Genoa then?"

The Fixer smiled. Withdrawing a fine, crinkled black rolled joint, he struck a piece of iron against flint. The spark lit the end. He took a deep drag and exhaled through his teeth and nostrils. The dank scent's origin. He yanked the dagger from his first victim's corpse to slit the begging patrolman's throat. He gathered the rest of his weapons.

"Never leave a good blade behind."

***

The Fixer was a bastard. Rebecca should not have been surprised given his slaughter of the night watchmen in Milan. Once outside the city's walls, he forced Rebecca to trudge alongside their horses. Blisters formed and popped, blood blossoming in her flat leather shoes. Echoes of Mama's beatings—the aches and bruises—trained her legs to withstand the labor. She refused to complain.

Although she had never visited Genoa, the distance could be covered between the sext and none hours by horse at full gallop. However, they camped in the woods at vespers to monitor the southwestern road. The Fixer wanted to ensure they were not followed. The city judges would be reeling by sunset with the discovery of four Signori di Notte butchered near the Wheel.

Rebecca shivered on a log as her companions tossed scraps of dried fish and hunks of bread crust at her feet. They took long pulls from canteens and offered her wine. She chewed with deliberation, although she was famished. Hunger was a constant friend as a child, so she knew how to savor her morsels. Bruises already formed, causing even the slightest movement to make her wince. She remained still, glaring at both the "Fixer" and the unnamed companion. The Fixer told the unnamed one to take the first watch, so Rebecca assumed his station was less significant.

The Fixer leaned against a tree trunk and smoked another black joint.

"Stop staring at me, Rebecca, and get some sleep."

The companion leaned behind a black locust and peered for signs of movement. When the Fixer closed his eyes, she gripped her blade. Being led into the dark by one, if not two, well-trained killers chilled her resolve. Treachery would be all too easy on the road.

When the Fixer began snoring, Rebecca snuck into the brush where the trees crowded the lack of path. She would bear east, arcing wide around Milan and on to the lake region. The republic grew each day, and with the new governor, it may yet absorb more lands. At least in the lake region, she could press farther east to independent Venice should the judges send riders to find her.

Life in Milan had its merits—gathering victuals in the central market or haggling with the innkeepers for good wine. Milan, with its tight living quarters for the common-folk, cypress-lined cart roads, and booming textile economy. Then again, those glimmers of a life were but a pale shadow of what she needed. Her profession in the stew, or reform in a convent, gripped her soul and twisted her guts. She may never see her fellow courtesans again, but they would march on without her. Harvesting olives in the mountains, yes, she'd till earth and orchard.

She picked up the pace, but a shadow invaded her path. The greasy haired companion barred her way.

"Stand aside," she said, drawing her dagger.

"My name is Azzo."

"I don't care." She advanced.

Azzo stepped backwards, but did not lower his hands.

"Come to Genoa, Rebecca Guarna. Your talents won't go to waste."

"Wish to see my talent now, Azzo?" Rebecca flicked the blade to usher him aside. He wouldn't be moved.

"You can kill naked, drunk, and unarmed men in the stew, but could you have dispatched those night watchmen?"

Rebecca squinted to read his expression. "When did you realize it was me killing the patrons?"

Azzo shifted his weight. Even in the dark, Rebecca sensed his satisfaction at discovering her identity.

"He's a knave, the Fixer, but you saw him earlier! He can train us to be an unstoppable force."

Another promised to the Fixer's training. The shine of his attention burnished before the promise could be fulfilled. Rebecca recalled the Spirit leaving the priest's eyes—she commanded real power, ever fleeting. The rewards. She must remember the rewards the Fixer promised.

"And the pay?"

"Mostly bread, but here." Azzo reached into his pocket and tossed her a small coin sack. She caught it and shook it open. Five silver grossi.

"Half my wages for tracking you. Keep it, Guarna. Steady pay begins in Genoa. Come train with me."

Rebecca considered the woods behind Azzo. He stood aside and shrugged. She bit the inside of her lip. Pocketing the silver, Rebecca sheathed her blade.

"What's he training us for?"

Azzo laughed, as carefree as a young boy playing games. Rebecca wanted to box his ears.

"To join his fraternity of assassins, the Sons of Saint George."

The operative word "fraternity" was not lost on her, but the romance of a secret society trained in combat, earning steady pay, stood in vast contradiction to her prior existence. A courtesan forced to entertain patrons stealing or selling her body for a dribble of coin over a decade. The fraternity couldn't be worse than slobbering patrons, the Fixer not as bad as living under the stifling thumb of Mama. And she wouldn't need to conceal her blade.

4

THE SONS OF SAINT GEORGE

The sight of the Genoan gates drove last night's misgivings from Rebecca's mind more than the small payment Azzo offered. She blinked fatigue and crusted sweat out of her vision to better examine the ancient port city. A breeze from the Ligurian Sea breathed through the docks, campaniles, and into the hills beyond the city center.

The Fixer, with Rebecca sitting behind Azzo in tow, weaved them around outcrops of homes that wreathed the city's outer border. Common folk. Rebecca gawked at the clusters of stone and mud-brick constructed homes. Each home enjoyed ample space between each dwelling, a luxury not afforded the residents of Milan. Two thousand Milanese crammed between the roads that partitioned each quarter or the central market. The Genoese could traipse over verdant slopes away from the bustle of the city for a quiet night's sleep. Rebecca craned her neck around Azzo to get a better view of the sea. The brine awoke a thrum inside her chest that she couldn't place. Joy, perhaps?

Riding at their leisure, Azzo took it upon himself to play guide. He pointed out drinking wells and a grand square for public gatherings.

"Here is the captain's palace," Azzo said, pointing to the most prominent three-story, U-shaped structure she ever laid eyes on. Rebecca counted thirty-two columns between the first two stories below statues of angels decorating the facade's brow. She felt eyes on her roving the expanse of the courtyard. The Republic of

Genoa's Head of State and his anthropomorphic marble sculptures stood sentry to all who passed the main road towards the sea.

"And here's the Cathedral of Saint Lorenzo."

Squeezing through a narrow side street, they passed under its imposing campanile. Adjacent to the palace, the cathedral boasted three arched entryways with a crest of its namesake carved above the center door. Rebecca thought the building shrugged into the sky.

"The Romans built that."

The Fixer led them towards the unmistakable trappings of a stable. The scent of horse shit and straw mingled with the brackish sea breeze. Rebecca dismounted with difficulty, her legs stiff from her first true horseback ride. While Azzo and the Fixer carried a brief exchange with the stable boys—all clad in black overcoats—Rebecca wandered to the promenade.

A fleet of galleys resided in the orb-shaped port. The Genoan coat of arms, the Red Cross painted on a snowy white canvas, littered the main sails and hoist lines. Oars caterpillared port and starboard sides, resting on the gentle rise of the tide or numerous docks. Gulls cawed at donkey carts guided by seafaring merchants toting wares aboard for trading posts. Men in tiny junk craft rowed about each vessel inspecting for wear and tear. Rebecca took a deep inhale, filling her belly. A flutter of joy returned. Why the sea compelled her so, she couldn't put words to it.

"First time?"

Azzo had joined her on the promenade.

Rebecca wished to sail beyond the docked galleys and into the vast yet intimate horizon.

"Where are they from?"

Azzo scanned the docks at the merchants. Genoese guards and dock administrators noted wares and directed foot traffic, but she referred to the foreign traders and sailors standing on terra firma.

"Valencia, Algiers, and Alexandria, most likely—all partners of Genoa. Let's go."

An about-face revealed the Palace of Saint George. Rebecca didn't know how she knew it, but she did. Azzo confirmed. She admired the rectangular white stone edifice and surprised herself at the recital of a silent prayer, hoping she made the right decision. The palace slumped in shadow with the rising sun at its back. She wished it to shine to take in its full effect. The Fixer waited for them at the mouth of an alleyway.

He weaved through homes Rebecca assumed were owned by statesmen or merchants residing so close to the port and administrative buildings. Passing several doorways, they arrived at a portico with stairs descending to the back loading platforms for the cellars. Rebecca counted four buildings until they stopped at a dilapidated double door with a carved facade. Beneath the grime of age, she could discern an engraved spearhead gripped by clawed talons.

The Fixer stepped into the dark. Rebecca hoped her companions couldn't hear her chewing the inside of her lip raw as she followed them inside. Her damp skin was met with the chill of being under marble, wood, and earth among the invisible, cool substrata wriggling with worms and bugs. She walked through a wall of cobwebs, mildew and dust spored the air like salt by the sea. A scratch and spark flamed as the Fixer lit a torch. The meager light illuminated a chipped and faded portrait of a mounted warrior stabbing a red serpent, jaws and claws snapping at the beast's hooves. Rebecca thought the red serpent's eyes glimmered alive in the torchlight.

The Fixer fingered a spot on the base of the portrait, and the frame issued dusty breath as it creaked open. She lost track of how many steps she tentatively placed until they arrived through an archway guarded by two sentries. They nodded at the Fixer, who ignored them. They exited into a wide tunnel with a vaulted ceiling.

Rebecca shuffled close behind her guides. A labyrinth of rooms vectored away from the central tunnel. As they passed the third or fourth threshold, the largest man Rebecca had ever laid eyes on lumbered from the doorway beyond them. The Fixer's wave was returned by a nod from the outline of the hulk. He crossed the main tunnel dragging a limp body by the wrist. Rebecca imagined blood staining the flagstones as they disappeared into another tunnel across the path, but the dark played tricks on the eyes. She startled at the Fixer examining her.

"Not all survive the training."

They entered the recently vacated room. There were small, square windows along the ceiling on the far wall casting sunlight onto a round metallic disc. The light scattered, brightening an armory. Rebecca examined pikes, maces, and swords along the walls. Various unknown instruments for the delivery of pain she could not name sat harmlessly on a wooden table above a pool of actual blood.

"You have demonstrated some proficiency with that blade of yours," the Fixer continued, taking a pike from the wooden rack along the wall.

"I killed four men with this blade," Rebecca retorted.

"Disarm me."

Rebecca could barely hold her head aloft due to exhaustion.

Azzo's words among the black locust grove echoed in her mind. She looked to him for guidance, but none came.

"I've never—"

The Fixer lunged. Rebecca juked aside, stumbling into a rack of swords. The blades clanged, unharmonious and metallic. She drew her blade.

"Four men with pikes wished to kill you naught one day ago," the Fixer said. "Will you be so ill prepared next time? Azzo!"

Azzo took his spot in the doorway. She was trapped unless she disarmed the Fixer. The trainer lowered the pike. Rebecca struck. He parried. The vibration against her hand and wrist, unsettling. The Fixer swiped her feet from under her and she fell to her ass. Gasping for breath, energy all but depleted, Rebecca lay unarmed and vulnerable at his feet.

"Death awaits those without fortitude," the Fixer said. He tossed Azzo the pike. Rebecca's vision darkened, the lack of sleep and hunger feeding on her winded lungs. "Your training has begun."

Fighting the fatigue for fear of being assaulted in her vulnerability, Rebecca's head lolled to the side, fading into an unconscious stupor.

***

Plup. Plup. Plup.

Condensation gathered and fell from the mortar between the brick ceiling. It dripped onto the cold stone floor, waking Rebecca. Her head throbbed behind her brow. The light from the refracted metallic mirror told her it was morn again. Had she been asleep for a full day? Peeling her cheek from the cold ground, she propped herself onto her arm, wincing. Cotton-tongued. Her lower back, tender, from where she hit the floor in the armory.

"You should eat."

She flinched. "Jesus!"

Azzo squatted to her left near the mahogany door of the empty room. Her eye was swollen, obscuring him from her vantage point.

"Sorry!"

He nudged a wooden bowl and not inconsiderable-sized cup near her cot. She examined the contents. Bone broth with a pig knuckle and red wine. The scent reached both nostrils and her stomach clenched. Her instincts told her to devour all of it. Her eyes said wait. She scanned the room. It was a stone cell with two rectangular windows similar to the armory—near the ceiling. The door behind Azzo appeared to be a flimsy wood. He must have sensed her hesitation, or feeling of claustrophobia, so he smiled and produced a second, identical meal. Sitting on the stone across from her, he tipped the contents to his lips and wiped the grease in his stubble on a sleeve.

Rebecca could not fret if it was tampered with any longer. She snatched the knuckle floating in the pool of fatty oil broth, and tore into it. Chewing with her mouth open, she had never tasted a more glorious piece of meat. Azzo ran a hand along the wall at his back.

"Did you notice the campanile on the northwestern corner? This is the foundation. The higher levels are a prison although the Genoans know it as a watchtower."

Rebecca hadn't discerned the palazzo's architecture in her shaded view, but took note. She desired to study her new environment as she studied the sea.

"Isn't this entire building a prison?" She gulped the broth dredges and swigged the decent red wine.

He tucked a lock of hair behind an ear. "There's a library, the armory, and Rustichello's study," Azzo continued. "A dozen tunnels."

She licked the pork fat coating her lips. She washed it down with the rest of the wine. Notes of currant. The vintage reminded her of a wine Leo shared with her when the judges hired him on retainer to serve the republic. Rebecca tried getting to her feet. Her side ached the worst, but she would live. Striding around the cell, one eye on Azzo's lanky limbs, she stretched her arms towards the ceiling.

"Rustichello?"

He smiled. "Of course! The Fixer. Do *not* call him 'Rustichello' though." Azzo lifted his sleeve to reveal a round burn on his forearm. "I overheard two sentries say his real name and learned he doesn't take kindly to the familiarity."

Rebecca hawk-eyed Azzo for discrepancies in his mannerisms and words. She appreciated the insights but hadn't determined his intentions.

"How many?"

Azzo's brow raised.

"Assassins."

He shrugged. "Twenty? Fifty? No idea. I was recruited before Christmas. Took over watch on you in the stews soon after."

Rebecca turned and kicked over a bowl sitting hidden beneath her cot. Pink water drenched the floor. A bloody rag lay nearby. She touched her face. Azzo must have cleaned her wounds while she slept. Rebecca went to her surcoat and withdrew the felt coin purse.

"Look, I don't need a friend, Azzo." She offered to return his pay.

Azzo lumbered to his feet. He stood a foot taller, deep crow's feet gathered by his eyes. She imagined his youth—a pampered son of the republic, not a care in the world to smile and laugh so liberally. Joining the Sons of Saint George could have been a laugh.

He gathered their bowls and cups and pressed her fingers away. Upon closer inspection, his eyes were ringed with dark bags and his neck was scarred. Or maybe he got into scrapes with unsavory characters.

"You will."

He jerked his head towards the tunnel. Rebecca draped her surcoat over her shoulders and followed him into the tunnel. They pushed deeper along a long arc. Like Azzo said, tunnels vectored out of sight on either side. None, save the armory, were lit.

"Where do these go?" She fell in pace with Azzo.

"All over the city, I gathered. Haven't explored 'em all."

A brick wall with a thick mahogany door framed by two torches lay at the end of the main tunnel. From inside the propped door, Rebecca took note of a desk. The Fixer's voice floated through the study and Azzo encouraged her to enter.

"Father Pio Rocco, Giancarlo Acorri, Bartolo Reale, Gennaio Milotti."

Wood paneled walls pressed a must of parchment and iron into her nostrils. Thick, thin, and tattered books languished on shelves. A massive tome was propped open on a stand, the pages displayed illustrations of human dissections. Between the shelves, maces, short swords, and flails hung on mounts, all giving the impression they were battle-tested. The dank scent perfumed the air.

Had candles not littered the room, she might not have discerned the Fixer pouring over a scroll of maps and missives at the desk. He repeated the names as the behemoth, corpse-dragging guard appeared in the doorway. His figure plugged any retreat. Chalk dust stained his lapel and hands. Rebecca felt tight-chested.

"Your four victims, Rebecca Guarna. Know what they had in common?"

Rebecca shifted her weight. The Fixer, or Azzo rather, keeping tabs on her kills, gave her a shudder. How oblivious, how vulnerable she must have been. Also, this blade expert who trained assassins allowed her to live. A flush warmed her cheeks. Azzo parked himself in a burlap armchair and picked at his fingernails. The Fixer lit another black joint and crossed his arms.

"Well?"

Rebecca's sole guess was the stews, but that couldn't be it. A safe guess to test the waters, so to speak, felt prudent.

"The patrons meant something to you?"

The Fixer choked a laugh through a haze. "They were my marks!" He slammed a hand flat against the desktop. "I'm assuming you've heard of the Lombard League. News must have circulated among the girls in the stew. Tell me."

Rebecca stifled a cough as the rank smoke filled the study, but it was the mention of the League that winded her. The Fixer's slight wouldn't go unmatched, but yes, he was correct. She knew the most powerful men in Lombardy. The consortium of businessmen profited from textiles, iron, herds, and wine; they were the economy of the republic. As the League, they became benefactors of whichever pope sat in Rome. Old money with unlimited resources and influence. They owned Milan.

"They were members of the League?"

"No," the Fixer said. "The League hired the Sons of Saint George to kill them. But *you* did it before my Sons; therefore, *you* cost me pay."

Rebecca puffed her chest. She wore defiance well even if it made her beholden to the Fixer.

"I did the League a favor, then."

"But not yourself. You're no one. You even cost young Azzo here his first contract." The Fixer pointed at Azzo with the stub of a joint. He shrugged to confirm the veracity of the claim. Rebecca bit her lip from laughing. Azzo could not have been far from her age, yet laughing in the Fixer's face with the mouth-breathing behemoth behind her wouldn't do.

"A coincidence. I'd have taken the Wheel had I known."

Rustichello laughed. He flicked the extinguished butt and lit another. Pointing at her with the rank burning paper.

"One should not be so lax when considering the Wheel." The Fixer offered a hand to Rebecca, encouraging her to sit. "The new governor, Matteo Visconti I, inherited the Lombard League, the judges, the entire republic from his granduncle. He hired us to purge the League of his family's rival—the della Torre family. There are more contracts. Earn what you cost me and then some, Rebecca, and we'll all profit. Do that, and you can stay on as the sole daughter of Saint George or go about your life. To the Wheel, to the north, wherever you'd like."

Rebecca's knowledge of the ruling elite and their political jockeying was scarce. She knew the governor, of course, and the League. Not a tanner, merchant, or builder withheld grumbles of their taxation. Matteo Visconti's granduncle took the governorship before her birth though. Rebecca considered the depths of the Fixer's proposition as he smoked through crooked teeth. One hiccup fueled her reticence.

"What's in it for the Sons of Saint George? Besides coin. Why kill for the League?"

A smirk plastered Rustichello's face, his eyes glassy. He reached into a drawer and withdrew Rebecca's blade in the sheath and her crumpled parchment. Her cheeks flushed, the rage welling inside her chest, praying he had not read the note.

"The Sons are proud champions of our namesake's legacy. Blessed by the pope." He made a sign of the cross. "We slay whichever demon plagues His Holiness. He depends on the League to extend the Papal States north. A last stand against Rudolf I, the Holy Roman Emperor. He depends on the Sons to defend his interests during strange times. And these are strange times, Rebecca."

Rebecca planted herself in the middle of two feuding elite families, the pope, and the Austrian emperor while inadvertently robbing an assassin-master of his pay, not once, but four times. All the while, her sincerest aim was to escape Mama and the convent.

"You have now learned—and seen—too much to leave here, Rebecca."

"Give me my blade."

He lifted the parchment, and her cheeks blushed. She clenched her fists and he noticed. Azzo sat erect at the edge of his seat.

"I took your blade because you failed to disarm me. You must take better care in defending against death."

She grew tired of his rhetoric. The blade and parchment, to a lesser degree, were the physical embodiment of her life. They appeared to be in captivity on his desk.

"Give me my effects, Rustichello."

It was the Fixer's turn to flush. He slammed the joint onto the floor and walked around the desk. Rebecca held her ground. The behemoth guard stepped into the room. The Fixer snatched the ancient text with the illustrations of dissections and slammed it shut. He spun around and smacked Azzo across the face.

The force of the massive book echoed in the study. Azzo slid off the chair and hit the floor with an involuntary whimper. Rustichello exhaled and scratched his neck beneath the saltpeter beard. Tossing the book onto his desk with a thud, he slid Rebecca's parchment across the tabletop. Dabbing the sweat from his brow, he retook his seat. Azzo moaned from all fours.

"Get up, Azzo."

She wished to offer an arm but worried the Fixer might punish Azzo again. Her fellow trainee dragged himself back into the chair, his cheek red and welted, tears streaming into his lap.

"Need I explain your predicament, Rebecca? Train as a proper assassin and earn your keep. Azzo can return you to the judges otherwise."

Life had to offer more, had to mean more than what others desired of her. She had nothing. She was nothing. Therefore, there was nothing to lose.

"I will train with the Sons of Saint George."

"Good. Dry your eyes, Azzo. Ride to Pavia. Kidnap the pastor of the Santa Maria Maggiore and deliver him here. *Un*scathed."

The Fixer signed a lined decree and rolled it. He held a red wax stick over flame, dripping the melted sealant onto the seam, then pressed his golden signet into the blob. Rebecca recognized the image. A spear tip gripped in a claw.

"And take Rebecca Guarna with you. Bring me the priest and you'll get your blade."

5

— · —

THE PRIEST OF SANTA MARIA MAGGIORE

A zzo shouted at Rebecca to find water. She sprinted from the altar into the sacristy, the side room where the priest prepared for mass. Azzo threw his cloak over the fire, threatening to consume the pastor's cloak along with the man they were supposed to deliver to the Fixer unscathed. She hurried to the nave, crystal water jug in hand, and doused the wailing target with abandon. Azzo stamped the last embers as the priest's screams subsided. He fainted. The prospect of burning alive too much. Azzo leered at Rebecca. She knew what he was thinking. Had they followed his plan, they would never have set the priest alight.

Azzo insisted they attend mass. Rebecca objected. They had debated on the entire ride from Genoa. Her fellow trainee believed they could negotiate with the pastor, encourage him to see reason.

Come along to Genoa, father, for your own good.

Fool.

As congregants ushered from the church, single file, to collect their palms, the pastor shook their hands. He chatted with the flock, calling each by name. As an infrequent mass attendee, Rebecca did not get the impression most priests greeted parishioners so warmly. Such a small town maintained its own customs. Once the pastor bid his final farewell and returned to the church, Rebecca intended to knock him unconscious, Azzo's plan be damned.

He'd survive a slight rough-up to face whatever the Fixer wanted. Rebecca ignored the line of thought as they neared the low-vaulted entryway. The morning sun dazzled. They shuffled forward to greet the priest. Scanning over the heads of tittering wives and town elders, Rebecca found a pair of striking blue eyes locked onto her. The congregant stood to the side, waiting to greet the priest. His blond-bristled hair parted neatly, he smirked at Rebecca. Azzo elbowed her as he blessed himself with holy water from the font. She followed suit without thinking.

She scanned the line for the blond parishioner with the nondescript face and subtle fox-like whiskers. He finished gathering his palms and departed for the square. The knot in Rebecca's stomach unclenched. She set her gaze back to the priest when someone jostled into her side.

An older man, swaying with each step, stomped his feet to regain his balance. He clutched a bundle of braided palms in one hand, a generous ash walking stick in another. His robe indicated threadbare poverty, and he stunk like wine. Rebecca scoffed. The drunk stumbled to greet the priest, whose brow crinkled. He held the braids to be blessed, which the pastor did.

"He makes a mockery of this place."

Azzo raised his brows and nodded in a noncommittal manner.

The words surprised Rebecca, sounding as if they came from someone else's mouth, considering her own beliefs.

It was Palm Sunday. Leo Salvagno brought her a twisted and tied cross at the end of last Easter season. It sat next to her rag pile in the stewhouse for a fortnight until he had forgotten about it. She assumed her own indifference mirrored the Void. God watched Jesus, His only son, ride into Jerusalem on the back of a donkey on Palm Sunday. The savior pushed towards his apocryphal demise willingly, the Father aloof. Somehow the drunk jostled opinions Rebecca would rather repress to the forefront of her mind.

They hung back from the retinue. Rebecca nodded to Azzo. Before he could argue, she hid behind a column. Following suit across the aisle, Azzo shot her a warning glance. She ignored his consternation. Let him negotiate. She'd be prepared to act. The priest bade his final farewells and returned inside. Rebecca waited until he was well into the aisle. She stepped between him and the door. He flinched at her appearance.

Azzo intervened. He emerged from the column, open-palmed.

"Father," he said. "We do not intend you harm."

The priest stumbled backwards, eyes darting between the two silhouettes, shadows against the sunlight streaming into his church.

"He said you'd come. Stay back!"

The priest scampered towards the altar. Rebecca beat Azzo to the aisle, but the priest stumbled. Azzo tugged on Rebecca's tunic, her head snapped back. She swung an open fist at his face, narrowly missing his cheek. The priest was not built for such vigorous movement. He gathered momentum in his flat-footedness and tripped over his own robes. Rebecca closed the gap. He reached in front of his torso to steady his fall and grabbed a candelabra. The metal candleholder snapped from the column. Face-planting on the flagstone, lit candles descended onto his back. His robe caught fire.

Rebecca froze, eye aghast, as the fire turned to a blaze. Azzo slammed past her shoulder. Blood pooled on the stone beneath the priest's face. He flipped over to reveal a broken nose. He blubbered a muffled cry at the sight—more like the heat—of his garments. Rebecca looked at Azzo apologetically; she meant to subdue him, not batter and burn him to death.

Her companion unclasped his cloak and threw it over the screaming priest. Azzo shoved her towards the altar and Rebecca retrieved the water from the sacristy. It was enough to smother the flames. The charred vestments smoked, casting an acrid scent to their nostrils. He fainted.

"He'll live," Rebecca said, more to assure herself than convince Azzo. In the panic to save his life, the companions failed to notice the remaining candelabras along the columns were extinguished.

Clap. Clap. Clap.

The drunk who knocked into Rebecca earlier stood in front of the closed doors. From this distance, Rebecca discerned an impairment with his eyes. Clouded, white orbs. He groped against

38

the back stone wall for a rope cord hanging on a metal hook. It led to the stained glass window, the sole source of dim light.

"The Fixer sent you, then? He's been wanting me for some time."

Rebecca realized what was amiss—he was blind.

He pulled the rope, and a black veil descended over the glass. It plunged the church into blackness.

"Get past me and I will travel with you."

Azzo's voice whispered. "He's the target."

Rebecca interpreted her companion's tone as disapproval at the trickery, as she felt it, too. Azzo moved Rebecca aside as he stumbled back into the center aisle. She clutched the back of the pew and snuck along the side aisle. They may as well flank the drunk. If he was drunk at all. Rebecca hoped the commotion with the false target hadn't roused any suspicion outside. Watchmen could still burst through the door, she reminded herself, even in a small town like Pavia. Azzo's ragged breath wheezed to her right. She wished she could silence him.

"I may be blind," the drunk said, words slurring. "But I saw you before mass concluded."

Who did the Fixer send them to kidnap? His voice cut a menacing timber in the dark. Rebecca's eyes adjusted, but she could still not perceive more than smudges. She bumped a table and gripped it to steady from alerting the blindman. A gasp sounded from behind her and to her right.

Wap.

Azzo moaned. She heard a thud and pew shake. With a few timid steps, masked by the commotion, Rebecca snatched braided palms from the table and crouched. A gentle swish of robe followed. She imagined hiding in Mama's brothel as a child. Too often had she scrunched her eyes closed and dreamed of being elsewhere, but the music of the stews painted a vivid picture.

Rebecca tossed a palm. The robe shifted closer. She tossed another, nearer her position. She could smell the wine on the priest's breath. She poised to jump, tossing one more palm. Unable to wait another second, Rebecca lunged. Wrong way. Swatting at air, the ash walking stick thumped into her ribs.

"I saw you before you left Genoa," the drunk said.

Rebecca tripped and tucked her head for impact. She hit the door! Her hands scrabbled for a knob. The drunk's feet clacked behind her, searching for her position. He must have realized her destination. Before he could prod her with the stick, Rebecca unlatched the handle and threw open a door. Light drowned the aisle. Up close, the drunk's eyes were not completely cloudy. He cocked his head sideways and examined Rebecca with a rueful smile.

Azzo stirred on the floor behind him, clutching his jaw. Rebecca prepared for another bout with the ash stick, but the drunk's shoulders deflated. He was more seasoned than the Fixer. The pauper withdrew a scroll from inside his robes and held it for her to examine. The Fixer's claw-and-spear seal, broken, the note read by its intended recipient. Duped yet again.

"Well, Rebecca Guarna," the drunk said, dropping the scroll. "A simple test, but you passed." He meandered back to the sacristy, swatting Azzo's boots from his path. Feeling guilty for the mishap with their plan, Rebecca offered Azzo a hand. She pulled him to his feet.

"Who was he?" Azzo asked.

Rebecca seized the discarded scroll. The Fixer's looping scrawl addressed the note to one "Father Lorenzo di Costa."

"Lorenzo di Costa."

Drunken Lorenzo returned from the antechamber with more wine. Chugging it, the pair watched him in disbelief until a massive belch echoed in the empty nave. He slumped sideways and blacked out upon impact. Rebecca gave Azzo the scroll, who pocketed it. Worried he died, they felt his shallow breath.

"Well, pick him up," Rebecca said. Azzo huffed, but complied.

Checking for a watchmen-free piazza, they trudged to the stables. The stout brick exterior and imposing facade of Santa Maria Maggiore stood garrison in the center of the town. The elongated archways and prominent belltower dwarfed the petite dwellings within the ancient outer defense walls. Father Lorenzo's bobbing head lolled side to side, supported by Rebecca, as they rode back to Genoa.

***

"The priest of Pavia." Rebecca and Azzo deposited Father Lorenzo into one of the Fixer's chairs. The old man continued snoring. "Unscathed."

The drunk priest earned no undue pity from Rebecca, but seeing such an older man in this state was pitiful. The Fixer disagreed. He slapped Lorenzo.

He woke in a groggy state. "Rustichello. Needed me that badly."

The Fixer snarled. "How did they do?" He pointed at Azzo and Rebecca.

"Terribly! Unsurprising though. I didn't train them."

The Fixer tossed Rebecca her blade. She sighed. The impregnable anxiety of being separated dissipated.

"No one has." The Fixer continued. "But you will then? Now that you're back."

Lorenzo stumbled into the Fixer's side table. He felt for the water tumbler. He managed to splash liquid over the floor and his hand before filling a cup. The Fixer pinched the brim of his nose and lit a joint.

After chugging the water, Father Lorenzo said, "Your body is a temple, Rustichello. You desecrate your mind with that indulgence."

Rebecca understood the Fixer's barked laughter to be at Father Lorenzo's hypocrisy.

"S'not good for me to be back here with them still out there. Hunting. Like we're game, mind you."

Rebecca and Azzo exchanged a glance. The Fixer refused to meet their questioning eyes.

"We have backlogged contracts. Plenty of coin to get lost in a wineskin or the consecrated blood of Christ. Whichever you prefer, Lorenzo."

Father Lorenzo cocked his head left then right. The gesture gave Rebecca the impression he was like a bird observing worms from a branch. The motion also offered him time to deliberate. His gaze lingered on Rebecca. She set her face, still as stone, appraising his clouded look.

"It should be me, the one who trains the first daughter of Saint George." The priest guzzled another cup of water. A smile twitched beneath his bristled beard. "I'll train them to end this feud. To no longer be the prey."

The Fixer knocked twice on his desk. He offered a broad smile with his arms open to Azzo and Rebecca. "Azzo and Rebecca, aspiring Sons of Saint George." The effect, more cloying than welcoming. Rebecca shivered in silence. "But don't fret, my dear Lorenzo—you won't be training them alone."

6

Coin, Blade, Corsair

Rebecca reported to the armory, unsure what to expect in the gathering. Azzo examined swords on the periphery, nodding in deference to a blabbering thick-necked Son. He reminded her of a pugilist that frequented Mama's brothel from time to time. Fat fingers and tree-branch wrists. Telltale signs of a fighter who beat in the skulls of others for pay. Father Lorenzo perched on a stool center floor, a porcelain bowl in his lap. He held a metal fleam and raised a wooden stick. A belt was wrapped around the forearm of another fresh face. He glared at Rebecca from beneath a broad shelf of a brow.

"So this is the quim we're to train, Lorenzo?"

Father Lorenzo raised his chin to the far left corner over Rebecca's shoulder. She nodded at his acknowledgment. The blood rose in her cheeks at the slight, but she drew satisfaction at the extra firm stick tap Lorenzo deployed against the bloodletting instrument. The fleam's pointed tooth punctured the bastard's exposed vein.

"*Rebecca*, Franco."

The leather belt forced blood to flow in an arched spout where Lorenzo caught it in the bowl. Rebecca was amazed at how Lorenzo managed with limited sight.

Franco winced.

"Yes, well, *Rebecca* won't survive her first day." He looked over his shoulder. "Take my odds, Carlo? Double or nothing on last night's contract."

The chatty Son laughed. He dug into a coin purse.

"You eliminated your contract because I distracted the chambermaid." Carlo produced two gold ducats and tucked them inside Lorenzo's robes. "Don't die, Rebecca."

Franco mimicked Carlo, depositing his bet into the priest's robe.

Emboldened by his dismissal and a chance to earn a coin, Rebecca said, "I'll take those odds." If anyone was to believe she could survive a single day in training, it may as well be her.

Carlo frowned in surprise.

"You don't have a single grossi to your name," Franco said.

Rebecca withdrew two silver pieces from Azzo's donated pay. She deposited it into Lorenzo's robe as the Sons did.

Azzo appeared at her shoulder.

"Rebecca, you don't have to lose that here. It was for you."

She dropped another grossi into Lorenzo's pocket.

"I'll survive longer than Azzo."

Rebecca may have slapped her fellow trainee. His shock turned to embarrassment as Franco and Carlo's laughter deepened. Azzo withdrew four grossi and added them to the pot. "On me."

"Enough," Lorenzo said. The porcelain bowl was full. He reached for a cup at his feet and snapped at Carlo. The Son added water until the white and green sticks of what appeared to be shit were submerged. He mashed the contents into a paste and applied it to Franco's nicked vein.

"Goose shit," Carlo said, confirming Rebecca's curiosity.

Franco removed the belt but held his arm above his head at Father Lorenzo's instruction.

The priest sticked his way to the weapon's rack along the far wall and took a longsword from the hanger. He faced the recruits and seasoned Sons, pointing the tip at a table to his right.

"Justice is blind."

Franco and Carlo nudged Rebecca and Azzo. Various swords and knives littered the surface along with two leather sheaths on display. Franco snubbed Rebecca and helped Azzo strap into his. Carlo offered a meek gesture to fit her with the other, but she declined. With furtive glances at Azzo, she snaked an arm through the holster and tightened the buckles against her rib cage. The sheath could hold six daggers with steel shorter than Rebecca's blade.

Lorenzo and the Sons peeled back their surcoats to reveal their own sheaths, equipped with blades. Franco withdrew a dagger by the eyelet ring on the pommel's end and spun it around his index finger. Rebecca noted the blade's palm length. When satisfied, Franco flipped and sheathed it. Azzo rolled his eyes.

"But we do not dole out justice," Lorenzo continued. "The Sons of Saint George are the instrument for the Lord's divine nature. Our efforts have been blessed by every pope since our fraternity's inception over a hundred years ago. Allow George's intervention to guide the tool in your hands. The blade, an extension of your corporeal form."

Lorenzo nodded. Carlo proceeded to name the various weapons. The mini throwing knives were passatore. He hefted a longsword that matched Lorenzo's and handed it to Rebecca. She forced an impassive countenance to conceal her doubts at wielding so much steel. Carlo whacked a cleaver into the wooden surface with a boisterous laugh, but a thin-as-a-needle, cross-pommeled blade caught Rebecca's eye.

"That's a stiletto," Carlo said, noticing the hunger in her eye. "The double blade and pin tip are ideal for close combat or executions. Especially with armored enemies."

Rebecca caught the stench of wine and stomach bile. Father Lorenzo leaned on the walking stick behind them. He stifled a belch. The priest knocked the stick against a massive chest beneath the table. Franco and Carlo dragged it out to reveal dozens of the silver, hand-length passatore. They fitted their sheaths.

"Here, put these on," Carlo said, shoving black sack cloths at the trainees.

Rebecca waited for Azzo to follow the instructions. The chiffon sack hugged his entire head and constricted around his neck loosely. He looked side to side and laughed. She slipped hers on. The sack was comfortable and comforting. The black darkened her vision, but did not obscure it. She knew it must serve a dual purpose—to conceal her identity.

"This is your operation, Carlo," Father Lorenzo said. "Do not fail. And, all bets aside, bring the recruits home alive if you can."

***

Rebecca ignored her elevated heart rate as they set off for the "operation." Carlo in the lead, Franco in the rear, they marched in silence through a tunnel she hadn't yet explored. She felt loose dirt for a path and tried not to bump into Azzo more than once. They walked for what felt like half an hour until fresher and cooler air met her covered face. She didn't notice a handle but heard the grinding of stone venting them into the night.

Once outside, Carlo resealed the door, invisible with no handle on the outside. Concealed to any passerby, Rebecca scanned the wall. Clever. They exited on the north side of the palace. The Sons crept through the city, weaving between narrow side streets, but maintaining a rough parallel to the promenade. Masts and flags flashed at the end of perpendicular alleys.

"You're both extra steel," Carlo said to Rebecca and Azzo. "I don't anticipate a fight, so keep the blades hidden unless I draw mine."

Carlo and Franco donned their black sacks.

"When do these corsairs not wish to fight, Carlo?" Franco asked. He flexed his gloved fingers.

Rebecca dried her palms. No wonder Franco bet she might die. She never encountered a pirate being from landlocked Milan.

Turning left, Carlo brought them to a sliver of a staircase that spit them onto a stone dock. The rectangular slab was cordoned from view of the dock by a stout building's jutted overhang, designed to obstruct the view of passing ships to the south. A single junk rocked with the gentle current, moored to a ring. They were last to arrive.

"Thibault?"

"Oui, Carlo."

Four corsairs with plumed hats and sweeping waistcoats, fastened to the neck, greeted them. Thibault clasped Carlo's hand. His face glistened in the torch light.

"You were supposed to come alone."

Thibault waved at the posse. "As were you."

Carlo clapped him on the shoulder, Thibault rocking to the side. "No honor among pirates, then."

"Nor Sons of Saint George," Thibault said.

Carlo stiffened. Rebecca could feel the static rising from his curly hairs. Azzo shifted his weight from shoulder to elbow, knee to foot. She wished he would stand still. Franco had positioned himself near the moored junk, hands loose at his hips.

"I don't recognize your crew," Carlo said. "All from Burgundy?"

Thibault shrugged.

The moonlight shifted. Masts and sails from docked ships cast the pirates into shadow. Rebecca squinted beneath her chiffon sack, unknowingly stepping forward to maintain her visual. The shift caused one pirate to reach for his sword hilt. Franco drew two throwing knives quicker than anyone noticed.

"Hold, hold, hold!" Carlo yelled.

Rebecca's sweat adhered the sack to her cheeks and mouth. The stench of body odor and swirl of brine on the stone slab nauseated her.

Thibault waved his companion to stand easy, cursing at him in their native tongue. The pirate released the hilt.

"We should get on with it," Thibault said. "Do we have the support of the Sons or not, Carlo?"

Carlo opened his surcoat to reveal a scroll protruding from his inner pocket. Thibault snatched it. Rebecca couldn't discern the insignia on the seal, but she would bet the entire ante from earlier that it was the claw-and-spear. Two pirates crowded over Thibault's shoulder to read the scrawl. Satisfied, Thibault snapped. They produced a wooden chest from the junk and dropped it at Carlo's feet. He reached for the metal key, but Thibault dropped it. Carlo scoffed at the disrespect but stooped to unlock the box. Rebecca forced herself to stay still but could not mistake the pile of gleaming gold. She'd recognize Ambrogino d'Oro, the currency of Governor Matteo Visconti I of Milan, anywhere. Leo Salvagno had gifted her a few over the years. Those coins were now deposited in Mama's account. She bit the inside of her cheek in a rankle of anger.

From one bended knee, Carlo whistled and relocked the chest. He looked at Thibault and said, "You always come through, Thibault—."

Rebecca sensed a change in the air, a breath amiss, before Carlo finished his thought. The pugilist drew a blade and sliced Thibault's heel tendon.

"They are navy!"

Thibault roared in pain and collapsed. The corsairs drew longswords, revealing the white tunic with a red cross splashed across their chests. The Genoan naval uniform.

Franco launched a passatore into a neck. The naval man gurgled a death rattle all too familiar to Rebecca. A longsword slashed Carlo, torso to jaw, ripping a red gash through his black tunic. Rebecca found drawing the passatore awkward, but managed quicker than Azzo. She threw a blade sidearmed, the steel whizzing over a sailor's shoulder. Her fellow trainee landed a solid kick to the assailant's chest who slid sideways into the port.

Rebecca drew her own blade, the familiar pommel melded to her grip. She joined Franco and slashed at the two remaining sailors. Stay alive. Why the navy was present did not matter. What the scroll said, irrelevant. Stay alive.

Franco parried a jab and gutted his opponent. It took all of Rebecca's strength to not lose her blade from blocking the longsword. Vibrations resonated through her hand, wrist, and forearm. She stumbled backwards into Azzo and they both tripped. Tangled in his limbs, she gazed at the raised sword and her assured end.

Two passatore thudded into the sailor's upper arm and temple. Franco drew two more knives and steadied his aim from the slab's edge. He launched them into the final man, who promptly sank.

Rebecca pushed free from Azzo. A curious wheezing and hacking replaced the clang of metal and grunts. Thibault. He clutched his throat, purple blood vessels splotched beneath his skin as his ankle bled freely. Eyes bloodshot and filled with terror. He tapped his chest, unable to suck air into his lungs.

Carlo clutched his chest and neck, still alive, but bleeding profusely. Franco sucked his teeth at Thibault's predicament. He shoved the scroll, key, and chest into Rebecca's arms.

"Azzo, get his legs. Let's go!"

Not until Thibault died did they get purchase on the slab and ascend the stairs. The sprint back to the palazzo was sporadic and labor-intensive. Azzo and Franco waddled all the way. Once beneath the palace, through the entrance the Fixer first brought Rebecca, Franco shouted for help.

The behemoth guard appeared first, covered in dust, sweat, and soot. He cradled Carlo with ease and delivered him to the armory. Franco sprinted away, shouting for Father Lorenzo and the Fixer, but Rebecca and Azzo stayed with Carlo. Azzo helped pull the sack off Carlo's head and opened his tunic. Rebecca had inflicted her fair share of gore in the stews, so she recognized a fatal injury when she saw one.

"Well?" the Fixer asked, appearing with Franco, Lorenzo hot on their heels. Father Lorenzo ran his hands over Carlo's savaged torso to his neck. Blood pooled on the table, dripping onto the floor. He placed a hand on Carlo's cheek and muttered a prayer.

"The capitano," Carlo rasped. "Father, he knew."

Azzo gripped Carlo's forearm. Franco handed the Fixer one of Carlo's blades. There would have been no way of discerning under the black sack or cover of nightfall, but the steel held a green hue. He nodded at Carlo. Rebecca wanted to know what Carlo meant by the "capitano" and the color, but before she could interject, the Fixer clasped Carlo's mouth and pinched his nose. He could not have been long for this world, but kicked his feet. The Son lifted a weak arm to the Fixer's hand, but his strength abandoned him.

The Fixer sighed. He lit a joint and handed Lorenzo the blade.

"He was dying," Azzo said. "You didn't need to kill him!"

The priest licked it with the tip of his tongue and spat.

"What happened, Franco?"

The Son recounted the night's affairs. The report filled in a few blanks that Rebecca wished she knew before the foray. Alessandro Boccanegra, the captain of the people, ruled Genoa, similar to the governor in Milan. Boccanegra controlled the navy. He sent the sailors undercover with Thibault to catch the Sons of Saint George. *Why* was still unclear to Rebecca. The Fixer opened the chest to examine the gold.

Franco ended his story by giving the Fixer the scroll. "We got the gold. Left no trace."

"Did you know?" Father Lorenzo asked, holding Carlo's green-tinged blade.

"Father," Franco said. "Carlo paid with his life."

"Did you know?"

"We told you before, Franco," the Fixer said.

Whatever explanation Franco would offer, Father Lorenzo showed no interest in hearing. Rebecca flinched at the crunching blows the priest delivered to his body with the walking stick. The old man moved with a precision and ferocity she could not have expected. In three strikes, Franco lay battered and moaning on the flagstone.

"Tomorrow, Franco," the priest said, wiping his brow. "You will empty the new path with Rebecca and Azzo."

The Fixer ordered Azzo to bring the gold to his study. Rebecca remained behind, unsure whether to dismiss herself back to the cell or wait for further instruction. Father Lorenzo produced a flask from somewhere inside his robes and took a deep draught. She decided to hoist Franco onto a stool since he saved her life on the slab. He eked out a word of gratitude from the corner of his lips.

Deciding it was time to leave, she strode for the door.

"Wait!"

Lorenzo dug into his robes and rummaged in his coin purse. He withdrew one gold ducat and tossed it in her general direction. Rebecca snatched it from the air.

"The customary winnings for your bet. You survived tonight, Rebecca," he said, taking another swig of his flask. "But will you survive the spear?"

7

—·—

STONE, SPEAR, GALLEY

S leep was not Rebecca's friend. The confrontation on the slab, Carlo's death, and the events afterwards in the armory refused to let her rest. She tossed and turned, crouched behind the wooden door—which had no lock—and fiddled with her blade. Passing time, she etched five tally marks on the wall. The Fixer, Father Lorenzo, Franco, Azzo, Behemoth. In a separate column, she etched one for Carlo. Pleased to have a gold ducat for surviving her first day, the coin was hardly a consolation if she landed in the same column as the fallen Son. She couldn't start anew. One ducat wouldn't pay her debt to the Fixer. Her eyes closed before sunrise long enough to feel drugged, not refreshed.

The door swung open, and with a jolt, she flew from the cot. In stepped the priest. He raised his chin.

"May I?" he asked, indicating to the blade.

Rebecca offered him the pommel. He ran three gnarled fingers over the flat blade. He did the same on the other side. She marveled at his delicacy given last night's strength.

"Cleanliness is holiness. You used your blade at the exchange?"

Rebecca held her breath. She prayed she hadn't broken any fraternity rules. She threw the passatore so poorly, and her blade, yet again, saved her life. She opened her mouth, but Lorenzo disappeared into the tunnel and beckoned someone she couldn't see. Behemoth appeared, bucket in hand, and doused her with frigid water. He grabbed another bucket from the tunnel. She retreated to the far wall but could not avoid a second or third splash.

"Auugh!"

"Your blade," Father Lorenzo said, "like your body, is an instrument of duty. It must be cleansed and maintained."

Behemoth returned with a bundle of clothes. She wiped the water from her bedraggled face, curls plastered her cheeks and neck.

"Dress, then follow us."

Once the door closed, Rebecca inspected the clothing. They were modest yet stitched to her dimensions. She didn't know if it was a coincidence or if they had measured her while she slept. She closed her eyes for a moment. The black breeches and white tunic tapered at the waist. She tied her hair into a tight, damp knot and examined the black leather boots. Glad to peel the sopping clothes from her skin, her odors were substantial. She hadn't missed the brothel, but a soak in the stew with wild sage and hyssop would wash the dank salt of the Ligurian Sea and curdled stench from her skin.

Torches lined the curved walls. The light led her into a storage room of sorts where Father Lorenzo sat at a table waiting. He wet her blade and flicked the excess beads off. She sat across from him.

"Salt and vinegar," he said, scrubbing a horsehair brush along the steel. "Now wash it again."

The blade shone already without the gore and blood of her victims. She dunked it into the bucket. Lorenzo dried it with an oilcloth. He dipped those gnarled fingertips into a small clay pot and dabbed the dry steel. The seed oil emitted a fatty, nut scent.

"Why were you bleeding Franco?"

Lorenzo nudged the cloth to her to dry her blade.

"To restore his humors. Franco was a choleric child." He unfurled a leather smith's tool belt and withdrew a metal rod. "We bleed before certain contracts."

He took the burnished blade and rested it, heel against rod. Dragging from base to tip, he alternated above, below, above, below.

"He saved our lives."

He lifted his hands as if to say he was unsurprised.

"Balance."

Lorenzo handed her the whetted blade. Rebecca sheathed it. Had she been born a boy, she may have apprenticed with the metal smiths at a forge. A tutor or master to impart wisdom. The priest intimidated her but impressed her with a font of knowledge.

"Thank you, Lorenzo."

"*Father* Lorenzo."

"If it's all the same to you—"

Lorenzo reached into his robe. Rebecca flinched. He smiled at the effect. Trying her hand at pushing boundaries was in her nature. She needled. Prodded. It was instinct. Why, she never could explain it. Instead of a passatore, Lorenzo withdrew a leather notebook and piece of charcoal.

"You produce too much heat, Rebecca. A natural temperament for this line of work." He thumbed to a blank page and peered over his nose. His scrawl was illegible. "Maybe your upbringing in the stews? The humidity? Am I correct? You have been with child before?"

How could he have known, Rebecca wondered?

"Once."

The reply slipped from her mouth in surprising haste. So much so, Rebecca's fingertips flew to her lips. Doctor Leo Salvagno spent more time sermonizing, obsessed with teaching her Scripture over the years than he did practicing medicine. For all she knew, the judges hired him to find the stewhouse killer because of his blind faith, rather than his medical know-how. Yet here, a celibate—to her knowledge—priest administered bloodletting and understood a woman's temperament. Had the Fixer not suffocated Carlo, he would have stitched his wound back together, she knew it.

He tapped her sheathed blade. "After every use."

Relieved that Franco joined them, Rebecca took note of the sweat pooled under her arms.

"Time to go, Rebecca."

She followed him to the source of Behemoth's dust-coating. Hard clacking of rock, silt, and stone echoed into the main tunnel. Behemoth loaded debris into a leather rucksack on Azzo's back. The tunnel was newly excavated. No torches lined its walls yet.

Rebecca sniffed Azzo. He smelled rank.

"*He* didn't douse you, then?" She nodded at Behemoth, who smiled.

"We are the *Sons* of Saint George, after all," Franco said, nudging her out of the way. He tossed her a rucksack and tapped Behemoth out. Franco filled her pack and Rebecca followed Azzo's lead.

They spent the day hiking to the top of the campanile, the watchtower-prison. Her thighs and lungs burned after two rounds. Before cresting the spiral staircase, they passed a row of indoor prison cells. As far as Rebecca could tell, they sat empty. At the top, Azzo turned her around and emptied the sack. He tossed the stones into the sea. As she did the same for him, he revealed what happened at the exchange.

"That scroll was safe passage. The Sons control the island of Corsica. The Fixer granted the corsairs access in exchange for the governor's new currency."

Governor Visconti sent his Ambrogino d'Oro all over the republic to compete with the florin.

"How do you know that?"

"Franco told me," he said, with a shrug. He offered her a waterskin. So Azzo didn't get doused and was granted an explanation for the night that could have killed her? Rebecca swished the water and spit it over the side. The sight of the vast sea washed the bitter taste from her mouth. From this vantage point, her gaze reached open waters beyond the naval fleet.

"I bet against you."

Azzo laughed. "I lived."

Franco had them ferry three more loads to the campanile and two into a storage room directly next to the Fixer's study. As they dislodged from the rucksacks, Azzo whispered.

"What do you think that hulking guard's name is?"

No one called him by name, if her memory served her correctly. She was at a loss.

"I knew a 'Bindo' from Pisa," he said. "Think it's that?"

She scowled at Azzo's playfulness.

"Maybe Franchesca? Vittoria?"

In spite of herself, Rebecca laughed. Azzo insisted he bore a woman's name. They traded options back and forth until Franco returned; Azzo even bet that his name was indeed female. Rebecca accepted his losing wager.

***

Franco guided them to a set of marble stairs. It sat on the opposite end of the tunnel as the Fixer's study. His hand searched in the dark for a thick, metal ring. A massive door creaked open. They spilled into an atrium. Marble columns wrapped a long staircase. A mezzanine draped the second story. Rebecca and Azzo ceased all laughing at the framed art of bishops, the Blessed Virgin Mary, and robed saints plastering every facade. Moonlight drenched the cavernous vestibule. They were in the palace, Genoa's central town hall.

"During the day," the Fixer's voice echoed. "The magistrate's arbitrage, bureaucrats hear pleas from sailors and slighted merchants. And Captain Boccanegra's spies politic and scheme. Scribes capture it all." He stepped from a column's shadows, Father Lorenzo at his heels. "At night, we have the run of the palace."

The priest unwrapped a bundle of cloth to reveal Carlo's blade. Franco accepted it and adhered it to the end of a spear. He donned a black sack and his wide-brimmed hat.

"To exist in the shadows," Lorenzo said, patting Franco's shoulder. "To hide in plain sight."

"Undetected by your target," the Fixer said. "Reach the grand meeting room." He pointed upstairs. The palazzo stood five stories from the basement at Rebecca's counting.

"Do not alert us," Lorenzo said.

Rebecca didn't understand, but by the look on Azzo's face, neither did he. She didn't dare ask for clarification.

"There is a portrait of Saint Sebastian adorning the wall next to your goal."

Franco handed Father Lorenzo the spear and produced another of his own from a side table. A bundle of mauve flowers and clay pots were also present. The Son guided Father Lorenzo upstairs. The priest called over his shoulder.

"One at a time."

The Fixer joined them.

"No weapons. Stealth. Azzo, you first."

He rubbed his hands together and set off. Rebecca had not been alone with the Fixer since he approached her at Mama's, and then she had the company of the usual patrons in the vicinity. He lit a joint, the skunked earthy scent unfazed him. Rebecca hated it. Should they speak? What would she say anyway? A shout above their heads saved her from chatting useless dribble. Another few breaths passed, followed by a booming thud. She imagined a scuffle. Had Azzo made it to the room?

"You should go."

Still, Rebecca didn't understand, but she didn't dare challenge the Fixer, especially after Carlo. She took the stairs with ease. The second story was all mezzanine—she assumed the meeting room had to be above her. As she found a staircase, another thought came to mind. Was the Fixer wrong? Carlo was suffering. How could Lorenzo have helped him? Even with stitches, he'd have bled out.

She stood at the end of a hallway. Rebecca clasped her mouth to prevent a gasp escaping her mouth a second time. The hallway was filled with figures in black surcoats, hats, and chiffon head sacks, standing in perfect stillness. Some faced the rectangular windows drenched in moonlight, others stared at her. Her shock subsided; there was no way they were real people. What stealth test would this have been if they could see her immediately?

To be safe, she darted from shadow to shadow, hugging the wall beneath the windows and avoiding open doorways. She tapped a figure, and as suspected, it was a marble statue. Even the busts were dressed in black chiffon sacks and hats. Deciding the bust needed them less than she did, Rebecca slipped a hat and mask and put them on. Now, she'd be dressed in all black. One advantage.

The carpet padded her steps. She faltered at a doorway. Peering through, she found another staircase. The next floor was staged, largely the same, except the windows were draped. She found a bust on the floor. Behind it lay Azzo. He was breathing but unconscious. She counted at least five razor-thin slices on his limbs and torso. No one in sight. She whispered his name. An err.

Two Sons she thought were statues lunged in her direction, both swiping through the air. She pressed against Azzo's inert body to avoid the first spear but wasn't as fortunate with the second. The Son's blade nicked her shoulder. She melted into the shadows behind another statue and the assailants returned to a frozen sentry. She waited for her heart rate to slow, her breath much too loud to press on.

Past another open door, this room was filled with desks and bookshelves, but no Saint Sebastian portrait. She remembered the martyr was depicted nude, staked to a tree, and littered with arrows. The wooden floorboard creaked. No carpet to muffle her steps. Three guards appeared, two from their places in the hallway and a third emerged from the depths of an offshoot room. She dropped to a knee but took another two slices. Biting her lip to stifle the pain, her eyes watered.

The Sons returned to their silent posts.

The penultimate floor was riddled in light. Every torch burned, the window frames bare to a cloudless night sky. Rebecca blinked to adjust. In the center of the hallway stood a single cloaked figure. She had no choice but to walk past. It remained immobile. The light and emptiness made her feel dread. Onto the final staircase, she arrived on the top floor. The hallway was pitch black, or nearly so. She understood the previous floor's purpose now—to obscure her vision. She couldn't discern a foot ahead.

That trick cost her. Panic set in as she bumped into an open door. A spear lanced the wall in front of her. Grateful the Sons' vision was as obscured as her own, she waited for the smudge of movement to reset. Although, as the Son tugged the spear free, the blade nicked her. How many Sons littered these halls? Or did they follow her as she ascended? There would be no way she could remember how many tally marks to add to her wall.

Rebecca groped in the dark until she rounded a corner and the moon reappeared. San Sebastian lay ahead. Was his painting wet? His visage appeared runny, out of focus. She stepped forward and the floor slanted. She righted her head to maintain a steadfastness she could not keep. So close. She must reach the room. Rebecca uttered a confused nonsensical word aloud and a flurry of Sons launched into motion. Mustering her wits, she ran. Her vision warbled, so she didn't know if she met her goal. A spear tagged her, this time the blunt end. She dropped to her knees, head to the ground shortly thereafter. Her vision blurred and she blacked out.

***

Rebecca awoke in her cell. Not for the pounding in her head, she was relieved to be alive. Stumbling into the tunnel, she winced at the jovial banter emanating from the armory. She stepped inside and wished she was still unconscious.

A dozen men chuckled, exchanging bawdy humor. One balanced a spear butt on his palm while another tried to knock it off, and a knot of black-clad ruffians raced Father Lorenzo in draining flagons of wine. The sense of joy felt jarring in the cold armory, a space she associated with the sarcastic Franco, somber Lorenzo, silent Behemoth. The Fixer, of course, was another matter.

She marched directly to Lorenzo, cutting a wide berth of Franco and Azzo. The latter was holding court with a few barefaced youths.

"You poisoned us."

Lorenzo wiped his mouth with the back of his hand.

"I poisoned you."

"How long was I out?"

"Four hours or so."

Rebecca took note of the purple and mauve streaks on his hands and felt silly nodding at a blind man.

"Carlo used a poisoned blade."

Lorenzo drank more wine, a twisted snarl on his lip.

"A technique for training. Not a contract."

Rebecca snorted. "What kind of hypocrisy is that?"

"Sons don't use weapons of the enemy," one of Lorenzo's drinking buddies mumbled.

The double standard fell a peg or two of concern at the comment. Had she heard him correctly?

"You should be proud," Lorenzo said. "You reached the meeting room. A valiant effort."

Mindful not to allow her impertinence overshadow a victory, she said, "Few have offered such a compliment to me, let alone have spoken it aloud."

Lorenzo grunted. "Better than Azzo."

She searched for him over the gathering, and they made eye contact. Azzo nodded.

"Are they all . . . you all . . . Sons?"

The drinking partner confirmed it with a laugh. She scanned the room—another eleven to etch on her wall.

Azzo, Franco, and a barefaced youth joined them.

"And we're ready to shove off," the fresh-faced youth said, "if you are, Rebecca."

"Shove off?"

"Rebecca!" Azzo said, gripping the Son around the shoulders. "This is Tommaso. We sailed together out of Naples. He's the first mate now."

"First mate?"

Tommaso laughed. "Of *The Corsican*. Our galley."

8

THE CORSICAN

Tommaso would not shut up. Rebecca glared at Azzo as if it were his fault for knowing such a talkative man. They followed the first mate to a straight and brief tunnel that revealed a dock. Gentle waves lapped the dinghies and junks moored to the Sons' private waterway. The sea beckoned underneath the portcullis in the distance.

"I need to finish unloading our wares for the market," Tommaso said. "Azzo said you might want to come along. I could use the help."

Azzo plunked into a dinghy and offered Rebecca his hand. Her fellow trainee knew her well already. The sea compelled her. The boat rocked with her first step, so she grabbed Azzo. With a laugh, Tommaso untied them and, nimble as a cat, jumped in.

"Want to row?"

Rebecca accepted the challenge. She took the center plank facing Azzo, Tommaso in the bow. With a shove, they were floating free. Rebecca gripped the oars. The dinghy rocked side to side, taking on a splash of water.

"Steady on!" Tommaso called.

"I've never done this before!"

"Nothing to fret." Azzo reassured her. "Keep your hands level."

Rebecca muscled the wooden spokes to comply. They leveled and she took her first stroke. Glad they weren't in the port yet, she fell into an easy rhythm before reaching the arched exit. With a heave, sweat gathered on her back and face. Open air. They glided on calm waters while passing the port's promenade. The Genoan fleet floated in eerie silence. Naval sentries patrolled the docks but took no notice or did not care for their presence. They passed a few junks, sailors tending to the marina.

The water, an onyx mass, twinkled under starlight. She closed her eyes and inhaled. Creaking wood. Rustle of cloth flags in a modest breeze. When she opened them, Azzo was smiling at her. She couldn't resist and allowed herself a grin. Tommaso jabbered on in hushed tones over her shoulder. Periodically, he instructed her to pull harder with her right or left hand to steer them on course.

As they arced starboard, other junks and rowboats departed the promenade. Like them, they held mixed company, but the women did not row. Like bees back to the hive, they were docking with the naval galleys.

"What are they doing?"

Tommaso and Azzo must have noticed, but neither offered a response. Rebecca held the oars in her lap and drew her blade.

"Rebecca!"

"I'll flip this dinghy," she said. "Do not lie to me, Azzo."

Tommaso said, "Rebecca, we're going to the Son's galley, *The Corsican*. The men have shore leave and we have more wares to unload. That's all."

"Those women are prostitutes?"

"For the navy," Tommaso said. "They send their jolly boats in for the company. Only the captain is aboard *The Corsican* tonight and he is expecting me. Here, I'll row us there." With some effort, they switched seats. "You can hold your blade to me, if you wish."

Rebecca felt more in control of the situation as she accepted Tommaso's offer. Concern plastered Azzo's face. She felt it was genuine, although it annoyed her that he had the privilege of not worrying how this late-night venture may be perceived by a woman.

After clearing the fleet, they sidled parallel to the dark side of the ship. Nothing but sea lay on their other side. Tommaso drew in an oar and tied them off on a metal ring. He bunnied along a metal ladder ascending the side of the vessel.

"Rebecca?" Azzo asked. "Stay here if you'd like. I can pass the crates down to you."

She sheathed her blade. "I'm coming."

At the top, Azzo swung a leg over the gunwale and offered a hand. Her ego refused to allow her to fall back into the sea, so she accepted.

"Welcome aboard, Rebecca!" Tommaso said. "Proud merchant vessel of the maritime republic and trading galley for the Sons of Saint George."

Azzo inspected a palette of crates. Rebecca ran her hand along the lines secured on the gunwale. The mizzenmast and main mast sails were furled, but the triangular Genoese flag, red with the thin white cross, rippled in the wind. The claw-and-spear crest was painted on the crow's nest. Doors towards the stern of the poop deck opened.

"Tommaso, what are you doing?"

The first mate rushed forward. "Captain, I'm unloading the final crates. I brought some help."

"Generous of you." The captain's voice rolled through the night air like gravel beneath cart wheels. He approached the trio in a slow march, inspecting the new faces on his ship. Streaks of white painted his beard, tied and twisted into matted bunches. His skin, leathery from the sun, melded into the oily folds of his black long coat and tricorn hat. Rebecca thought his presence alone put Thibault the Corsair to shame.

"Why not have the longshoreman finish?"

"The men needed leave. I volunteered so they'd have more time ashore." Tommaso introduced Azzo and Rebecca. "This is Captain Marchetto."

Marchetto squinted at the guests. "I promoted you to first mate, not nursemaid." He pursed his lips and put his hands on his belt near a curved sword unlike the ones Rebecca learned about in the armory.

"Yes, captain."

"Come to my cabin."

The trio followed him through the doors. He stared at the gallery windows and spoke to the glass. Maps and quills littered his meeting desk along with a sextant and compass. A massive ledger lay open with the heading "Captain's Log."

"Care to earn some coin, recruits?"

Rebecca and Azzo looked to Tommaso, who shrugged.

"Come," Marchetto continued. He offered a looking glass over his shoulder. Rebecca stepped forward since Azzo froze. She took the glass and aimed it where the captain pointed. With an eye on another merchant vessel flying unfamiliar colors, she could feel his gaze resting on her.

"Those are merchants from Alexandria. Sea rats. We tangled with them leaving Algiers last summer. There's too damn many of 'em. I'd like nothing more'n to raid that bedeviled city and set it ablaze. Every ware they sell to the Genoese vendors, is a profit loss for the Sons of Saint George. Get it?"

Rebecca offered Azzo the glass. He inspected the ship.

"What did you have in mind?" Rebecca asked.

Whatever image wavered in Marchetto's mind, he refocused his eyes and inspected Rebecca's face. His gaze made her uncomfortable, but she did not look away.

"What did you say your name was, girlie?"

"Rebecca," she said. "Rebecca Guarna."

He grunted. "Guarna." The captain thudded to a cabinet. He tossed a felt sack onto the desk, the unmistakable jangle of coin rattled around the cabin. "Get aboard. Destroy their cargo."

Azzo laughed. "What about the Fixer? We can't do that without his permission."

Marchetto drew his curved blade and pressed it against Azzo's chest. "On my honor as a member of the Sons, I can do whatever I damn well please, boy! Especially aboard my vessel. Rustichello's domain is his hiding hole beneath the palazzo. Mine, the open sea. Do you question that?"

Azzo shook his head. "No, captain!"

"Oh," Marchetto said. He chuckled, the gravel bass jangling like the coins on the desk. Rebecca pressed her blade to his ribs, catching him unaware.

"Captain," Tommaso said. "Rebecca. Allow me to counsel reason."

Rebecca dropped her blade after the captain lowered his sword.

"Will you take my offer, Guarna, or not? You can take your friend and my first mate with you."

Azzo returned to the other side of the table to consult Rebecca out of earshot of the captain. "We can walk away."

Captain Marchetto laughed. Tommaso's expression remained neutral. Rebecca considered the offer. She didn't want to piss off the Fixer, but Marchetto said he had less control on the sea.

"Your men are ashore?" Rebecca said.

"A perfect alibi," Marchetto said. "No doubt they've spilled from the palazzo and are frequenting every brothel in Genoa. Consider this—that ship is operating on a skeleton crew. Their men are on shore leave as well."

Rebecca sheathed her blade. She raised a brow at Azzo. Before he could argue, she asked the captain, "How should we destroy their wares?"

"Burn it, dump it, steal it—I don't care!"

Back at the dinghy, Azzo asked, "How will we get aboard without them noticing?"

Rebecca knew the answer and before the men and their lecherous, simpleminded schemes could voice it. "We have the perfect cover," she said. "Me."

***

Tommaso rowed them back towards the naval fleet and around a galley. Once out of sight, they rowed towards their target, giving the appearance they came from the promenade. Rebecca didn't question why or how a lady's tunic and overdress were aboard *The Corsican* but changed before setting off. She sat in the bow while

Azzo whispered a litany of ways this sabotage mission could go sideways.

"Oh, shut it, Azzo!"

Tommaso agreed. No use fretting on a charted course until the sea swallowed you and the planks splintered. The youth was growing on Rebecca.

Pretending to be a courtesan was within her wheelhouse. If Father Lorenzo could poison them with prejudice, then they could sneak about an enemy galley and destroy the cargo. The Fixer be damned also. Not until they made final approach did Rebecca consider the captain's plan omitted one detail—what cargo did the Alexandrians carry?

"Let's do this," Tommaso said.

He hailed the merchant vessel. The night watch held a torch and peered at them over the gunwale. He shouted in a foreign tongue. Tommaso replied in the same language, miming and pointing at Rebecca.

What could go wrong?

After more shouting and quiet deliberation, drag lines were tossed over and the boys affixed them to the bow and stern. The merchants hoisted the dinghy level with the deck and assisted Rebecca aboard. Azzo and Tommaso were forced to stay aboard. She didn't show her concern, but it was their first hiccup. Not anticipating going alone, she'd need to figure this out with haste.

The ship wasn't much different than Captain Marchetto's galley. Rigging, masts, and crates. The night watchmen led her to the doors beneath the forecastle. A wave of sound shocked her as the tween deck bustled with activity. The commotion—or more accurately, a party—disproved the captain's assertion of a skeleton crew. Rebecca hid her fear behind her most charming smile.

Barrels of ale flowed and sailors danced with one another. Rebecca was pleased to see other courtesans entertaining the Alexandrians, wooing their coin as payment before escorting them to private quarters. Captain Marchetto said to find the cargo, search between the deck and hold. Rebecca pretended to know a few of the entertainers and skirted her way to their group.

Safety in numbers. She struck up a conversation and joined in the laughter. No one seemed to understand one another, so the language of the night was physical.

Rebecca tossed back the barley ale and joined in the dance. She fit right in. Genuinely enjoying the night, she waved off the more aggressive sailors until she spotted her target. Hanging on the edge of the festivity, a sailor swayed alone. She looped a hand through his arm and he guffawed with sincere joy at her company. There, near midship, was a staircase. Rebecca inched them closer.

He made some grabbing gesture at his face and said, "Bella." He pointed at her. She thanked him for the compliment and found his accent stilted. He spoke in some southern, regional dialect reminiscent of Azzo's parlance. Rebecca grabbed a wooden jug of ale and shoved it in his hand. Once downstairs, the drunken sailor became more confident. She giggled at his searching hands and swatted them away playfully. From this level, the stomping above echoed and commingled with fornicating below. Rebecca spotted her target—three large bins filled with a beige grain.

Her consort took a sip of ale, and she encouraged the entire jug back until he drained it. With a laugh, his eyelids drooped and he stumbled. Rebecca also laughed and helped him rest against a bin. He reached for her to join him but passed out.

"That was easy."

Rebecca ran around the bins, looking for a solution. If she set fire to it, the innocent women upstairs could get hurt, or die. She couldn't steal the bins because they had to have held hundreds of stones worth of millet. She stopped running around and tried to consider another solution.

"Rebecca!" a voice whispered from behind her.

She jumped. Azzo's face peered into the hold from a porthole. Clutching her chest, she sprinted over to him.

"What're you doing, Azzo?"

"I came to warn you! Tommaso says to hurry. The navy arrived—routine harbor inspections. Are you almost finished?"

She explained the predicament and watched him work through the problem while hanging on the metal clamps. The ship rocked and her stomach turned. If the navy boarded them, she would be trapped or swept into the group to be ejected from the ship.

"Dump it!"

"I can't lift these bins," she said. "Are you blind?"

Azzo scoffed. He stuck his arm through the porthole and pointed at the wall. "Those leather sheets are for filling the bins. They act like a funnel. Attach the eye loops onto the bin and fold an end through that porthole. Use the pulley to hoist one side and tilt the grain out to sea."

Rebecca glared at Azzo as he smiled and nodded, pleased at his own idea. His optimism annoyed her. Yet it may be her best option.

She sprinted to the far wall and unhooked a sheet. It was the same width as the bin with metal grommets along the lining. They matched the hooks on the end of each bin! She fastened it, Azzo encouraging her along the way. Rebecca pushed the opposite end through the porthole on the starboard side. Back near Azzo, she jumped to catch the pulley rope. Tying it off with the bin hovering complete, but how to tip it?

Before she could solve that problem, her amorous sailor woke. She ran back around the bin before he could realize what was happening and kicked him in the head. He flopped to the ground unconscious.

"Nice kick," Azzo whispered. "Rebecca, hurry."

Rebecca grunted in frustration. She took a breath. As if it made the most sense all along, she jumped onto the bin and grabbed the rim. Her body weight tipped it enough and the millet began flowing over the leather and through the porthole. The pulley ropes creaked but held. Hanging with her toes grazing the floor, she prayed it didn't snap. Azzo cheered. When most of the millet was drained, she let go. The bin wobbled, much lighter, and the pulley squeaked in relief. She rigged the second bin with the sheet and hoisted it into the air, repeating the process.

The music stuttered and the stomping became less rhythmic. Had the navy boarded? She held on until the second bin couldn't be emptied anymore.

"One more!" she said.

"Good! Get out as soon as it's empty."

Rebecca hadn't even considered that. When the third bin was hoisted, and Rebecca hung on its lip, a sailor and courtesan emerged from the hold. She smiled at the postcoital pair. The sailor shouted. The commotion upstairs must have distracted reinforcements, but he drew a sword. She let go of the half-emptied bin and squared off. He swiped. She ducked. The courtesan shrieked and sprinted upstairs.

Rebecca and the sailor circled the bins, feinting either direction. Her faux lover stirred from the floor. As he lumbered to his feet, Rebecca tackled him into the sailor. She jumped back onto the bin. As the two men fumbled, she successfully finished her job. With a quick glance through the porthole, now devoid of Azzo's face, Rebecca made for the stairs. She got halfway when a hand grabbed her ankle. She slammed her knees and yelled. With a donkey kick, she was free.

As she suspected, the Genoese navy port inspectors arrived and crashed the party. She was directed topside. Looking like she was supposed to be there, she steadied her pace to a walk and made it to the deck. Sailors were lined up showing safe passage scrolls to the inspectors, while the courtesans and their handlers were shoving off in the jolly boat. Tommaso's dinghy was no longer visible port side, but she couldn't imagine they abandoned her. Since joining the Sons of Saint George, she had been involved with two acts of piracy. They could have left her. She advanced to the gunwale as the sailor from below erupted onto the deck.

In the confusion, he broke through the crowd and charged, short sword drawn. Throwing all caution to the wind, Rebecca sprinted. In her final stride, the blade tip sliced her back, so sharp she knew it happened not by the sting of the wound, but the fresh air meeting her skin. Rebecca jumped. As she dove, upside down, she spotted Tommaso and Azzo severing the drag lines from the dinghy.

The plunge into the frigid water forced another silent prayer from her lips. Back bleeding liberally, she hoped her companions would fish her from the "drink," as Tommaso called it, because Rebecca couldn't swim.

9

THE FIRST CONTRACT

Lorenzo stitched her wound while she laid belly-down in Captain Marchetto's medical bay. The cabin held rough tools such as saws and braces for amputations and exotic liquids in vials such as mercury to treat syphilis. Azzo heated coals in a bed warmer and Tommaso wrapped it in thick burlap. They draped the heated fabric from Rebecca's feet to midsection to restore her heat. Marchetto barked them away once the priest had all he needed for the procedure.

The cold plunge, which did wonders to numb the pain, was wearing off. She squeezed her hands into fists, which still shook. The navy's inspection timing of the Alexandrian vessel was miraculous. She learned Azzo had dove in to recover her. Vinegar stung her back and Rebecca bit a roll of cloth from a prone, shirtless position. She yelped as the hook and fishing twine pierced her neck.

"You're doing well, Rebecca," Lorenzo said. "More wine?"

She groaned. "No, get on with it."

"Lucky Azzo retrieved me from the palazzo and not Rustichello. He's horrid with stitching."

When Azzo and Tommaso dragged her into Marchetto's medical bay, shivering and cursing, she begged Azzo to avoid alerting the Fixer. The sword scraped her midsection over her shoulder blade and curved onto her lower neck. Marchetto forced a flagon of wine to her lips to calm the nerves while Azzo retrieved the priest.

Rebecca grimaced as he snipped the final stitch. "Aren't you the Son's medical expert?"

"It had nothing to do with that sack of coin Marchetto offered you?"

Rebecca forgot about their pay. The sabotage was a success. The captain cackled like a fool when Tommaso relayed their exploit. Lorenzo dabbed honey along his stitchwork.

"In truth, father, I had Carlo in mind."

The dabbing paused. "Ah, I see. You will not succumb to this."

"Good." Rebecca untensed her shoulders. "Thank you."

"Yes, good," he said, clearing his throat.

Rebecca wasn't sure he would come with the festivities ashore and the Sons' debauchery. When the drink got a hold on someone, in her experience, it took root. Revealed the true nature of good people. Her distrust in men like Father Lorenzo di Costa was not unfounded. A modest skepticism was essential to preserve her own fragile self-respect. Even if the priest dispelled her reticence of clergymen at each turn.

"Well, I hate to disturb the mind of my injured patient, but you should know now rather than later—the Fixer intended you and Azzo to destroy the Alexandrian cargo."

Rebecca propped herself onto her elbows, emboldened by the wine and Lorenzo's partial blindness.

"He what? Why didn't he just tell us?"

Lorenzo shielded her bare chest with the ripped tunic.

"Consider it a test of your temperament."

Rebecca scoffed. "I could have died!"

Lorenzo gathered the equipment. "You did not." Using his walking stick to balance, he left Rebecca at the table. She sat, careful not to stretch her left side more than necessary, and pulled the tunic overhead.

"Father?"

"Yes?"

"Azzo and I—may we keep Marchetto's payment?"

Lorenzo laughed and shook his head. "Will be our secret." As he stepped over the lintel, Rebecca had another thought.

"And father?"

He turned his head.

"Please don't tell *him* about my injury."

Lorenzo knocked the top of the stick on the cabin's doorframe and left her alone to finish dressing.

Topside, Rebecca joined the captain as he supervised Tommaso and Azzo loading the final crates in a jolly boat. They'd need the extra space now with Father Lorenzo. The captain gave her the felt sack and said, "Guarna."

Pleased, she couldn't wait to divvy it between her and Azzo back ashore. The men assisted her over the gunwale and aboard the landing boat. Marchetto squinted at her the entire time. The way he said her name, as if in disbelief, unsettled Rebecca. The injury and the pay distracted her from caring more than she needed.

Azzo rowed. Rebecca leaned one hand against the splash board. "What's in the crates?"

Tommaso flicked open a blade and wedged it between the lid. Hairy, green flower buds emitted an earthen scent. Rebecca rubbed her hand over the bundle, packed tightly in the crate. The whiskered plants were more rough and less wooly.

"Is this what the Fixer smokes?"

Tommaso laughed and Father Lorenzo *tsk*ed.

"Calls it 'hashisha,'" Tommaso said. He patted another box. "We sell the stalks for rope, fabric, tinderboxes. The navy always needs rope. Textile merchants haggle for it, too."

Rebecca smelled a conical flower. "The Fixer found a purpose for the buds."

Tommaso resealed the crate. Back through the portcullis and moored on the dock, the Sons already unloaded the other crates before their tangle on the Alexandrian vessel. They disembarked as the Sons who had shore leave stumbled, bleary-eyed and disheveled, to the jolly boat. Rebecca and Azzo received a round of applause and claps on the back. Rebecca bit her inner lip so hard, she drew blood. Yet she was pleased with the praise. After all parties were deboarded and boarded, Rebecca spotted a curious exchange when Azzo tossed his friend the mooring line.

Tommaso pointed across his chest with two fingers, then gripped the air, fashioning his fist into the shape of a *C*, and finally, pointed his thumb upwards. The other Sons didn't notice, and when Tommaso caught Rebecca's quizzical gaze, he dropped his hand in haste.

Back in the tunnel, Rebecca stayed on Azzo's heels all the way to his cell. She nudged him inside, showing him the sack. He closed the door behind her.

"Great work out there, Rebecca. Let's count it—"

Rebecca shoved him in the chest. "The fuck was that?"

His naivete was showing again. The same pained mask from her bet against his life. The blow jostled her tender torso and neck, but it felt good to inflict pain on another. The tricks and the secrets. Where could she expect honesty in Genoa?

"Rebecca, what are you talking about?"

She mimicked the gestures as best she could. Azzo flushed.

"You could trust me, you know. I helped you with the millet."

"I don't trust you. Not you, not that stupid boy, not the Fixer."

Azzo sat on his cot while she paced. "Hand signals from our sailing days. Tommaso said 'there'd be trouble on *The Corsican*, but nothing to worry about.'" Azzo mimed the same hand gestures.

"What trouble?"

Azzo shrugged. "You saw the Sons—common drunkards. They make the privateers we sailed with look like priests . . . well, not like Father Lorenzo. Holy ones."

Rebecca turned the sack over. She couldn't sustain the argument after their ordeal. They counted five ducats, twenty-two silver pfennigs, and seven florins in silence.

"Even split."

"You were injured," Azzo said. "You should—"

"Even split." Rebecca gathered her half and stomped out of Azzo's cell. She longed for solitude and sleep but needed to hide her pay. The rocks from the storeroom near the Fixer's office could work. Once she paid her debt, and survived training, she wanted to keep her options open. This surprise pay should not go to the Sons, but her future, whatever that may be. She tucked the coin sack under her cot for now and started towards the storeroom. Franco and Azzo emerged from the latter's cell, intercepting her stride.

"Guarna," Franco said. "Fixer needs to see you."

With no choice but to fall in line, Rebecca kept some distance from Azzo so he wouldn't be tempted to engage her. They passed Behemoth standing sentry outside the Fixer's study and she could tell Azzo tried to get her attention, no doubt to evoke a smile from their previous bet.

The Fixer smoothed a scroll onto his desk and propped it open with candleholders so he could light a joint. Franco cleared his throat when they entered and the assassin-master dismissed him.

"The Lombard League sent word. Come. Sit."

They sat in silence, Rebecca on the edge of her seat to avoid pressing against her wound, while the Fixer traced the curvature of the letters with a thumb. He finished his joint.

"Did Marchetto pay you?" He asked Rebecca.

"No."

Lying to the Fixer was easier than breathing. She prayed Azzo would not deceive her.

As if the Fixer read her mind, he asked, "Azzo, did he pay you?"

"No. Fortunate to escape with our lives."

Shut up, Azzo.

"You have three days. Kidnap Giuseppe Banco and bring him here. The merchant is planning to escape Milan in three days. The League wants him questioned."

The Fixer dismissed them to continue training with Father Lorenzo. Rebecca appreciated not being left in the dark for this contract even if she needed to split the payment with Azzo once again. The pay, if they were successful, was substantive.

"Three hundred gold ducats for the della Torre sympathizer," the Fixer said. "When we extract what they need."

A third of her payment to the Fixer. Azzo's secret hand signals with Tommaso were all but forgotten.

The next three days consisted of more stealth training through the palace at night followed by hours of throwing daggers in the armory. Straw-filled sacks of cloth were jammed atop scattered logs throughout the training room. The weapons racks were dragged to one side. She didn't kill any of the patrons in the stews by throwing a blade. This felt like the first real training exercise. She felt dumb at the memory of missing the naval officer on the slab.

Lorenzo observed. He coached. He yelled and swatted with his stick as one blade after another clanged around onto the floor. Azzo was the quicker draw, releasing a blade before she got the comfort of her grip. After two or three rounds, though, Rebecca proved to be the better aim.

During evening stealth routines, scabs still itchy, fine slices from before their sabotage mission, Rebecca asked Lorenzo about Banco.

"He's a spice trader," Lorenzo said. "The League must want control of his routes."

Rebecca felt like a swindler. The Fixer demanded his lost pay. She failed miserably at kidnapping Lorenzo in Pavia. If she failed, she may have to yet turn over her earned coin from Marchetto. Each evening, Lorenzo reapplied fresh honey to her wound. Old wounds, hollow scars came to mind.

The Breaking Wheel. Thoughts of Mama, of escaping the convent, and Leo. She'd be traveling backwards by going to Milan. There was nothing to be done about those worries now. She owed a debt she must shed. Lorenzo insisted she needed to rebuild her gumption, so she received extra pork, broth, and a warm loaf of bread every day. A full belly and the knowledge that she'd be wearing a black sack to conceal her identity put the dread aside.

Six hours before Azzo and Rebecca were to ride north with Franco as their handler for the operation, Rebecca was escorted into the Fixer's study. Father Lorenzo leaned on the windowsill.

Without pretense, the Fixer said, "Azzo is dead."

Lorenzo stared at a fixed point in the corner. Rebecca's shoulders knotted. She met with Azzo that morn after stealth training. He hadn't fared well. Lorenzo fetched Behemoth to apply honey to his new slices. The spears! They were laced with poison. Would the Sons have him killed for poor performance during training? Azzo wasn't that inept.

"The spear."

Father Lorenzo nodded. "Yes, he succumbed to the poison."

Heat rose in Rebecca's face. Her hand twitched to her thigh holster. The act wasn't lost on the Fixer. He placed both palms on his desk and narrowed his eyes, goading her to act rashly.

"You killed him," Rebecca said. "You all killed him."

Azzo wanted to become a Son—she was forced to. He wanted to be her friend, and the Fixer's announcement rang indifferent.

"Rebecca," Lorenzo said. "The Sons may be complicit, but not at fault. Death awaits us all, especially those without the fortitude to persist."

Rebecca kicked the book pedestal over. "Don't you dare imply he was weak, Lorenzo."

The Fixer stood. Behemoth filled the doorframe. Backed into the corner, Rebecca drew her blade.

"I won't do it. I won't kidnap Banco."

"Volta," the Fixer said, discouraging his sentry from responding to her outburst. So his name was "Volta," not Franchesca. The losing bet she'd never collect from Azzo.

"Azzo chose this path," the Fixer continued. "I own you, lest you forget. I may collect my due or send you back to the judges in Milan any time I desire."

"Your threats don't scare me, Rustichello."

It was the Fixer's turn to trash his study. He smashed a clay pot of ink against the wall above Rebecca's heads. She felt the beads of oak gall splatter her head and tunic. She held her ground.

"As sure as hell and damnation awaits us Sons, I swear it, you will fulfill this contract. No amount of fucking will release you from my debt, Rebecca. Marchetto's pittance isn't even enough to buy your freedom."

Rebecca snarled at the Fixer. Bastard. With his little boys and their secret club. From the safety of his study, he sat there with an unlit joint between his fingers and judged her for a past she would never have chosen.

"We are blades for hire, Rebecca. There has been no offense, no irreparable damage. Bring me Banco."

She wanted to sheath her blade, but Volta the Behemoth stood too near. Father Lorenzo cleared his throat. "Give us a moment, Rustichello. I need to warm my bones. Rebecca." He offered his elbow.

She accepted it and allowed the priest to lead her from the study. They walked in silence through the atrium. Rebecca thought it bold of Lorenzo to pass scribes, magistrates, and common Genoans in the town hall's midday flurry of activity. Rebecca glared at a portly scribe sprint to the stairs Azzo ascended for stealth training at the twenty-fourth hour last night. He clutched scrolls filled with machinations or trade records, seafaring ventures or contracts.

Father Lorenzo steered her in a wide arc around in the courtyard, passing the port's promenade and pausing to gaze at the palazzo's facade. Artists were painting on scaffolding. Cherubs and golden visages of saints filled the arches on the second and third stories.

"Do you know the story of Saint George?"

Doctor Salvagno never mentioned George in his religious ramblings, but Rebecca knew the fraternity's namesake slayed a dragon.

"He enlisted in the Roman army. A Cappadocian. He rose through the ranks, his valor recognized across the empire as the 'soldier christened by the divine hand of God.' The King of Silene hired him to slay a winged, fire-breathing beast who captured his daughter. He refused the eucharist until he returned home victorious. Had he failed, he would have forfeited the eternal banquet of God's gifts. Spear locked against claw, faith against wanton evil. He returned the princess and his courage shook the foundation of the earth."

Rebecca studied Lorenzo's wizened face for a conviction in his retelling of George's exploits. No matter how brave or ferocious the deed, she struggled to believe what he did.

"I envy his stout heart, father."

Lorenzo guided them towards the sea. "You're wrong."

Rebecca dislodged her arm from Father Lorenzo's elbow. He shook his head and uttered a sigh of exasperation. She didn't realize she offended him. "You doubt my admiration for Saint George?"

"I doubt your lack of conviction." He continued, "You possess the courage to walk towards the great serpent. To vanquish your dragons. You could be a leader among men. The sole daughter of the Sons of Saint George!"

A legacy. A legend. Rebecca mourned her lost child. A lost legacy of sorts. The most authentic continuance of her spirit. Yet the notion the Sons of Saint George could provide more for her than a means to pay a debt appealed to a quieter dream, basked in shadow in the far recesses of her imagination.

They made their way back towards the palace. She sensed he meant for them to reach the stables because they didn't reenter. Father Lorenzo believed in her. Saw potential where others saw an empty vessel. If Azzo was dead, she could at least honor his memory and persist. Gazing upon the fresco, she returned her focus to Banco. Kidnap him. Earn her freedom.

Franco waited in the stables. Rebecca mounted a tawny, her light kit already packed. The priest walked them back outside, guiding the horses by the reins. As he handed Rebecca hers, he lowered his voice so Franco could not hear. His warning caught her by surprise, but before she could question him, Lorenzo slapped her tawny to begin the gallop to Milan.

10

— • —

Banco, the Spice Trader

S talking the piazza mercanti, Milan's central market, felt as comfortable as Rebecca's new tunic and black overcoat. So not comfortable. Franco refused her wish to wear the black chiffon mask and in good counsel—they were among a crowded square midday. Hiding in plain sight was the wiser disguise. Loathe as she was to admit it, Rebecca would have felt more confident operating from a place of certainty with the Sons. Not a full-fledged assassin, no longer a courtesan. Banco, at least, knew his place.

The trader's voice cut above the jabbering hawkers. He yelled at sheepish vendors as customers haggled. Mounds of viridian, auburn, and sunflower spices in burlap sacks perfumed the market. Rebecca pretended to be interested in the butcher's cuts while Franco examined their target from the baker's stall.

Rebecca kept tabs on the fellow Son as she stalked Banco. Franco's main priority was to observe her, which muddied Father Lorenzo's warning.

Beware the enemy.

She valued his counsel, but who was her enemy? Or had he meant the enemy of the Sons? The Lombard League? With Azzo gone, her isolation grew. Rebecca never had a friend. Leo couldn't fill that role, not with their history and his intentions. Zita doted on her; Maria and Paula were petty extensions of Mama. Confused, a tug at her forearm broke her concentration.

"Rebecca?"

Zita, the matronly courtesan from Mama's brothel, appeared. As if Rebecca's thoughts produced her.

"It is you!" Zita pulled her into a tight embrace. "We thought you died."

Rebecca squirmed free. "Zita, keep your voice down." She peered around but could not spot Franco. Banco still cowed his hawkers. She pulled Zita past a stall and into a side alley. Not that Banco knew her, but she couldn't take a chance at making a scene.

"Rebecca, what are you doing?"

Rebecca smoothed Zita's cape and outer dress. "I can't tell you how it pleases me to see you. Is everything okay at Martina's?"

Zita patted Rebecca's cheek. "Yes, yes. We're all fine. Business is better without that stew killer terrorizing patrons! Your doctor has taken to Paula now that you're gone, though."

What did Zita expect? Rebecca to cry? The last anyone saw of her, Mama had the Signori di Notte lead her to the Breaking Wheel. Of course, Leo did not wait for her to resurface. Zita misunderstood the change behind Rebecca's eyes, because she gripped her shoulders in dear concern.

As Rebecca considered setting her straight, a black gloved hand curled around Zita's mouth, stifling a terror-filled scream from alerting the market. Franco rammed his blade into Zita's back, twisting until the matronly courtesan expired.

"What the hell are you doing?"

Franco rested Zita's body against the wall with care and held a single finger in Rebecca's face. His dagger, drenched in crimson, hung at the ready in his other hand. She faltered. Rebecca witnessed his accuracy before and did not wish to die today.

"This is your fault," Franco said, shoving her back towards the market. "Do not allow Banco to escape. I will dispose of her."

Rebecca couldn't argue, but also she couldn't move.

"Go!"

A cold sweat prickled Rebecca's face and neck. A quick backwards glance showed Franco dragging Zita to a doorway. She retched. A passerby jumped aside to avoid the stomach splatter.

Recovering, she stumbled through the market. She spotted Banco pressing on towards the cart road. She hung back but kept him in sight as he strode beyond a group of city dredgers. A section of the breaker wall guiding the Naviglio Pavese needed repair.

She found Banco about to board his carriage. A man in a crimson surcoat whispered in his ear, near enough that Rebecca thought they were embracing. He patted Banco's belly and the trader laughed. Her quarry loaded into the carriage, and the man in the crimson surcoat waved the driver on. Rebecca held her breath. She hid behind a corner to confirm her fear. Doctor Salvagno nodded to a passing group as he crossed the canal bridge, away from Rebecca's target.

Enemies indeed.

With no time to lose, Rebecca sprinted across the alley, back towards the market to collect her horse. If she rode past the non-stewhouse inns and taverns, she would reach the southern gate before Banco did in his carriage.

She urged her beast along between the taverns, marveling the horse's speed and strength. Weary travelers jumped aside to avoid her charge. The horse path ran perpendicular to the cypress-lined carriage road and Rebecca was ahead. Her goal was in reach; she passed through the gate without obstruction.

The Ticino River flowed southeast, so Rebecca banked away from the water. Barreling through strawberry trees, mud flecked her vision. Iron gray clouds dropped fresh rain.

Hidden among a hemlock grove, she calmed her tawny. From this vantage point, it would be impossible for her to miss the carriage. She dismounted and drew two blades. While Rebecca knelt in the mud, the rain turned to sheets. Sodden clopping reached her ears. An advance guard didn't ride with Banco, so her only obstacle was the driver. She could intimidate him and avoid bloodshed.

Rebecca barred the path. As she launched the first passatore, intending to scare the driver, she spotted a mauve and green boutonniere on his lapel. The blade landed in his shoulder by mistake.

Committed now, she sprinted at the slowing horses. Launching another blade, this time, from near enough killing the man.

She climbed atop the front seat and gathered her blades. The spice trader had ample time to arm himself. Rebecca needed to disarm and bind him. The extra horses would aid in delivering him back to Genoa.

Rebecca ripped the door open and jumped inside with a guttural yell. Dressed in finery, a chaperon hat of expensive fabric, silver rings adorning fingers, Banco slumped on the felt seat. She closed the door and sat across from a dead man.

He could have been asleep or in a drunken stupor, but his chest didn't rise or fall. She punched the door. If she couldn't kidnap him, she'd at least make a profit. Rebecca snatched the rings from his fingers and tore open his coat. His coin purse held some heft, so she pocketed it. Banco had no need. Should she return to Milan and find Franco or head straight to Genoa?

As she left the carriage, she decided to cut the horses free. Walking back around towards her tawny, she didn't hear the footsteps behind her in the mud until it was too late. With a thud, a burst of stars obscured her vision as a black bag slipped over her head.

***

Rebecca's lungs expanded rapidly, terror flooding her mind. Her last memory was slopping around in the mud. Now, torchlight flickered through the black cloth bag obscuring her vision. She turned her head side to side. The muscles in her neck and shoulders hurt as well. Unsure how long she was unconscious, her wrists were tied behind her back and ankles bound to the legs of a chair.

Feet shuffled somewhere to her right. The figure shifted past her concealed sight line. Squinting did nothing to reveal their presence. A booming, baritone of a voice rattled her eardrums.

"Confess, woman. Who hired you to kill Giuseppe Banco?"

Banco. That's right. He was her target. The images of his limp figure came back to her. She didn't recognize the voice. Shallow breaths sucked the cloth against her nostrils.

A hand gripped the chair and plunged her backwards, her world turned horizontal. Blood rushed to her sinus cavity, pressure mounted behind her eye sockets. Somewhere to her left, water was being displaced and dribbled onto the floor. The muted light flickered.

"Who hired you?"

Rebecca wiggled clasped fingers and toes, her sole resistance. The silence yawned and the torture began.

Water poured over her face, permeating the bag and invading each nostril. She yelped, which was an error. The liquid seeped inside her mouth and throat. Gagging, Rebecca could not draw breath. Shaking her head did nothing to prevent the searing pain.

The water stopped. The chair legs were back on the floor. Water beaded on her cheeks and drained through the cloth. She choked and spluttered. She needed to avoid the water again. "He was already dead."

"Lies. We saw you kill the driver. Who hired you?"

Beware the enemy.

Lorenzo's warning nagged at her predicament. Who was torturing her and could she resist them forever? How long until she succumbed?

The chair was dropped backwards again and Rebecca screamed and shook to no effect. The water clogged her cavities. Choking. Her lungs seared.

"We will kill your partner," the voice warned as it righted her again. The water took much longer to seep out of her nose and ears. Rebecca struggled to shake the cloth from her mouth.

Was Franco's life worth saving? He killed Zita. She might still survive this if she turned him over.

Brain on fire, saliva coating her tongue, viscous and thick, Rebecca gagged. She mumbled, "I work alone."

A hollow laugh. "I will ask you but once more," the voice said. The chair dropped back. "Who hired you?"

For whatever reason, her choice in the Fixer's study—*train and pay me back or be returned to the judges*—came to mind. That being the case, she had nothing to lose. Now, she had a path, but would die before amounting to more. The decision was simple. Rebecca clamped her mouth shut, drawing what breath she could through her nose.

The water stifled and burned. She uttered a silent prayer to a God she did not know as she felt her consciousness leaving again. And then, it stopped.

A splash. A massive hand gripped the top of her head, peeling the bag from her skin, pulling hair with it. She squinted.

Volta the Behemoth stood before her. Waterlogged, her brain didn't register his presence. Had she never heard him speak?

"You?"

Flint scratched behind her and claps echoed in the chamber. Although her sense of smell was still muted, the dank must of hemp buds reached her nose.

"You have no idea how satisfying it is to know you are to be trusted, Rebecca Guarna."

The Fixer walked around, joint clasped between his teeth. Volta lit another torch and leaned against the doorframe. A bucket sat by his feet. Rebecca's stomach turned. The room spun.

Taking a deep drag on the joint, the Fixer slapped Rebecca to keep her awake.

"Saint George was martyred for refusing to sacrifice a lamb to a pagan god. You put the Sons ahead of your own interests."

She struggled against her bonds, wishing to strangle him. She feared all strength left her body though and she'd be useless once freed. He laughed.

"Son of a bitch!"

Fixer snapped at Volta. The guard tossed the Fixer a cloth sack. He dumped it at her feet. Banco's coins and rings.

"We are not common thieves. I'm not training poor brigands, stealing for bread."

Volta cut Rebecca's bonds, one arm at a time.

"Why not kill me then?"

The Fixer continued to patronize her. "I may have use for a daughter yet. Since you allowed Banco to die, I'll be keeping these along with your cut from Marchetto. You understand? To reduce your debt."

Franco appeared in the doorway behind Behemoth. Rebecca struck at her supposed "handler."

"Bastard!"

In her thrashing, she rocked the chair and it toppled sideways. The Fixer raised his brows at Franco, who snarled at her.

"It was your fault the quim died, Rebecca! You jeopardized my operation."

The slam to the flagstone hurt, her body already fighting to stay alert. She howled.

Ignoring Franco, she spoke to the Fixer. "Take my coin, torture me. Double my debt for all I care; let me kill him!"

The Fixer jerked his head at Volta. Behemoth scooped her from the floor, feet still bound. He carried her back to her cell and released her from the chair once inside. No more fight in her, Rebecca crawled to her cot. With Behemoth gone, she cried.

Jerking, ragged sobs racked her throat. Her lungs, waterlogged as they were, rattled inside her chest. The sobs turned to dry heaves, but she wasn't sure when she ate last. This lasted until the gentle drip of condensation cast her into the slippery realm between sleep and consciousness.

Rebecca woke hours later. The tiny basement window at the ceiling of her cell was black. Unfazed by the hard flagstone, Rebecca heard whispers in the tunnel. One resembled that of a woman.

She crawled on her hands and knees to the door. Behemoth hadn't latched it properly. Rebecca forced three fingers in the crack and peered into the dark. Two silhouettes walked past. One was a man of average build in an overcoat, but that only ruled out Behemoth and Lorenzo. The other, decidedly a woman.

Rebecca strained to catch a glimpse of the visitor or a snatch of conversation, but feared being discovered. She pressed an ear in the crack. Maybe she overheard "for this to end" or "coming to an end." She couldn't be certain.

Before further investigation, the man threw his hands in the air and scoffed. He stomped back towards Rebecca's cell. Rebecca flattened herself against the wall and waited until the steps faded. She returned to the crack. The woman stood still. She seemed to be watching the man stomp away. She disappeared into a tunnel. Rebecca shut her door and flopped onto her cot.

11

— • —

SKELETONS BENEATH THE CATHEDRAL

Rebecca allowed herself to wallow for two days and nights. She wrapped her single, rough linen blanket around her shoulders and hugged it to her chest. The faux hug brought her a simple comfort. Volta delivered meals, yet she ignored them. Instead, she etched tallies on her wall. Eleven for the Sons who took shore leave, one for Captain Marchetto on *The Corsican*, and one with Carlo's tally for Azzo. Where to put the woman?

She doubted it even occurred. The midnight exchange in the tunnel could have been a fever dream. After the fear of being drowned and near suffocation, Rebecca questioned her water-logged mind.

"Are you finished moping?" Father Lorenzo stood in the door-way. He took a deep draught of wine and swayed. "Like you, hate you, be indifferent. This game is not personal. Why choose to care what people think of you?"

"I didn't realize my life was a game to you."

He drained the cup and threw it on the ground.

"Well, come on."

Rebecca shed her blanket and followed. She swayed, not realizing how famished her body was. The priest led her to the new tunnel she and Azzo cleared. She hesitated at the mouth, but Lorenzo shoved a torch in her hand and grabbed her arm, hell-bent on pressing forward. Unlike the water passage, this tunnel's floor was still uneven dirt. They both stumbled a few times. Fortunately, their trip was brief.

A draft lifted dust and the subtle scent of incense from the walls and floor. Lorenzo guided Rebecca in a circle, lighting wall mounted candelabras as they went. Between each bracket were stacked rows of coffins. Each was occupied. Not that she had visited numerous crypts in her past, but this one bore no elaborate burial ornaments. No gold-plated decor or hand-painted family insignias adorned each tomb. In the center of the room, three skeletal remains covered large tables.

"We are beneath the cathedral."

Rebecca examined the ceiling. Besides corner joists, there were no indications they were below the church. Another passageway lay across the entryway.

"Father Lorenzo brought me to the crypt beneath the Cathedral of Saint Lorenzo. Do you feel special here?"

His laugh sounded slurred. Lorenzo sauntered to a marble chest and pushed the heavy lid back. He withdrew a sealed clay pot and uncorked it with his teeth. Rebecca accepted it after he took a sip. The wine reheated her throat and stomach.

At closer inspection, each skeleton was in varying degrees of decomposition. One, clean-boned. Meat still clung to the other, tendons clung to joints, skin liked baked parchment. The third still had hair and eyes.

"You share Saint Lorenzo's sense of humor," Lorenzo said. "He was burned alive on a grate and, in his final breaths, directed his executioner to turn him over. He had finished cooking on that side."

In lieu of her recent torture, and the remains in front of her, Rebecca didn't find the story amusing. By the looks of the tear that leaked from his eye, neither did he.

"Who is the enemy, father? That's why you brought me here, right?"

Lorenzo cleared his throat and stood opposite Rebecca. He placed his hands on the table between the bodies. She guessed he knew what was before him and where everything was in this crypt.

"I'm going to teach you how to kill a man."

Rebecca grew impatient. "Have you forgotten? I've taken souls already. That's why I'm being trained."

He chuckled. "Souls? Have you discovered your faith, Rebecca Guarna? Guiding innocent spirits to be reunited with the Lord?"

She slammed her fist on the table. Bones rattled, echoing an eerie tinkle around the tunnels. Why was he being so difficult?

"You're being trained to do as the Fixer commands. You owe him a debt. I wish to show you what you need to survive."

Rebecca took another draught from the wine and offered it to the priest. Without hesitation, he accepted. After his fill, Lorenzo drew a knife from inside his humble vestment. Rebecca did not wear her passatore sheath, but her own blade rested against her outer thigh. He told her she wouldn't need it, although her hand hung nearby while he rummaged in the marble chest again. Lorenzo dropped a bouquet of mauve flowers and forest green leaves onto a skeleton.

"Do not underestimate Emperor Rudolf. He cannot deploy his full army south from his Habsburg stronghold without declaring war on Pope Honorius. He desires to absorb the republic yet operates in the shadows. His answer to the Sons of Saint George is the Nightshade Brotherhood."

Two months prior, Rebecca's world was much smaller. Her biggest concern was Mama's fist. Slobbering patrons and Leo's desire to send her to a convent were equally alarming. However, being entangled in a fraternity of assassins who pledged allegiance to the wealthiest family in Milan in service to the pope was unimaginable.

"Nightshade Brotherhood. The Sons of Saint George," Rebecca said, contempt wavering in her throat. "Next you'll tell me a story about the Secret Order of Good Friend Knights."

"Do not jest. The Brotherhood are a fearsome, elite squad of killers," Lorenzo said. He tossed the bouquet at her. "Their signature method of destruction—Atropa Belladonna."

Rebecca recognized it from Carlo's dagger and their stealth training; she felt its effects and Azzo succumbed to its power.

"The driver," she said. "Banco's driver wore this on his lapel."

Lorenzo nodded. "The Brotherhood got to Banco before us. Whatever he knew, they needed it to go to the grave."

Not expecting the truth, Rebecca was pleased by Lorenzo treating her like an adult. His honesty didn't deter her, however, from keeping a secret of her own. Doctor Salvagno saw Banco off from the piazza mercanti. Did he poison the spice trader? She found it difficult to believe given his investigation into the stewhouse killer, but her patron's personal life held mysteries shielded from Rebecca.

She noticed Lorenzo studying her body language—he stared at the point over her shoulder. Rebecca checked behind her, in case, but nothing appeared out of place. She decided not to disclose Leo's presence in spite of Lorenzo's directness.

"Franco was impressed with your throwing skills. Perhaps you perform better under a sense of urgency."

Rebecca shook her head. Franco killed Zita, disposed of her body, and found time to watch her fumble the kidnapping. Was he the one to knock her unconscious, too?

Lorenzo proceeded to point to susceptible anatomy with the knife. A well-placed cut to those locations would draw excessive bleeding and diminish the strength of any foe. Below the arm, inside the thigh, under the neck. The priest demonstrated how to hold the blade for optimal slices or jabs. She copied his motions and committed the guidance to memory.

"Why use the poison in training, but not for contracts?"

"The blade, Saint George's legacy, is the only honorable means to deliver a death blow." Lorenzo replaced the bouquet in the marble chest. "Tonight, you will practice. Get some food in you—recover your strength for now."

They returned to the main tunnel and Rebecca decided to play into the priest's honesty. She asked him about a woman who may have visited the palazzo before. He faltered in his step, but Rebecca considered the uneven floor—and his drunkenness—could have contributed to that.

"No," he said. "No woman would be permitted to step foot beneath the palazzo. Well, no *other* woman." He patted her guiding arm.

***

That night, Lorenzo sent Rebecca to retrieve her sparring partner. He said he was in the storeroom near the Fixer's study—and not to worry—the Fixer wasn't present.

She found Volta constructing a smaller shed of sorts using the stones Rebecca and Azzo deposited there. Crates were stacked against the stone foundation for a size comparison. His brow covered in sweat, he laughed when he saw her.

"Come with me, shit for brains."

He spun around, moving with a speed she hadn't anticipated for a lumbering hulk. It took every ounce of nerve and willpower not to flinch.

"What did you call me?"

Rebecca drew him towards the armory. Lorenzo tossed Volta a wooden sword when he arrived. Rebecca squared off. He snarled. The practice blade looked like it was smithed for a child in his hand. Volta's size reduced the space Rebecca could maneuver, but she circled with care.

She swung first. He blocked it with a forearm. Rebecca swiped at his feet. Surprisingly nimble, he danced away. Annoyed by his defiance to respect the exercise, Rebecca launched a flurry of swipes and jabs, mimicking Lorenzo's instructions in the crypt. Volta parried or blocked most, but took a hard jab to the inner thigh. With a swipe, the flat of his blade slapped her hip.

Rebecca limped away, biting her lip. Volta advanced. His blows threatened to crush her skull. Fatigue from her recent torture set in, but she kept breathing. Rebecca drew her blade to double her blocking strength. Lorenzo shouted.

Volta's sour sweat stench filled her nostrils. With a twist, she disarmed him. He caught her wooden blade with a bare hand and threw it aside. Rebecca kicked him in the testes and punched him in the bridge of his nose with her pommel.

"Enough!"

Volta dropped to his knees. Lorenzo stepped forward to distract Rebecca from making a mistake.

"Don't allow anger to cheapen your honor."

Even kneeling, Volta was near eye-level with Rebecca. Blood flowed over his mouth, resentment burned in his gaze. She couldn't care less. Had Lorenzo not intervened, would she have struck him down? Most likely, yes. She could live with humiliating him though. Rebecca sheathed her blade and left. Father Lorenzo caught her in Azzo's cell, pacing.

"If you encounter a member of the Nightshade Brotherhood, remember this training. Deliver their body to the crypt, for I wish to dissect it."

"Does it bother you? As a priest."

Lorenzo found the rickety chair in the corner and sat. He folded his hands in his lap.

"Can you continue on this path, Rebecca?"

"I—"

"Because the way of the blade is not for all."

Had he meant it as a slight to Azzo's memory? To her being a woman? There was no hard edge to his tone, yet she felt antagonized.

"I regret killing those men," she said. "The patrons."

He withdrew a thick-roped wooden cross from his robes and thumbed the rough effigy. Lorenzo blessed himself. "May their souls be at rest, then." He closed his eyes and nodded.

"But not what they represented."

"It does not."

Direct. Honest. Again, Rebecca valued the priest. She gave him the truth and he returned it. "How come?"

"For the same reason you do not mourn the loss of those patrons. Hypocrites. False faithfuls bereft of principles. We uphold the teachings of Christ in our word and deed. You are part of this tradition now, as you have taken up George's cause."

"I wish to continue."

Lorenzo blessed her with the cross. Rebecca accepted whatever silent prayer he made. "Amen."

Rebecca called after him. "Father? May I visit the cathedral? My friend Zita deserves a prayer."

"Yes."

Rebecca's penitent moment was not a conversion of faith, but an acceptance of Lorenzo's endorsement. He cared for her opinions. Not some patron. Not some Void. He validated her existence. She hoped it was the priest and not the wine speaking.

12

— • —

"Repent! Pray for Forgiveness"

Father Lorenzo escorted her to the cathedral. Rebecca sensed she was allowed to leave the palazzo on sanctioned contracts, but this straddled official business. He left her in the vestibule and wandered the streets to do whatever it was an assassin-training priest did. Rebecca blessed herself from the font and picked a pew. She genuflected before kneeling on an uncushioned tuffet. Candles were lit, but she was alone.

Rebecca sighed. A prayer for Zita's soul was worth breaking her silence with God. Unsure how to begin, she studied the altar, gaze fixed on nothing in particular.

Her mind wandered and the words wouldn't come. Was thinking clearly so challenging? When her father left her and Mama, they took refuge in the Basilica of Saint Ambrose. Nuns fed and clothed them. In her naivete, she was encouraged to pray and did often. Little whispered requests. Intentions for Papa to return. Hope rekindled for a better future until the sisters discovered Mama's nocturnal activities. Mama pleaded she only wished to earn enough coin to repay their generosity, but the abbess cast them out by the next morn.

Lord, have mercy on Zita. It was my fault she's gone. Don't barre her way into your kingdom for my sins. And if you care, take pity on Azzo. He meant well.

Having lingered long enough, Rebecca genuflected again. Her blade was sheathed against her inner thigh, the old parchment from youth tucked inside the hidden pocket. There was no secretive way she could steal a horse from the Sons' stable, thus she decided to stowaway on a merchant ship. Her penitent moment was no conversion of faith. It was time to leave Genoa.

As she reached the font, the vestibule doors opened. In walked the Fixer. Her heart sank. She arranged her face from disappointment to surprise, which was not altogether suspicious.

"Lorenzo said you were here. Walk with me."

The Fixer guided her along the sanctuary's perimeter. He couldn't have known she was going to escape. Was he mad she left the palazzo? She studied his profile and kept a passive tone.

"I hope it's okay that I came to pray."

"I don't give a shit," he said with a wave, "I need your help."

Rebecca stopped walking. If he needed her help, it must be serious. Asking for favors didn't align with his demanding nature. He rolled his eyes and snapped her to rejoin his pace.

"I need information," he continued. "A vintner returned from Burgundy this night. I suspect he's secured a trade agreement. We know it was between the della Torre family and the emperor, but I must know the other details. Are they moving wine into, or out, of the republic? What is their shipping route—by land or sea?" He rattled off each unknown, gesturing with a joint in his hand.

Rebecca was going to make it easy for him. She was about to flee moments before. "Why not send Franco?"

"He's on another assignment. This contract requires a lighter touch. Use whatever creative extraction techniques you can think of, but avoid killing him if you can."

The Fixer leered. She knew what that look meant, all women did. Rebecca wished to pluck his eyes from their sockets.

"What's his name?"

"Giulio Panza. He'll be staying in the podesta's manor in Milan."

Interrogate a vintner by seducing him while he resided in the civilian administrator's manor, one of the most heavily guarded homes in Milan.

"Will this reduce my debt?"

The Fixer laughed. "I'll pay you if you collect the intelligence I need."

Given Lorenzo's recent honesty, she figured it was worth a shot to push her luck with the Fixer. "How many Sons are there?

"You know I can't tell you." He lowered his voice and looked around the empty church. "If you're captured by the della Torres or the Brotherhood, that is too sensitive. Even after your brave performance with Volta."

She guaranteed her success. Lorenzo escorted Rebecca back to the palazzo. Since she accepted the Fixer's request, the priest prepared her. He unrolled a map of the city center of Milan. Rebecca recognized the gates and cart path; she spotted the piazza mercanti and the canal. She knew where the podesta's manor was in the northwestern quarters.

"It's good to get acquainted with your destination, especially when you're familiar with a place. You take alleys, bridges, and inns for granted until you find yourself in a dire situation."

Rebecca nodded. "Yes, I agree." She had considered this to a lesser extent when she killed the patrons; however, the stew quarters were well contained.

"Changed your mind about running?"

Rebecca froze. She often struggled when confronted with the truth directly. The big lies were simple—hiding her identity as the stewhouse killer—because no one asked her about her role. But so direct a question disarmed her. There was no denying it.

"I don't have two grossi to my name, and I refuse to sell myself for coin ever again."

"Nice to be needed." Lorenzo rolled the map. The same steadfast commitment to Rebecca's success did not reside in his hands. They shook like Rebecca's thighs after her first stair sprints several weeks prior. "If you get into trouble, get to the roof."

Warmth emanated from the priest. Rebecca felt it from behind his opaque eyes. He tapped the staging table in the armory with the rolled parchment. She was ordered to leave her blade and the passatore sheath behind, concealing only two throwing knives for protection.

"Don't die, Rebecca."

***

Rebecca balanced on the catwalk between the second-story terrace and adjoining residence. She found herself on the manor's roof much sooner than she'd have hoped. Crimson stained hands struggled to tie the rope around the stone archway. Shouts followed her outside. The fall wouldn't kill her, but she needed her legs intact to flee. Escaping the Signori di Notte proved to be more difficult than entering the manor.

The Fixer hired a troupe of courtesans from Genoa to travel with Rebecca as part of her cover. And the girls brought the charm. As tenants took their aftersupper stroll, enjoying the sunset, around the modest piazza, the night watchmen did as expected—allowed the courtesans access to the manor. Entertainment for the master and his guests meant the possibility of attention for them.

Rebecca kissed Podesta Antonio Marti's servant on the cheek for leading them upstairs. Not quite Lorenzo's age, the administrator's attendant blushed at her affection. Rebecca hoped she didn't need to kill this kindly old man, but if seducing Panza wasn't as simple, she would do what must be done to get away.

The servant led them to a great room. The guests cheered at the arrival of female companionship. Rebecca froze in the doorway. On the other side of the room, Doctor Leonardo Salvagno was in a heated debate with another guest. Neither cared to examine the courtesans closely.

Run? she thought. He didn't notice; she could turn tail and wait outside for Panza to leave. No. She couldn't interrogate anyone on the street. But what was he doing there?

Rebecca greeted two guests who hung near the far wall. With her back towards Leo, she allowed one guest to pull her in close by the waist, even placing a palm on his chest. He guffawed at his friend like a favored idiot who won some grand prize.

"Giulio?"

She took a chance. Without knowing who all the guests were, or her target, Rebecca had to be aggressive.

His smile faltered.

"Panza hired you? Figures." He let her go and pointed. "He's leaving with the doctor."

Rebecca found the servant and asked where she could freshen before returning to the party. He led her to a small cupboard where a burnished silver pot sat between two large candelabras. She waited for his steps to fade, and bolted for the staircase. Pausing between family crests and portraits of dead ancestors, she most decidedly heard the shuffle of steps and muted voices. Rebecca took the stairs and drew one passatore from the folds of her dress. There was no way she'd put herself in such danger without being armed.

The voices came from the room at the end of the hallway. The door was ajar, so Rebecca leaned against the wall. She didn't recognize the stern tone to Leo's demands. Quick to passion, in her experience, not anger, Rebecca thought he sounded cruel.

"Make this easy for us all, Panza."

"The city magistrate's have no right to meddle in my business ventures, Salvagno!"

"You know who I report to," Leo said through clenched teeth. "Do you wish to go the same way as Banco?"

Was Leo threatening Panza with poison?

Panza cackled in disdain. "There's a comparison. Was it a loss? Giuseppe wasn't moving product on my volume. Imagine the profit."

"The judges will find out, Panza. The duty will come due."

"Send for one of those whores, Leonardo. You need to release that stress."

Feet shifted. Rebecca couldn't tell if they were finished whatever conversation needed to be had or about to scuffle. She bolted towards the door and slipped inside. It was a study, not unlike the Fixer's, filled with a large wooden desk and bookshelves. No weapons or books on dissection though. She peered through the crack. A crimson coat walked past and she heard the next door open and close.

Panza, or Leo?

What did she know? Enough intelligence to bring the Fixer? She couldn't guarantee time with both. Maybe she didn't need to though. Her suspicions outweighed her debt.

Rebecca took a left in the hallway. She steadied her breath and entered the room.

"What do you want with Giulio Panza, Leo?"

Leo startled. He dropped his crimson surcoat. The learned patron of her youth looked aged. What color was left in his face drained. The gray creeped higher than his temples and deep-set bags ringed his eyes.

"Rebecca! I thought you were dead." He gripped her into a one-sided embrace. Holding her at arm's length to inspect a supposed dead woman. Rebecca reminded herself not to trust him. She needed to be in charge of this situation.

"Convenient. How's Maria?"

He let her go. "I came back for you. Martina told me you died with those night watchmen by the Wheel."

Rebecca gripped the passatore so hard she felt the metal cut into her palm. "And yet they never found my body. Did you not wonder?"

Tears sparkled in his eyes. "I did, but what did I know? Thank the Lord you're alive." He blessed himself.

Rebecca squared her hips. The grip of her sole weapon was damp with sweat. She wanted to be prepared in case his veneer of faith slipped. "Are you working with them?"

"With who?"

'Don't lie to me, Leo. I heard you with Panza. Did you kill Banco for the emperor?"

Leo blanched again. The note of severity returned to his voice, although he took a seat on the edge of the bed. "How do you know about that business? Who have you spoken to?"

A confirmation? The years of accepting his coin for her time and companionship spilled to the surface. Rebecca wiped her eyes with an open palm. He reached for her face, but she stepped away. She couldn't care less about the della Torres or Viscontis, the pope or the emperor. The League bore no more weight on her mind than the Nightshade Brotherhood. But the man who taught her Scripture, who nurtured her intimately, was not who she believed him to be.

Rebecca blinked the tears away. She strode to the bedside table. A glass of wine sat on a serving tray with a bouquet of mauve flowers. The evidence she needed to verify her suspicions. Leo stood between her and the door. His head hung to the side, examining her discovery.

She brandished the throwing knife. "Get away from me!"

He advanced. "Rebecca, please! Calm down. Let's discuss this."

She swiped. Leo leaned backwards.

If Leo poisoned Panza earlier, she might not have much time to question him. Yet, with Leo cornering her, she felt like a little girl trapped in the brothel again, not a young woman who received the Sons' training.

He rushed her, and this time Rebecca slashed his forehead. Leo fingered his bleeding face.

"No damage has been done that cannot be undone. Just put down the blade, Rebecca."

Unwilling to fully commit, she drove the passatore into his shoulder. He groaned and fell, tumbling with Rebecca on top of him. Rebecca stumbled free and into the hallway.

She sprinted to the last door and flung it open. Panza sat writing in a ledger. A glass of wine sat on the desk. Rebecca knocked it over.

"What the hell are you doing, woman!"

"Did you drink that?"

"I've asked you a question! And why do you have blood on your hands? Who the hell are you?"

Rebecca didn't have time to waste. The belladonna worked fast on Banco. Could it be ingested? She slapped him. He jumped to his feet and raised a fist, but froze as Rebecca stole the stiletto from his waistband.

"You have been poisoned and you're going to die. With haste, tell me how you're transporting your wine. A sea route?"

The surprise and the sting of her slap faded. She recognized the realization in his demeanor. She was a threat.

Panza yelled, "Guards!"

He shouted as Rebecca chased him around the desk. She tried to silence him. Panza threw the ledger and ink pot at her. Rebecca scurried to the door. The roof! The party guests, unfazed by the commotion in Leo's room, now quieted at the yelling. Panza followed Rebecca to the hallway, screaming for the administrator to send his guards upstairs. It didn't take long for the men-at-arms to reach the bottom landing. Leo reappeared, injured and rueful. He shouted as Rebecca bolted past him.

"Repent! Pray for forgiveness, Rebecca."

She returned to the study. Forcing the window open, she squeezed through and dropped onto the terrace. The parapets were short enough that she could swing a leg over.

Rebecca tripped on a coil of rope as the shouts followed her from the window. She threaded it over her head and one shoulder, the motion tugged at her scabbed back and neck wound. A guard appeared.

"Halt!"

Rebecca dodged a swipe and rolled. From her back, she threw the stiletto into his throat. He clutched at the blade, choking his last breaths. A second guard bounded from the wraparound patio. In one swift motion, Rebecca cleared the distance to her blade, yanked it from the throat, and dropped to a knee. The guard charged into her flying blade and hit the ground with a thud. She collected her new knife, proud to save it.

With stained and shaking hands, Rebecca tied off the rope around a catwalk. She leaned back and rappelled the brief side face, shimmying the last few feet to the ground. Her hands were rope-burned in the process. The narrow alley adjacent to the piazza led to a canal. A mound of stonework waited to be constructed into a section of degraded fortification. The canal had been drained and diverted, so Rebecca jumped into the muddy shallows. She waited until dusk.

When shouts subsided and her knees ached, Rebecca returned to the stable. Her dress caked in mud, hair a frizzled mess, she had at least cleaned her hands in the canal. Tossing a grossi to the stable boy, she led her horse to the southern gate. The beast stamped against the evening brisk. Amazed at her good fortune, she'd be clear of Milan in mere minutes.

Clear of the city boundary, a chorus of crickets set the pace of their trot until the horse slowed to an unsteady gait. A wheezing constricted its breath. She couldn't dismount swift enough as it faltered and collapsed. Rebecca stood by, impotent, as throat muscles contracted and the tawny's tongue fell from its mouth. The horse was dead.

"What the hell?"

She scanned the road, but no sign of ambush came. She tugged her travel kit free, jostled open to reveal a bouquet of belladonna. Rebecca gripped the needle-thin blade all the way back on the long walk to Genoa.

13

— · —

The Sea, the Sea, the Ligurian Sea

"D o you realize how critical that intelligence was?"

Veins bulged in the Fixer's forehead and neck. Rebecca could pinch them if she desired. She fixated on the tender spot below his jaw, a weak point Lorenzo taught her to target. Obviously, she understood he wanted Panza's shipping routes and trade partners. But she didn't know Doctor Salvagno would be present in the manor!

"The Nightshade Brotherhood closes in on us, Rustichello," Father Lorenzo said, his words slurred. "Your arrogance should not deflect the real threat."

"Shut the fuck up, Lorenzo!" The Fixer brandished a joint at the priest. "Have another drink."

Rebecca turned her gaze from her drunk trainer to the vase the Fixer ordered to be set on his desk. It was filled with water and the bouquet from her saddlebag. She felt foolish, double dumb for injuring Leo.

"No, Rebecca," he continued. "You clearly do not, or you would have acquired what I requested." He lit the joint and took a deep inhale.

"For eight and one hundred years," Lorenzo said, not to be silenced, "the Sons of Saint George have maintained order for a dozen popes. You should be pleased at our first daughter's progress. She is uninitiated."

Rebecca didn't know if Lorenzo complimented or belittled her. She valued his defense, but not at the cost of her integrity. She was trying.

"Lorenzo, you are correct," the Fixer smiled nonchalantly. He threw his hands into the air as if the priest declared the sky was blue. "And as an uninitiated woman, I should not have expected her to follow simple orders. Volta!"

Rebecca shot to her feet. Lorenzo stepped forward and placed a hand on her shoulder. She interpreted the gesture as a means to steady her nerves, yet Behemoth's presence in the crowded study evoked claustrophobia. She shook free of the priest and tried to run.

"Bind her hands and gag her."

Volta did as he was commanded. All resistance was futile pinned against his torso in a vise. She was carried to the drainage tunnel while the Fixer smoked and Lorenzo protested. The Fixer refused to take the blind man aboard the dinghy as Volta rowed them past the fleet and to *The Corsican*.

"Evening, Fixer!" A familiar voice called to their dinghy, now tied to the galley. "What business do you have aboard *The Corsican?*"

The Fixer laughed. "We are all Sons, Tommaso. Are you denying me leave?"

"The Captain is not aboard tonight."

"Are you not first mate?"

Rebecca imagined they deliberated because a beat later, they were granted permission to board. Once on the merchant ship's deck, Rebecca hoisted like a sack of millet, Tommaso inspected all three new arrivals.

Sailors-on-watch greeted them in confusion. Tommaso approached the Fixer. "With all due respect as it is to be given a man of your leadership, why is the woman bound?"

Rebecca's tunic was soaked in sweat. It cascaded along her spine; she bit her lip so hard, a chunk of skin lodged between her teeth. Warm tinny blood saturated her tongue.

"We all play a role among the fraternity."

The Fixer commanded Volta to untie her. She struggled against him, but his vise-grip kept her immobile. Tommaso's face was obscured by the lantern in his hand.

"Better?"

Tommaso's demeanor relaxed. "It would depend on which manner of role you intend to play tonight, sir."

Rebecca could see the uncertainty in Tommaso's expression, but the hierarchy among Captain Marchetto's ship and the Fixer was unclear. She tried to break Volta's grip once more with no success.

When the sailors stood by assessing the Fixer from a safe distance, he returned to Rebecca. The stench of the hemp and his smug face broached her personal space. He groped for the sheath at her thigh. Rebecca struggled and grunted through the gag. Drool trickled onto her chin and her hair flew wild. Volta restrained her so the Fixer could finish what he started.

He unsheathed her blade, her sole possession of incalculable value, and examined it under Tommaso's light.

"Crude."

Rebecca snarled and squirmed. She would rather not have her throat slit by her own weapon, the extension of her arm. She already paid for it with her previous life.

"You failed to reduce your debt," the Fixer said, strolling to the gunwale. "You defied my command."

Rebecca inched her hands along Volta's sweaty, swarthy forearm and wrist until she grabbed his little finger with both hands. She ripped it backwards, cracking the bone clean. He roared in pain and released her.

The Fixer shook his head at her act of defiance. Too slow, she could not stop him from dropping her blade into the sea. Without hesitation, without heeding the cries of Tommaso or the sailors, she jumped over the gunwale and plunged into the inky waters.

"Man overboard!"

The shouting muted beneath the surface. Her hair and tunic swirled in the motionless black. Breathless, Rebecca clung to hope. Paddling to remain submerged, pumping, lungs screaming for air, her blade was lost to the cold and the dark and the depths.

She accepted the watery grave, to go with her blade to the long sleep, when a thick rope slapped the water above her head. She kicked and fought against the crushing traitor of a sea that swallowed her blade and grabbed hold. As she broke the surface, peals of laughter filled her ears. Tommaso and the sailors hoisted her over the gunwale.

The Fixer's cackling, fake and patronizing, was the sole clamor aboard. Until, in her chattering mess, she joined him. Stuttering, sobbing laughter escaped Rebecca's mouth. She had little cause for true joy in the stews. The palazzo contained fear and ambiguity. Her laughter erupted from grief, her fury, and the sea.

***

High in the mast-head,
  the steward cries; wind quiets breath,
  cold cuts him to the quick. And tears away,
  swallowed in the sea; for he will never again lay eyes on thee.

Rebecca took in a familiar sight, yet she didn't place it at once. Humming continued behind her, and a hand patted her hair gently. Too numb to recoil, she rolled over to face Tommaso. He offered a rueful smile seated next to the table where Lorenzo stitched her back and neck. Her arms and legs were bound, but not by ropes. She was wrapped in a quilt, and the coal pan rested on her chest.

"What do you sing?"

"Have you never heard a 'chanty' before?"

The rhythmic pulse of the galley and the warmth of the coal pan soothed Rebecca's nerves enough to care about Tommaso's query.

"Should I know what that is?"

He cast his sight to the porthole, mind no longer in the medical cabin. "The captain hired Azzo and me in Naples. We didn't know each other then. Corsairs know the best tunes."

Rebecca forgot Azzo knew Tommaso before joining the Sons. So the captain introduced them to the Fixer and their training killed Azzo.

"How long have you been at sea?

He checked the coals. Satisfied they did their duty, he removed the pan so Rebecca could prop herself on an elbow.

"So long I can't recall my mother's scent." Tommaso gave Rebecca her sheath. "The Sons on *The Corsican* respect you. Jumping into the Ligurian is not for the faint of spirit."

Rebecca gripped the leather, custom cut and stitched and now defunct. It was still there. She withdrew the parchment. "Can you read?"

Tommaso accepted the note. "Some letters, yes."

"Read it."

Tommaso began, "Dear daughter, if you forget my face, my voice, my—"

"Tickly chin hairs," Rebecca interjected.

He smiled and refocused.

You may never forgive me, but my heart belongs to you and the great wide world. You cannot follow. One day you'll be grown, tall enough to reach the figs from your mother's counter, and on that day, you will understand.

"Farewell, my little fig," Tommaso said, tears welling in his eyes.

"Yours," Rebecca finished. "B. Renucci."

Tommaso gave her the parchment back. Rebecca tucked it into the sheath. "I come from nothing. That blade was all I am."

When her clothes dried and the chill receded, Tommaso rowed her to the drainage tunnel. He bade her farewell for *The Corsican* intended to sail away on a trading expedition. He assured her they would return soon.

Rebecca was spent. Hollow. "B. Renucci" was correct—she couldn't recall his chin hairs. He was as distant and featureless as the Lord. Her world tumbled from security to the brothel, fast. The deep well of resentment forced her name change from Renucci to Guarna. Even Mama agreed. She became Signora Martina Guarna. The one time they were of accord.

Yet Papa was right. Her heart yearned for adventure. Why else would she kill those patrons? Run away to join a secret order of assassins? They shared that call. But did she know for sure? Just because he wrote it didn't mean it was true. The Fixer might have buried her past by tossing the blade into the sea, but one person could bring the past to the light. Rebecca crumpled the letter. She held the parchment over the torch in the tunnel. Watching it burn gave her no closure, but she knew how to begin that process.

14

— • —

George, Friend of a Foe

Rebecca hurled blade after blade into wooden practice logs. The exercise of positioning the thick, barkless timber in their stands earned a sweat. She launched steel passatore after passatore at the marks. Splintering, clanging, thudding, the eyelet knives drummed a racket on her ears. Varied techniques yielded varied results.

Rebecca windmilled her arms. She flung a blade sidearmed, overhead, underhanded. By nightfall, she settled into a rhythm. Drawing the knives became smoother.

Don't leave a blade behind.

The command echoed between her ears. She gathered the six knives after each were tossed and reset. Near the twenty-fourth hour, Rebecca decided it was time. She attempted running away once and was cornered in the cathedral. A visit to Milan with the intention of returning felt reasonable.

She snuck towards her escape route—the first tunnel she arrived in. If she must maim a stable boy to steal a horse, so be it. She was armed with a full sheath. There was not a chance she'd walk to Milan. On the way, stalking the shadows, reminiscent of another woman, Rebecca froze. The specter who argued with the unknown man at twilight. Had she been real? Damp, stone halls swallowed her presence as they threatened to swallow Rebecca's will.

She counted nine offshoot paths from the main arched tunnel in her time among the Sons. The outflow to the dock, the new path to the crypt, and her escape route to the palazzo's rear facade were known. She stood at an unknown tunnel entrance near her destination. Whispers slithered through the dark. A cry.

In case she imagined it, Rebecca held her breath. The cry came again. An intuition urged her forward, taking a step into the yawning depths. She kicked a piece of hard debris. Rebecca felt blindly on the dirt path. Father Lorenzo's walking stick.

She lit a torch and pressed into the curving pathway. Glad to be armed with the ash bo, she readied for whatever lay ahead. As Rebecca considered the tunnel may never cease, the moaning grew louder. Pausing again at the threshold, she lit the torches. Fresh tinder set aflame quickly.

Her eyes adjusted to a semicircular chamber. The light cast shadows over a mound in the center of the space. Made of earth and ringed with animal skulls, it rose to waist height. A round basin had been hollowed in the center of the conical peak. An altar, draped with red and white linens, was set with a wooden chalice and crucifix. She ran her fingers over the cloth and a chill tingled her spine.

A moan croaked from behind the altar. Rebecca's grip on the torch faltered, but she caught it before it extinguished. Her pulse raced. Bracing for what lay around the altar, she found Father Lorenzo. He slumped against the wall, chin in his chest, surrounded by wineskins and pots.

"Father!"

He mumbled and knocked over a pot. Rebecca squatted to inspect him. His eyelids threatened to close. "Why do you drink so, Lorenzo?"

"Rebecca."

She hoisted him to his feet, bumping her shoulder on a wooden framed painting behind the altar. Guiding him back to the mound, she flopped the priest over to look around.

"What is this place?" She patted Lorenzo's cheek. "Father, are you with me?"

He puked. Rebecca jumped to avoid the mess.

"Water."

She followed his finger and returned to the backside of the altar. Among the wine stood a waterskin. While the priest swished his mouth clean, Rebecca turned her attention back to the painting. It was a triptych upon closer inspection. They were nailed into the stone wall, mounted in a way to accommodate the chamber's curve.

The left-hand panel depicted a familiar icon—Saint George in full battle armor, red cross blazoned on his chest. But in this rendering, his horse lay slain and serpents surrounded the hero. Tiny flames sparked from their fanged mouths.

"George's tomb."

Rebecca spun. Lorenzo leaned his head against the mound and caught his breath. He nodded as if to say his drunken proclamation was true.

"He's buried here?"

Lorenzo pointed to the painting. Rebecca inspected the center panel. George lay propped against a massive tree trunk in the woods, eyes closed. A towering figure administered to his wounds. Not a man, but not quite a beast, his visage sent shivers along Rebecca's spine. His head and torso were that of a man, yet his waist to his feet were a billy goat. He tipped a cup of red liquid into George's mouth.

"Hundred years ago, the emperor laid claim to Rome, betraying the peace treaty with Pope Alexander," Lorenzo said. "He decreed certain artifacts be secreted away before the emperor desecrated them. His most trusted crusaders delivered George's body here."

Her engorged sense of dread did not prevent Rebecca from examining the final panel. George, alive and well, stood in a semicircular chamber. Chalice in one hand, crusader's sword in another, he presided over three prostrated knights. Swords at their hips, two wore white tunics with the Genoan red cross, the third with a black tunic and white cross. In the shadows to George's left stood the half-man, half-goat figure. Beneath him read, *Faunus.*

Rebecca assumed the name of the Fixer's assassins to be more of a spiritual inspiration. Although, the presence of George's remains proved the most obvious of conclusions supported by the known facts.

"The Sons of Saint George have always safeguarded the pope's wishes?"

"Indeed," Lorenzo said. He got to his feet and held out a hand. Rebecca forgot she held his walking stick. "Take me to the crypt below the cathedral."

Pleased to depart the chill and stale air of the tomb, Rebecca guided him through the curving tunnel. As they reached the chamber below the cathedral, Rebecca scanned each detail and found the skeletal remains missing from the table were replaced by a bundle of rags. They resembled her bed in the stew.

The priest swung himself onto the table.

"You are no help to yourself when you are like this."

Lorenzo grunted. "Why do you care, Rebecca? Weren't you leaving?"

Father Lorenzo's uncanny ability to sense what is unsaid silenced Rebecca. She decided she would go even if he guessed her intention.

"You asked if I could live with this—training killers to take God's most precious gift," Lorenzo continued. "The guilt is staggering."

"Sleep this melancholia away." Rebecca patted his forearm. She dried his forehead with her sleeve. Lorenzo closed his eyes to sleep an uncomfortable rest on the table. Rebecca turned to leave, but he grabbed her arm. A warmth rose in her cheeks at his firm but gentle grip.

***

Rebecca paced in the back alley outside the stewhouse. She shot furtive glances at the curtained windows but kept her head obscured by the wide-brimmed hat. Figures cut across the candlelight. Patrons, drinking and cloying, the girls flirting and dancing to the rhythmic lute and vielle.

After each kill, Rebecca went home. It was instinctual. For all the pain and resentment Rebecca fostered over the years, the stewhouse felt like a sanctuary. She'd wash the blood of her victims from her hands and entertain guests. The tenuous dance between murder and normalcy, a burden inherited from her parents, could not last forever. The Fixer saw to it. Before him, Mama turned her over to the Signori di Notte and her fate—the Breaking Wheel. The toll came due.

She retained no kinship with the brothel yet needed to return somewhere familiar after the death of her blade. A comfort like Lorenzo's encouraging grip or Tommaso's coal pan in opposition to the devouring sea. Rebecca slipped in on the arm of a patron, overcoat drawn high. The brothel heaved with life. Patrons guffawed, laughter bounced off the walls. She could taste the familiar perfume of wine, sweat, and sex.

Maria sat in a patron's lap. Rebecca was pleased that it was not Leo. She did not recognize the woman behind the bar, and the twang of guilt for Zita's death choked in her throat. Franco's toll was due. She would collect. Edging past the lutenist and sawing bowstring of the vielle player, she scanned the bar.

On the second story, Rebecca inspected each stew to no avail, therefore, she must confront the door at the end of the hall. With a deep inhale, she turned the knob. Mama was seated, brushing her hair. The signora twisted round as the door closed.

The brush clunked to the floor.

"Rebecca!"

Face white as fresh parchment, she scooped the brush as if the horsehair and wood provided sufficient defense against her murderous daughter. Rebecca stifled an insincere laugh. She turtled forward, hands raised. The memory of the Breaking Wheel and stolen treasure creaked to the forefront of her mind. The impulse to sling a passatore into Mama's face surged, but a degree of control was essential. If she were to get what she came for.

"Yes, I'm alive."

"What are you doing? Back away! You must go! At once, or I'll—"

Rebecca removed her hat so Mama could envy her flowing curls. She made sure no tears tracked her cheeks or riding grime coated her face. A shadow of satisfaction plagued Rebecca. Mama presented her full attention—a distinction she failed to do when her daughter was a little girl.

"How—"

"I'm here for what you owe me."

Mama laughed. "I owe you nothing! You left a wake of gutted men throughout the stewhouses. Did you think I was going to sit by and let you run amok killing our patrons?"

The signora cared first and foremost about profit. Rebecca cut across the rhetoric and to the point.

"Yes, I should have died on the Wheel," Rebecca said. "But what I am owed does not sit in the city depository."

Martina strode to her night table. She drew a small shiv and pointed it at Rebecca. "I will not hesitate."

Rebecca opened her overcoat to reveal the sheath. Mama's face crumpled. She desired nothing more than to intimidate Martina, but if it came to blows, the signora stood outmatched.

"Why did Papa leave us?"

Mama shook her head. "We haven't recovered since you left. Then Zita disappeared. If I knew where that wench got to, I'd strangle her."

Rebecca drew a blade. Her fury may have been misplaced, but the callous remark still raked her patience.

"Why, woman?"

Mama cowered. "You think I know?" The puny blade hung limp.

She was pleased that Mama was forced to confront two ghosts of her past. But she refused to concede from getting what she came for. "He left you, too, Mama." Rebecca sheathed the blade.

Martina sat, dropping the blade on the night table.

"The 'bastards were grinding him down', as he'd like to say. To be fair, the merchant guild underpaid for his fruit. You don't remember?"

Papa's note called her his little fig.

"Go on."

Mama crossed her arms. "He met some captain, a vagrant. Promised him riches. He said they'd sail east from Corsica. Blegh, the idiot."

Rebecca's mind raced. She knew a captain who sailed from Corsica. Then again, this was years ago.

"What does that mean? Why would he sail east?"

"If I knew, I would know, Rebecca. He left and I kept our miserable brat fed and watered."

Rebecca's curiosity ebbed and her resentment resurfaced. She would be lying had she not considered killing Mama. This woman, whose life was in Rebecca's hands, made her youth miserable. Martina didn't appear happy or content. She reveled in the hardships that women bore in Milan. The profit eased the pain. Rebecca wished to kill her, but not today.

"B. Renucci. What was his given name?"

Martina refused to meet her gaze. She stared in defiance out the window. "Some things must be kept in the past. Now get the hell out of here, Rebecca, unless you wish to visit the Breaking Wheel."

There was nothing more Rebecca desired from Martina. Back on the streets of Milan, she sauntered along the cypress-lined carriage road, reins in hand, contemplating Mama's empty threat. The pity at their shared abandonment stung the corners of her eyes. An interminable chasm between Papa's deception and the loss of her blade threaten to unleash enough tears to fill the new canal.

She bit her lip, the tried-and-true method to stymie her catharsis. The pain swelled and held the tears at bay. Milan sat still under the morose, dim light of the moon. As she reached the southeastern gate, a figure clad in black shifted along the defense wall. Rebecca plunged her hand inside her overcoat, but would need to think quicker to talk her way out of a run-in with the night watchmen.

The guard barred the path and removed his wide-brimmed hat. She drew a passatore and launched it at the ghost from her past.

Azzo screamed in a futile attempt to stop the blade from reaching its target.

15

FAVORED SON

Azzo groaned. The blade struck his shoulder at an odd angle. Rebecca knelt to inspect her work, proud of her reflexes. The fellow trainee who was supposed to be dead winced as he tugged the passatore free.

"The Fixer told me you were dead."

Rebecca stood. "He told me *you* were dead."

"Didn't hit bone."

Needing time to gather her thoughts, Rebecca reined in the horses. In the process, she kept the throwing knife in her gloved hand. Azzo might be injured, but could he be trusted?

"Following me?"

He ripped fabric from his tunic and held it on the wound. He struggled to fish a needle and thread from his kit. Azzo offered her the needle with a grimace. She accepted it and tied the thread. He pinched the slit closed as Rebecca poorly reseamed his skin. Arm sutured, Azzo got to his feet, and accepted the reins.

"My assignment brought me here."

"Father Lorenzo should redo that."

He agreed. The pair walked their mounts out of Milan. She kept him on her right so her blade hand remained vigilant and accessible. He proceeded to explain the Fixer's suspicions. Genoa's captain of the people, Alessandro Boccanegra, encroached on the Sons of Saint George, which she knew from their botched exchange with Carlo and Thibault. He desired access to the fraternity's ways to gain their support, but Rustichello could not

118

comply due to their agreement with the Lombard League. The Fixer needed an ear and eye proximate to Boccanegra.

"But why you? What have you been doing?"

"I joined his guard, collecting intelligence." Azzo pursed his lips. He held back. Under the pressure of her glare, he continued, "Boccanegra has certain appetites. Coaxing what the Fixer wanted to know from him took a special touch."

Rebecca knew shame. The early years in the stewhouse bred confusion. As she matured, her carnal obligations became pleasurable. A hotbed for shame and anger to grow. Azzo's face reflected those feelings.

"Truth be told, I didn't learn much. That's why I'm here. Tommaso said you rode to Milan. I hoped to meet in private."

A revelation too irksome. She held the passatore to Azzo's collarbone. It was her turn to barre the path forward.

"Tommaso knew you were alive?"

He winced again as he raised empty palms. "My safety depended on his silence, Rebecca. Don't interpret his omission as a personal offense."

Azzo convinced her to join the Sons among the sycamore trees not far from where they now stood. She required convincing again. Sheathing her blade, a test would do.

"Prove I can trust you, Azzo. Help me board *The Corsican* without the Fixer knowing. Before it sails away."

He raised his brows beneath the curtain of greasy locks.

"I must speak with its captain," she said. "Or at least read his ledgers."

***

Rebecca sifted through the crates in the Fixer's storeroom. She searched for an empty box large enough to cramp into. Tommaso kept watch in the tunnel while Azzo shifted each chest.

"Why didn't you leave your mama sooner?"

Rebecca opened the lid to a chest full of Ambrogino d'Oro coins. Her eyes swam in the gold reflected in the torchlight at Azzo's inquiry. He posed a question she often considered over the years, but in light of their current pursuit, it became apparent.

"Mama never abandoned me."

Grateful he could not see her blush at the childish remark, Azzo grunted. He peered over her shoulder at the coins.

"To be loved by those most dear is a luxury." Azzo scooped coins by the fistful and dropped them with a clink. "Curious."

Rebecca found their crate. The trio navigated it to the drainage tunnel and onto a dinghy. She squatted inside, hugging her knees, while the boys rowed past the fleet to the galley.

A voice hailed their vessel. Rebecca didn't bother to ask what would happen to smugglers according to Genoese law. They weren't carrying contraband and she was a willing participant. However, the navy ruled these waters. She bit her lip. They lingered. The Son assured the watchman they returned ware crates on a routine shore run. Not till Tommaso offered coin for passage did they begin rowing again.

A gentle knock tapped the crate and Azzo's voice said, "Docking now, Rebecca."

The lid creaked open. Tommaso disappeared over the gunwale before Rebecca could amble out and onto the iron ladder. Azzo would remain behind; he informed Rebecca that the first mate searched for clear passage. Even with the Sons ashore, the captain lurked among his galley.

Rebecca reached the deck. Prowling, head on a swivel, she turned the knob to the captain's quarters. Holding her breath, no sound but the creaking of wood in the swelling current greeted her. The night sky cast dim shadows over the sparse cabin. The ledger. She dashed to the desk. Leather-bound and inviting, it lay open.

Rebecca scratched flint to stone and lit a candle. The first page listed where the galley made port. Genoa. Dated yesterday morn. Famagusta. Tunis. She flipped back to the beginning and thumbed through several pages at a time.

The first passage she scanned read:

We do not have the manpower to seize the bank. The island is protected by sheer rock face and shallows. Rustichello's dream is a fool's errand. He should be so fortunate to waylay his query through Thibault. Franco's arrangement was a boon if a trifle.

Rebecca had no idea what bank on an island Captain Marchetto wrote about. Regardless, not far enough back. Any mention of her father would be years prior, not months. Where was the list of conscripted men? She slammed the ledger and searched along the shelf. A half dozen others like it sat inviting her to explore. The sea air permeated the wooden hull and that inexplicable calling nagged her heart.

She tugged another volume from the shelf and cracked it open. Must met her nose. Lists of traded wares, quantities, and values sold or traded littered the entirety of its pages. She tossed it aside and pulled another. This one was full of maps of foreign ports and sea passage routes. She kept checking the door, but no movement or sound came. Rebecca dropped a volume at the disturbance behind her.

"Permission was not granted to board, little girl."

Rebecca's heart slammed against her chest. She flew to her feet, near tipping the candle onto the desk. Captain Marchetto emerged from the shadows in the corner. He sat on the edge of his seat, appraising her. He rested his forearms on the pommel of his cutlass.

"Requesting permission—"

"Not granted." He tossed the blade onto the table between them. "Take it."

Rebecca snatched the pommel. She held it loose in the air between them.

"What does the sole daughter of Saint George search for in my ledgers?" Marchetto drew another blade, his boots thudding as he blocked the exit. Rebecca circled to maintain the table between them. Why not try?

"Did you know my father?"

"Aren't you a waif like Azzo?" Marchetto laughed. "I don't know you, Guarna."

The captain challenged the Fixer's authority before, so he possessed some degree of autonomy aboard the galley. Rebecca needed another option. Some leverage. She considered her plan as they rowed through the port, crouched inside the crate. Coming to blows with the captain was least desirable, so she gambled trust.

"Renucci. My family name is Renucci."

Marchetto's face was hidden in shadow. He tilted his head.

"And what do you, Renucci, have to offer for the information you seek?"

Rebecca's heart skipped again. An admission? If he spoke true, Rebecca possessed nothing. Her blade rested at the bottom of the sea, and she accrued no coin beyond what she paid towards her debt. Trading her honor for the riches of men was no longer in her repertoire either. A pillaging assassin-captain must have the same base desires as all the other tramps Rebecca encountered.

"Once my debt is paid, I may go as I please."

Marchetto pointed his blade. He stalked towards the desk. Rebecca backed into a chair to keep him in view.

"Can you now? Will Rustichello allow it?"

Rebecca didn't know what the Fixer would allow, but she had to believe he'd be good for his word.

"I'll join your crew. Name your term of service."

He mocked her. "A deal with the devil for the knowledge of the father." Marchetto lunged. She parried. He swatted and she shuffled. They crossed blades over the desk. "A dangerous agreement. I knew the fruit merchant."

But would he divulge more? If she bested him with the cutlass, perhaps . . .

He swung. Rebecca jumped backwards and fled through the cabin door. Marchetto on her heels, she braced. Circling on the deck, the pair dueled beneath the furled sails. Tommaso appeared above and behind the captain on the stern deck. Azzo, unaware of Rebecca's predicament, shouted from the dinghy to inquire of their progress.

"Did he sail with you?"

Marchetto's tight slashes and swipes forced her into the mast. She rolled sideways.

"Captain!" Tommaso called, but the captain shooed his first mate.

Rebecca dropped to a knee and reached for a passatore. The captain punched her in the shoulder. The blow sent a ripple of pain through her semi-healed wound. She could not draw the throwing knife.

"Does your offer still stand, Rebecca Renucci?"

Marchetto slashed. Rebecca parried, the angle of steel meeting steel opening the captain's chest to a striking position. She grabbed a rope tied off on the gunwale and launched her feet into the air. Her kick landed in his gut. Rebecca brought her blade to the back of his neck. He laughed. Dropping his blade on the deck, Rebecca allowed him to stand erect.

Rebecca looked the captain directly in the eyes. For much of her life, she found this simple act to be a challenge unless in the context of seducing a patron. The intimacy of it chafed. The instinct to protect her inner thoughts, somehow transparent in the unseeing tether between her hazel eyes, an exchange she did not wish to offer others. Rebecca transmitted her most honest self, her truest intent, when she held the gaze of another. So with her nod, a palpable connection formed as if they grasped hands or shared an embrace.

"Benito Renucci conscripted with my sailors. We deposited him at Famagusta. Genoa and Venice battled for the fate of Tyre. He chartered passage east with corsairs to pillage in the chaos."

Marchetto grabbed her hand. She acquiesced, drawn in by learning of her father's fate. Benito. The nondescript signature of a stranger's name, now revealed.

Tommaso shouted. He sprinted to mid-deck, but in her trance, Rebecca didn't feel the blade in her palm. The captain drew blood. He did the same to his own and clamped their hands together.

"Benito was never to be seen again."

Disappointment painted Tommaso's face. "Captain, bringing a woman onto the crew would be most unlucky. We've seen all manners of fits of men too long upon the open water, but never her cackle. That mad laughter when she emerged from the drink . . . sent shivers in my bones."

Rebecca snarled at Tommaso. The Fixer humiliated her. Tommaso's insult hurt less than the revelation of her father's destiny, life's cruel joke. The captain clapped his first mate on the shoulder and sauntered to his cabin.

"A bond sowed in blood."

As Rebecca swung her leg over the gunwale, the captain said, "You have a valiant heart, Rebecca. Pay your debts to the Fixer, then I'll be expecting you."

Tommaso berated her all the way back to the drainage tunnel. He revealed his intention to sully her value as a crewmate was to protect her from a mistake. Azzo wrapped her hand and shook his head. She scoffed at the patronage.

"Don't judge me. I needed to know."

Wanting to run away from her decision, she stalked the dock. Rebecca would need time to process the revelation and desired to be alone. She turned back to see Azzo and Tommaso embracing, lingering, cheek to cheek. They broke apart when they realized she was watching.

Tommaso scowled at her and pushed off to return to the galley.

Azzo said, "Please, Rebecca, not a word about—"

Rebecca leveled her gaze with him, the man she believed dead until a few days ago. He convinced Tommaso to bring her aboard *The Corsican* without question. The tempest inside Rebecca settled with the mystery of her father uncovered. Who was she to unleash a squall on Azzo and Tommaso's harmony? She gripped his shoulders.

"You have my full confidence, Azzo."

A toothless smile played beneath his stubble. He looked as though he wished to hug her. Regret for her bargain with Captain Marchetto and learning Benito's name exhausted Rebecca.

Fighting sleep, Rebecca muttered a silent prayer. Could she now trust Azzo? *The Fixer lied to them both about the other's fate.* For the time being, Rebecca chose to believe in the favored Son of Saint George.

16

—·—

Don't Feed the Devil in Your Home

"**A**re you certain you can live with your pact?"

Rebecca held a finger to her lips. Five restless nights tossing and turning on her cot debating the same question later and she wanted Azzo to drop it. Nightmares grip her unconscious mind, each the same—rope strangled her of their own accord. Looping and constricting her arms, legs, and torso. She woke, without fail, tangled in her blanket. The suffocating sensation left her drenched. A different sweat than from their sparring session.

Father Lorenzo prayed on his rope rosary. He wished to build their training around Rebecca's momentum of disarming Captain Marchetto. Rebecca swore the priest to secrecy from the Fixer, which he agreed to, given her assistance in the crypt. Although the nature of her visit was not revealed nor inquired about.

The dank scent of hashisha preceded the Fixer's arrival, Volta in tow. Both wore wide shit-eating grins that turned Rebecca's stomach. She worried about what tidings they may bring with such glee.

Tommaso appeared in Volta's shadow. He clutched a scroll and wore the same scowl from the other day.

"I smell the sea," Father Lorenzo said.

"You smell desperation," the Fixer said. "Spite and hubris."

Tommaso handed Rebecca his missive. She handed Azzo her blade and unfurled it. Looking to the room for permission to review it, the Fixer waved her on. Azzo scrutinized Tommaso's face for any outward indication.

The scroll was a contract.

"You are to serve one full expedition, port to port, under the honorable Captain Marchetto's command," Tommaso said. "You will appear alive and fit to serve *The Corsican* upon the successful fulfillment of your debts in accordance with your agreement. At which time, your prior employer, Rustichello da Pisa," Tommaso said, nodding at the Fixer, "will release you and hold no further obligation of your talents."

The Fixer barked an insincere laugh at this point, which Volta mimicked. His baritone cackle reverberated on the metal in the armory.

Tommaso finished reciting what lay written in red ink in Rebecca's hands. "The captain retains no liability for Rebecca (Renucci) Guarna should you suffer death, shipwreck, or failure to secure satisfactory chattel, wares, or loot. All profit is for the good of *The Corsican*. These are your terms."

Rebecca followed the proclamation to the end where, with a flourish, the captain signed the letter, again in red ink. She suspected it was their shared blood.

"Is that all?" she asked. "Must I sign?"

"You already have," Tommaso said, confirming her assumption. "You may keep this copy for your records."

"This," the Fixer said. "Is a generous agreement. From Tangier to Alexandria. You will not choose where *The Corsican* ventures. Women are not held in such high regard at those trading posts as they are here in Genoa."

Rebecca flushed. She regretted giving Azzo the blade.

"My parents warned me as a child," Father Lorenzo said. "The Prince of Darkness is ever-present. Don't feed him as a guest in our home."

Rebecca tucked the contract in her tunic. The adage irked her. She gathered a spear from the rack to have a task to do with her hands. The Fixer pressed into her personal space. He whispered,

"I own you, Rebecca; your debt, unpaid. Marchetto will not have you until this is through."

Tommaso took his leave. Rebecca tapped Azzo's blade with the spear, wishing to avoid any more threats or cryptic warnings. More importantly, she had no desire to explain her father, that is, if the captain didn't already divulge that detail to the Fixer.

Father Lorenzo dismissed them after a few more rigorous bouts. On the way back to her cell, Rebecca had an idea. She buttoned her black surcoat waist to neck and donned her black chiffon mask. Returning to the armory, she searched among the leather whetting straps on the walls and on the pile of rods on each table until she found a rucksack. The same she wore to shuttle debris to the campanile. Rebecca edged to the storeroom, stopping in each tunnel mouth to conceal her movement. No one would fault her for extra exercise.

Inside the storeroom, she stuffed the ruck with hemp buds until they were so squashed she could not fit any more. Rebecca took the stairs, two at a stride. At the top, she dumped the hashisha buds into the sea. The wind felt refreshing against the sheen of sweat on Rebecca's skin. She snuck to the storeroom again and refilled the ruck. Beyond the crate sat another chest. Inside were more Ambrogino d'Oro coins.

What did Carlo say about the Milanese coins those months ago on the slab? The Sons of Saint George were helping Governor Visconti dilute the florin? Then why were so many in the Fixer's storeroom and not at market? Not to get sidetracked from her intent—reduce Rustichello's precious joint stash—she sprinted back to the campanile twice more before returning the ruck to the armory.

Rebecca brought a bowl to the spigot, the water cool and clean. She couldn't fret about the contract with Marchetto. The time would come and she'd be prepared. Her father, for his little worth, yearned for the sea. Rebecca accepted that part of him in her. At least she didn't have a family to leave behind, only her past.

A clamoring and thud erupted from the tunnel to her left, echoing around the vaulted ceiling. She dropped the bowl. Drawing a passatore, Rebecca tread with care into the dark. She reached the portrait of Saint George, the first she encountered on the day after the Fixer saved her from the Signori di Notte. She steadied her breath and opened the frame.

Her eyes adjusted to find a wriggling, struggling figure sprawled at the bottom of the stairs. Rebecca lost her footing, windmilling her arms to stay erect. The floor was covered in gold coins, a chest upturned when the figure fell down the stairs.

She recognized Franco as he crawled to her. Black liquid trailed behind him.

"Rebecca!"

Stooping to help him, Rebecca maintained caution. She didn't know where he was injured, but on closer inspection, she couldn't decipher where it was the worst. He was stabbed in multiple locations. He clenched his teeth and struggled to swallow. Terror painted his eyes.

"George's . . . devil . . . inside . . . inside . . ."

Rebecca's hands were covered in blood. She could feel its warmth. Even if she could carry or drag him to Father Lorenzo, would he survive his wounds? She looked at the coins. Enough to start over. She had a sheath full of passatore, and when he died, no witnesses. She could run. Franco killed Zita. Who would mourn his loss?

Don't feed the devil in our home.

"Damn you, Lorenzo." She draped his arm around her shoulder. "Come on! I'll get you to the priest. Franco, walk!"

The Son shook violently. He mumbled and muttered about the devil being present until he could not draw enough breath to complete a sentence. Rebecca urged him to stay quiet. His ramblings disconcerted her spirit. She needed to leave him for assistance when he collapsed to his knees. Sprinting ahead, she woke Azzo. The commotion drew the Fixer and Father Lorenzo from the study, but Rebecca didn't care. If they were to save Franco, they'd need to be swift.

With the group, they lugged an incoherent Franco onto a table in the armory. Lorenzo barked orders. Azzo gathered clean water and a small medical kit from Lorenzo's quarters. The Fixer cut open Franco's tunic and breeches. As Rebecca suspected, he was covered with stab wounds. She guided Lorenzo's hands to feel each one. He squinted and held his head to the right.

"The . . . dragon . . . George's . . . inside . . ."

Now in the light, it was clear to Rebecca that Franco's breathing was irregular. "Is he poisoned, too, father?" Rebecca asked.

"No," the priest said. "This isn't belladonna. It's something else." He took the Son's hand and began to pray.

The Fixer gripped Lorenzo's shoulder. "You can't save him?"

The priest continued his prayer until Franco ceased taking in breath. His chest spasmed. He clasped his throat, mouth moaning in silent pain until he turned purple. A blood vessel burst in his eye. He twitched.

Rustichello rested a hand on his chest. Rebecca and Azzo watched in horror as the periods of stillness expanded between twitches. Franco's head limped to the side, his spirit expired.

The Fixer poked Lorenzo in the chest. "Figure out what caused this. If it is the Nightshade Brotherhood, I must know."

Lorenzo shook his head. "It isn't belladonna."

"Prove it."

***

Lorenzo enlisted Rebecca's aid to dissect Franco. She stood in the crypt. The recently deceased replaced the skeletons on the table. The priest had Rebecca bring extra torches and lit every candelabra. Azzo filled a brazier with logs.

Rebecca inspected his workstation. In addition to needle-thin knives and saws, there was a mallet and clamps. Lorenzo fingered an odd wooden-handled device. A crank adjusted the aperture of the two pincers.

Azzo delivered a tome to Lorenzo. "From the Fixer." The same book Rustichello smacked him with months prior. It felt like another lifetime. She flipped to the page Lorenzo described—a study of the armpit. Connected by a network of lines, cherry-sized stones beaded together. Lorenzo laid the pincer device on the page and advised Rebecca on how to adjust the depth. She did so until it encapsulated the largest, hand-drawn cherry-bead.

"Azzo," Lorenzo said. "You're dismissed."

He left them.

"You may vomit. It is acceptable." Lorenzo indicated to the corpse. "Avoid Franco."

Rebecca steeled her mind. She could handle blood. Pain—inflicting it or suffering—fine. The gruesome nature of Franco's death and the prospect of investigating his interior repulsed her. She reached into the marble chest, hand grasping in the dark.

"They are gone."

He was right. The wine pots were absent.

"The real work," he said, "as you reminded me, Rebecca, begins when you're sober. I have not had undiluted wine since your venture to Milan. To see your mother."

First Azzo, now Lorenzo. Both surprised her in the most unexpected and pleasant ways. Even scowling Tommaso's disapproval rang of a veiled concern. They made an effort—what? For her? No, she decided. Lorenzo could not hold a steady hand to train them if he continued to drink as he did. Azzo and Tommaso's motive, selfish. The sawing of metal on bone drove Rebecca's thoughts back to the nude Franco.

She dabbed sweat from Lorenzo's brow as he labored to lacerate a Y shape on the departed's chest. He caught his breath and affixed the clamps. Rebecca pressed the torso to the table, full weight behind her elbows, as Lorenzo cranked. The chest bones creaked. A crack. One final twist. His body split open like budding arnica in the morning light.

Rebecca stared into the abyss. The intimate knowledge of Franco's innards stared back. She puked.

"You missed Franco, I hope?"

Rebecca grunted.

"Good. The difficult part is over. Before we excavate what I hope will prove my theory, let us measure and record the stab wounds."

Rebecca thumbed to a blank page in the tome. As Lorenzo instructed, she noted how many, how large, and the location for each and every stab wound. They worked in tandem. He insisted on feeling every puncture. Twice he started and asked Rebecca to double-check their measurements.

"What is your theory, father?"

Lorenzo laid his hands over Franco. He closed his eyes. The logs in the brazier crackled, and Rebecca fidgeted. The stench of her sick mixed with Franco's insides.

"Review your notes. Tell me if you notice a pattern."

Rebecca ran her charcoal-covered index finger down the list. She did it again, this time, her finger stopped halfway. She conferred with the body. Removing a passatore from her sheath, she came within a hair's breadth from inserting it into a wound, but the priest stopped her.

"Which wound are you testing?"

She let him know, and he allowed her to continue. Pleased, Rebecca said, "A passatore stabbed Franco."

Lorenzo grunted in approval.

"But your theory is that he died of other causes."

"How come?"

"Though many, these injuries would not kill—only wound."

Lorenzo clapped her on the shoulder. "Shall we test my theory?"

This tested more than his theory—it tested Rebecca's will to remain conscious. He probed, snipped, and cut skin away, then hammered, flayed, and tugged. The cherry-like beads sat on the table.

"Recall, Franco struggled to draw breath," he said. "Lungs draw air to the body." He pointed to the double, meaty sacks beneath the rib cage. "These nodes," he said, pointing to the beads. "They control your humors. If the humors have been damaged by toxin, they send cool waters throughout the vital tissue such as the lungs. The cooling effect could suffocate the victim."

"Victim?"

Lorenzo ignored her question. "I must compare the weight of his lungs against that of another's to know for certain."

Rebecca took more measurements as instructed.

"Well?"

Lorenzo held Franco's hand. "Well, what?"

"If you suspect he was killed by toxin, then stabbed by a Son to conceal it, what do we do?"

"Rebecca, not a word to Rustichello or Azzo or anyone. We need more evidence either way. It is for our safety."

Lorenzo made a note in his own journal before they met the Fixer in the study. The priest relayed their process to Rustichello. He requested to keep the body an additional day to finish examinations; however, the cause of death was most certainly not belladonna.

Rebecca held her tongue.

17

— · —

PHYSICIAN, LOVER, INVESTIGATOR

Rebecca left Father Lorenzo alone with his thoughts and Franco's body. When he emerged from the crypt a day later, she inquired as to his investigation. The priest burned belladonna and soft tissue. He measured organs. Lorenzo whined about needing undiluted wine. Rebecca encouraged him to remain sober.

"Not a word to anyone," he said.

Rebecca could live with the secrecy. Why not? Father Lorenzo showed her compassion, trained her, and welcomed her into his process for solving this mystery. He cared about her opinion, her faith. The Void still stood on uneven ground in her estimation as the Lord's spirit was sown in stony earth that was Rebecca's heart.

"I have a favor to ask."

She agreed before he could explain. Dispose of Franco's body, save the pieces stored in the marble chest. Rebecca shivered. Which pieces did the priest keep? She gathered a bolt of burlap and rope from the storeroom. Rebecca didn't think she could lift Franco's remains alone, so she set off to find Azzo. Lorenzo didn't say anything about working alone.

She paused outside the Fixer's study. Raised voices rumbled from behind the mahogany door. Rustichello berated someone. Shadows of pacing feet disrupted the light. Before she could discern who took the Fixer's wrath or stride away back towards Lorenzo's charge, the door opened. Azzo bumped into her, leaving at speed.

"Rebecca! I was just coming to find you."

"As was I, you."

"It must wait. Come in."

Dread settled in her chest. As she guessed, the Fixer paced. He smoked. Candle butts and scraps of parchment littered the floor.

"You've been summoned," he said. The Fixer ceased pacing. "On the orders of Alessandro Boccanegra, captain of the people."

Rebecca didn't bother hiding her alarm. She looked at Azzo for clarity. He squeezed her forearm.

"Trust me, Rebecca. Alessandro does not wish you harm."

"I'm no one," Rebecca said. "And I owe the captain nothing."

The Fixer laughed. "On that we agree. As your keeper, of sorts, I've been summoned also. You have not paid your debt, therefore it is in my best interest to represent you."

"I won't go."

The Fixer stubbed his joint. "We go now."

Azzo reassured her. "I made Alessandro a deal."

The Fixer shoved past the pair and scoffed. "Have you grown fond of Boccanegra, Azzo? Your charge was to extract intelligence, not fall in love." He trudged from his office.

Rebecca and Azzo kept pace through the tunnel and into the crypt pathway. She deposited the burlap and rope on the table beside Franco's dissected corpse. Rustichello paused.

"I'll expect a full report on Lorenzo's findings when our business in the palace is concluded."

Rebecca grunted. She'd never betray the priest's confidence. She took note of Franco's dismembered hand and foot. She had her suspicions as to why Lorenzo kept those parts of the fallen Son.

The path continued beneath the city, between the cathedral and the captain's palace. Similar to the sloping tunnel into the town hall, they emerged into a secret doorway to the captain's quarters. However, Rustichello had them exit through the cathedral and walk through the city. The captain must not have been aware of the underground connection between the two buildings.

Rebecca recalled the palace from her first ride into Genoa. Its columns and statues patronized and bullied residents. The eyes of whoever sat behind its marble and grandeur must have done the same.

The Fixer turned to Rebecca once they reached the courtyard and said, "Not a word about our deeds, girl. Deny all contracts if you know what is good for you."

Rebecca resented the Fixer for his assumptions. Of course she would not implicate the Sons or her deeds. Armed guards greeted the trio beneath the outdoor vestibule.

"Master Azzo," one said. "This way."

It was Rebecca's turn to raise her brows at her fellow trainee. He ignored her questioning gaze, jaw clenched. Led to a marble staircase of the same design as the main atrium in the Palazzo of Saint George, they ascended in silence.

The guards opened the double doors and shepherded them through. Two sealed the door behind them and one announced their arrival to the man seated on an elaborately carved wooden chair.

"Rustichello da Pisa, Azzo of Napoli, and the woman," the sentryman said.

Rebecca stifled her disdain, her voice choked in the back of her throat at the sight of the captain's guest. Standing to his side, left arm in a cloth sling, Doctor Leonardo Salvagno studied the trio.

The Fixer stamped with every step, huffing and rolling his eyes at the summons. His defiance fueled Rebecca's confidence. How much power did the captain hold over them? Was she shielded by the Sons of Saint George? Was the captain in league with the Nightshade Brotherhood as Leo was? Rebecca regretted not divulging this discovery with the Fixer. It may be the crucial detail that would save their lives.

"I've desired to meet you for some time, Rustichello da Pisa," the captain said. "Arresting this girl pulled you from your hideout."

"Genoa has been my home for years. And you're wrong."

The captain was much younger than Rebecca expected. An elected official, he lorded over them as if he were born in this hall. She reminded herself he must be of noble class to attain this office—never doubting a rise to importance or power. His gaze lingered on Azzo longer than the Fixer or Rebecca. Azzo kept his eyes trained on the wall behind Boccanegra.

"Wrong?"

The Fixer drew a joint from his inner pocket. He sniffed it. He examined it in the light. Walking to the wall, he lit his hemp indulgence in a torch. After a deep drag and saunter back to his trainees, the Fixer clarified.

"My ward is not under arrest. We have come voluntarily."

The captain bowed. "Our fair city's enmity with Pisa aside, Rustichello, the good doctor here, has posed serious questions." He indicated to Leo. "I wish to resolve the matter."

"I'll determine the gravity of his questions," the Fixer said.

Doctor Salvagno bowed to the captain. He paced across the room and faced Rebecca.

"My name is Doctor Leonardo Salvagno. Milan's magistrates employed me to identify a murderer in our fair city."

"Then what are you doing in Genoa?" the Fixer asked. "Doctor." Disdain coated his voice.

Rebecca knew the doctor to be tender, naive, spiritual to the point of infuriation. How he'd fare against the raging Fixer was yet unknown.

Leonardo smiled. He paced and made a show of pulling a silver object from his tunic. A passatore. Rebecca's stomach plummeted. She replayed their struggle in the podesta's manor over in her head and realized her error. She left a blade behind—in his shoulder. Leo handed the weapon to Boccanegra.

"A passatore, if I'm not mistaken. My colleague, Giulio Panza, suggested I might find its owner in Genoa."

"Do you recognize this weapon, Rustichello?" the captain asked, brandishing the blade.

"Tool," the Fixer corrected him.

"What did you say?"

The Fixer finished his joint and flicked the stub at Leo's feet. Through his exhale, he expanded on his comment. "That is a tool, Alessandro. Not a weapon."

Boccanegra stomped across the room and held the throwing dagger in the Fixer's face. "Do you recognize this *tool*, Rustichello da Pisa, guest in my palace, guest in my city?"

The Fixer turned his head.

Leonardo placed a gentle hand on the captain's arm. The gesture, reminiscent of Rebecca's years acting as his favorite courtesan.

"Four men," Leo said. "Father Pio Rocco, Giancarlo Acorri, Bartolo Reale, and Gennaio Milotti were slain in the stewhouses in Milan, but not by a passatore. By my merit as a doctor, I'm left to wonder."

Sweat beaded at Rebecca's brow and beneath her armpits. She desired to rub her face dry, but dared not move. Leo didn't wish to pursue her assault on him in the manor, but came knocking for her prior indiscretions.

"By all means," the Fixer said. "Enlighten us with your wonderings, doctor."

Rebecca groaned in silence. *Shut up.* Yet his barking might be all that stood between truth and the Breaking Wheel.

"Were they committed by the same hand?"

Smug, self-satisfied, Boccanegra's face invited a fist Rebecca wanted to offer. The captain slammed the passatore on the table and retook his seat. His guards poked their heads into the room at the elevated voices and disturbance, but he waved them off.

"Captain," Azzo said. "I do not see the relevance of our presence and the doctor's line of questioning. If we may confer in private, I'm sure—"

Leonardo held his right hand in the air to interject. Boccanegra deferred to him.

The doctor rounded on Rebecca. "Did you kill those men? Upstanding, faithful members of society?"

The generous allowance in his description of the lecherous patrons set off a fuse that had been coiled for ten years. Rebecca didn't need a tool or weapon—she wished to throttle Leo to death with her bare hands.

"Lechers! Hypocrites! They feigned piety. Be truthful, Leo."

The Fixer's gaze narrowed. Too furious to notice the subtle change in demeanor, Rebecca 's anger distorted her vision. Leo pressed forward, bearing down so close to her she could smell the leather and shaving putty.

"Would you believe me, Signore Boccanegra, that this woman was a common whore prior to her time in Rustichello's employ?"

"And what is the manner of her duties?" Boccanegra interjected. "I wish to know."

Leo cut across him. "But you are no common whore, are you, Rebecca Guarna? Did you kill those men?"

"You're a fool," she said.

"Did you kill them?"

"Man of faith," she mocked.

"Do you deny it?"

"I never loved you!"

The silence buzzed. Rebecca didn't recognize the doctor before her. As the most intimate male relationship she ever experienced—a blend of father, mentor, and lover—spewed vitriol in her face, her heart grew cold. She wouldn't admit it, but she longed for his trite recounting of Scripture. If he took aim to wound her character, she would do the same.

"How could I? I never desired a child. When the bleeding stopped and my belly grew, Zita helped me purge your seed from my womb. A tumble down the stairs worked. The memory of your touch disgusts me, vile swine. Fine! I admit it—you have discovered the truth."

The Fixer gripped her arm. Azzo opened his mouth to interject. Boccanegra, half-seated, half-standing, watched mouth agape.

"I was your whore. Nothing more, nothing less. My relationship to Rustichello is the same as it was to you, doctor."

The Fixer cleared his throat. "A lover's spat! The matter is settled."

Boccanegra stood. "Doctor." He gathered the passatore. "Did you get what you needed?"

The vein in Leonardo's temple pulsed. Again, Rebecca felt him crumble, the illusion of their tryst shattered. He bowed to the captain.

"I apologize for wasting your time, captain."

"On the contrary," Boccanegra said, offering the throwing knife to the Fixer. "I desired an audience with Rustichello. Although our fleet sits in the harbor, Pisa will be mine. Do not forget it, friend."

"Should you wish to parlay again, Alessandro," Rustichello said, accepting it with an air of curiosity. "You may meet me on *The Corsican*. I prefer open water to the luxuries of court." He bowed. "I take it we are dismissed?"

Boccanegra dismissed them with a wave.

Rebecca's face burned with humiliation, but she held her head aloft. She refused to give Leo, or the other men, the satisfaction of seeing her downtrodden.

The Fixer insisted they take a circuitous route back to the palazzo. The captain's guards blatantly followed them. They weaved to the street behind the palace and descended the dilapidated staircase where Rebecca first entered the hidden network of tunnels. Behind the painting that doubled as a secret entrance painting, the clang of wood and metal scraped stone. The hidden tunnel felt alive.

Three blond figures in red and brown surcoats emerged from the armory. Before Rebecca could get a clear look, the Fixer flung the passatore into the nearest man. "Nightshade brothers. Kill them!"

Rebecca and Azzo drew blades and gave chase. They bolted deeper underground as Father Lorenzo stumbled from the armory, clutching his gut. Blood seeped through his fingers, crimson smeared his face.

"Father!" Rebecca said, gripping his shoulder to ease him to the ground.

"The Austrians!" He slipped his notebook into Azzo's hand. "Stop them."

Breath ragged, the priest dismissed them with a nod.

"Circle the building," Rebecca said. "I'll drive them outside."

Azzo did as she commanded. Fury coursed through Rebecca's veins, plunging her farther into the black. She assumed each portage was protected, their training halls a bastion of safety. That assumption proved wrong. She closed her mouth to quiet her breathing. Her pace, however, betrayed her whereabouts.

A fist swung around the curve and into her mouth. It wasn't the worst punch she'd ever endured, but the surprise in the dark jostled her. Rebecca lanced forward and stabbed air. A foot pinned the blade against the wall. Footsteps of his accomplice scampered away. She drew a second knife and lodged it in the attacker's thigh—into his major artery. His scream pierced the claustrophobic tunnel.

Rebecca stabbed the injured Austrian twice in the heart and jumped over his dying body. Sprinting in earnest to deliver justice, Rebecca felt the floor elevate. Dim light illuminated a figure reaching the top of a ladder. She squinted at the light above from double doors.

Rebecca swung a leg over the ledge and squinted to get her bearings. She faced a galley, elevated on massive beech tree trunks. The keel hung above wood shavings. Coils of rope awaited their fate as mast line, anchor ties, and ladder material. The workshop opened to greet the port, sea air filling her nose. Woodworkers and engineers toiled atop the galley. A stack of oars toppled and Rebecca ducked in time to avoid a handle bashing in her skull.

The Austrian swung again. Rebecca's shoulder bounced off the hull. She launched a blade, which thudded into the wood. He jabbed at her gut and swiped in long, sweeping arcs. The rough-hewn floorboards offered a treacherous purchase. She stumbled into the pride of Genoa's craftsmanship again. The Austrian laughed. Rebecca recognized his nondescript face beneath the cruel mask. He pressed the battering ram at her and turned tail. She caught the oar with an *oomph*.

The Austrian, with Rebecca in hot pursuit, spilled out of the workshop. Groups of Genoese piled logs into small bonfires along the street. Each fire sat in front of a home. They weaved through the crowd, Rebecca bumping into a priest.

Prayers to Saint Joseph, Jesus's earthly father, interrupted. She followed the blazes dotting the piazza. The Feast Day commemorated Joseph's paternal instinct to protect a pregnant Mary against their cold reception in Bethlehem. Rebecca rumbled through the citizens of the republic to keep her target in sight.

She spotted him. He leered through flames of a roaring bonfire, watching, waiting for her to close the lead. The Austrian lifted a hood and sealed his palms in mock prayer. The disguise was brilliant. How could she kill a priest among the faithful in broad daylight?

Smiling, he sauntered past children, blessing them, offering a nod to other clergymen. Rebecca kept pace with her head lowered. The crowd swelled. Sweat burned her eyes. Ignoring shouts of indignation as she pushed people from her way, Rebecca spotted him. He boarded a carriage, and with a final smirk, the driver whipped the horses onto the Piazza Raffaele de Ferrari. Rebecca startled penitent families with a shout.

She lost him.

Rebecca ignored curious and outraged faces as she sprinted back to the palace. She pounded the basement stairs, nearly winded as she reached the armory. Father Lorenzo was laid out on a table, his robe front opened to his waist. The Fixer, Volta, and Azzo crowded round. She jumped over spears and swords from the overturned racks. A man in his prime would have succumbed to so many stab wounds.

"We couldn't stitch him in time," Azzo said.

The priest died clutching his rosary.

"Can I have a moment?"

Volta and Azzo left. The Fixer patted her shoulder and told her to report to his study when she was ready.

Lorenzo alone, the vision fading from his pale blue eyes, saw Rebecca for what she was, for what she could be. He valued her existence. She wasn't convinced the Void had a plan for her or that she deserved His love. But she suspected the priest, in his most quiet, private heart, believed in salvation.

Rebecca made the sign of the cross and prayed his spirit did not linger, that the Lord did not protest his merit. The foul circumstances of his death should account for a reasonable judgment.

She pocketed his rosary and closed Lorenzo's eyes.

"Amen."

18
— · —

THE LAST CONTRACT

"**S**omeone was followed!"

Azzo stormed in the Fixer's study. Rebecca threaded the rosary through her fingers, letting the coarse rope bristle in her palm. She sat on the windowsill. Lorenzo once sat here surveying the vase filled with Atropa Belladonna on the Fixer's desk. Was his spirit wandering the palazzo or had it passed through Death's veil?

The stench of a joint broke Rebecca's reverie. Volta appeared in the doorway and Azzo rounded on him.

"And where were *you*?"

Rebecca gave Azzo credit for poking Behemoth in the chest. She understood his frustration, but preferred not to pick a fight with Volta unarmed.

"I do not answer to you, boy," Volta said. He raised a forearm the thickness of Rebecca's thigh, but the Fixer halted him. Azzo's chest swelled and he glared at the threat.

"He was on assignment," the Fixer said. "Receiving this." He held a scroll aloft.

"On assignment," Rebecca said. She waved the smoke from her view and brandished the rosary. "How come Father Lorenzo was left unprotected? How many Sons of Saint George do you command, Rustichello?"

The Fixer grimaced. In the wake of Lorenzo's death, Rebecca threw caution to the wind. Azzo could not be punished for her choice. The priest would not shield them from the assassin-master. Rebecca felt exposed. Raw. If she suffered in Lorenzo's absence, then Rustichello needed to be laid bare also.

He poured four cups of wine and encouraged the group to accept his offer. He raised his glass. "Wrong question, Rebecca, but I must admit, you are correct. Let us take a moment to honor Lorenzo. His death is our loss. He was my oldest—and dearest—friend."

Volta followed suit. Azzo watched Rebecca for approval before taking the cup from the desk. She took a cup and examined its contents. The Fixer sucked it through his teeth.

"Eleven Sons sail *The Corsican*," the Fixer said. "Several are on sensitive assignments. Like I told you before, I cannot divulge the entire whereabouts or count. How could I risk their lives? What I can say is that the rest are on the island."

Azzo glanced at Rebecca, eyes wide. She drained her cup and pressed the advantage. Nothing like death to loosen lips.

"Which island?"

Volta laughed. "Isn't that obvious?"

"You three represent our strength in Genoa," the Fixer continued. "And right now, there are bodies in our tunnels. Austrian bodies."

Leadership and assertiveness were not part and parcel; however, direction of any sort was welcomed in moments of uncertainty. The sting of Lorenzo's death hurt, but Rebecca hungered for guidance.

"I'll search them," Volta said.

"Good," the Fixer said. "Bring them to the crypt."

"We were *all* followed, Azzo," Rebecca said. "I recognized one of the Brothers, the one that got away."

The room fell silent. Rebecca described his bristling blond hair, the robin's egg eyes, a round jaw. When Azzo and Rebecca arrived in Pavia to kidnap Lorenzo—she did not utter his name—a parishioner gathered his palms and waited to say his farewell to the pastor. He startled Rebecca at his frank appraisal, watching them linger in the vestibule. The same smirking face infiltrated the palazzo, killed Lorenzo, and escaped by impersonating a priest.

"The Austrian's been tailing us since Pavia?" Azzo said.

"Jesus," the Fixer said. "Yes, all of us by the sounds of it. The emperor is thorough. He saw your faces?"

Although the question was redundant, Azzo and Rebecca's silence was tacit assent. Another uncomfortable truth nagged at Rebecca. If there was ever a time to choose transparency, then it was the present.

"Doctor Salvagno," she said.

"Rebecca," Azzo cut across her. "You don't have to—"

She patted his forearm. "I believe he is working with the Nightshade Brotherhood." Rebecca told them about the belladonna bouquet in his room at Podesta Marti's manor. Azzo groaned. She appreciated the support. Her embarrassment at exposing so much of their intimate history felt fresh as the split lip she sported. She ignored Volta's confused looks, but the Fixer offered a somber nod.

"We must act fast then," he said. "There's but one solution to the Nightshade Brotherhood—eradicate the della Torre family."

"Hear, hear," Volta said.

The Fixer unfurled the scroll and turned it to face his audience. Rebecca and Azzo stepped forward to read it. "The Lombard League has issued an order to sever the head of the snake, Corrado della Torre. The patriarch will be at his Lake Como estate, Primaluna."

Azzo's temper cooled, but Rebecca could not discern the look in which he appraised the scroll. "This order arrived, when?"

The Fixer lit another joint and squinted at the favored son through a haze. "In the night. Right, Volta?"

Behemoth grunted. Rebecca thought he'd still like to strike Azzo for his accusatory poke. Whatever Azzo's reservations, he kept them to himself. The Fixer turned to Rebecca.

"I take it you need no coddling? Kill Corrado, the Nightshade Brotherhood has no reason to pursue us. With the emperor's lackey gone, the Lombard League reigns supreme. Rebecca, the bounty would satisfy your debt."

Rebecca believed him. Somewhere in the depths of her core, a kindling of faith ignited because of Lorenzo's example. The Nightshade Brotherhood would not cease until the della Torre-Visconti feud ended definitively. A purpose beyond herself. The Fixer gave her that chance. She could unburden the yoke of debt, prove she is worth more than coin, and avenge Lorenzo di Costa. One final contract.

Azzo offered nothing but warning behind his curtain of locks. She skimmed the scroll again. It was not signed by the Lombard League or Matteo Visconti I, but one "C.P." Rebecca slammed her cup onto the desk.

"When must I depart?"

Rebecca ignored Azzo's consternation. A shadow of a smile lingered behind the Fixer's beard. She knew he waited for a sign of weakness, for a recoil in her gut decision. She would not give anyone the satisfaction of misgivings. This contract was hers. She earned it. She would deliver a resounding success. He gave her less than a week to prepare. Rebecca could do it. She had to.

"I expect results."

The Fixer dismissed them. Volta shoved past the trainees, fast becoming full-fledged Sons of Saint George, to recover the Austrians and lay Father Lorenzo in the crypt. Rebecca mimed "ma che vuoi"—*what's wrong?*—at her disgruntled compatriot. He held a finger to his lips and nodded to the spiral staircase. She sprinted to maintain pace with his strides. At the top, Azzo peered into the prison cells. He leaned against the parapet. Alessandro Boccanegra's fleet shifted listless in the harbor.

"Something doesn't feel right, Rebecca."

A pit formed in her stomach. She didn't want to hear naysaying when there were preparations to be made.

"You don't believe I can fulfill the contract?"

Azzo scoffed. "Of course that's not my belief. You're more than capable." He smacked her upper arm with the back of his hand. "The Nightshade Brotherhood infiltrate the palazzo, kill Father

Lorenzo, *and* another contract arrives in the night from the Lombard League? Convenient, isn't it?"

Rebecca rested her forearms on the parapet. "What are you saying? I have a chance to be free of Rustichello's debt. Do I forfeit the contract for coincidence?"

Dinghies and jolly boats cut wide berths around galleys as slate-gray clouds gathered overhead.

"I don't know. And who is C.P.?" A spring shower rolled over the promenade and spittled against the tower's stone room. The rain beaded on their cheeks. Azzo wiped a tear away and sighed. "Poor Lorenzo."

"You convinced me to come to Genoa, not Rustichello." Rebecca held out a hand. He clasped it. "Just wish me luck."

"In bocca al lupo, Rebecca." *Into the wolf's mouth.*

"Crepi il lupo." *May the wolf die.*

***

The esteemed guests of Signore Corrado della Torre reveled at his verdant estate nestled in the mountains east of Lake Como. The Primaluna region offered seclusion for plotting, security for the waning influence of his family in the republic of Milan.

Notes from strings, horns, and wind instruments drifted onto the grounds, punctuating the last of the spring day's twittering birdsong. The villa's stone walls swelled with decadence. Cooks poured over cauldrons and cutting boards as the waitstaff shuttled dishes throughout the various nooks and crannies of the stone villa. Wine flowed from cellar to cup, noble men and ladies laughing at their good fortune for imbibing the host's generosity, fit to please Bacchus, the god of wine himself.

Rebecca's thighs ached as she perched inside della Torre's smoking room. Thick drapery obscured the fading light. She positioned her black-clad figure in the shadows of a wooden armoire, hidden in plain sight among the gaudy decor. Azzo insisted she travel at night on backroads in full garb—black tunic, surcoat, and wide-brimmed hat, the black chiffon mask pulled over her head the entire ride. She cursed the Austrian in silence for making her face in Pavia.

The Lombard League's intelligence pointed to a gathering of premier conspirators under the guise of Corrado's party. Guests languished on the finest upholstery while schemes developed to disrupt Visconti rule. Rebecca's task—eliminate Corrado and his son, Florimondo.

Florimondo, Corrado's heir, arrived first. His cheekbones breathed haughtiness into a resting expression. He positioned the leather chairs into a semicircle around a low card table. Rebecca held her breath as he passed between the towering armoire and his father's desk. She heard a glass decanter open, liquid slosh into a cup, and the son gulp with a self-satisfied smack. Florimondo opened the door, clueless to her presence.

Two men entered, the cackles of laughter slipped past. A shawm trilled and naker drums beat the end of a frivolous tune. Florimondo welcomed the guests and poured drinks. The door swung open once more, berthing the host and guest of honor, chattering like girls in the stew. The Lombard League—C.P., Rebecca corrected herself—instructed the Sons of Saint George not to kill Podesta Antonio Marti, who would be present. He was their inside man. Matteo Visconti was one step closer to securing absolute control over the republic using this mole.

She kept her head lowered, well-worn boots planted to the floor. Rebecca resented her fluttering heartbeat. Reliant on hearing alone, she steadied her breath and recited a generic, silent prayer. The heft of bodies and positions of voices painted an image in her mind.

"Gentlemen," said a booming voice. "Welcome to Primaluna! Allow me to introduce the man of the hour—Condottiero Amerigo di Narbona. We raise our glasses to your promotion, sir."

"Cent'anni!" *A hundred years*, the room said in unison, tossing back their drink.

"With your appointment," Corrado continued, "the emperor's army will swell and the Ghibellines will be neutered."

A new voice responded, presumably Amerigo's, interrupting a nagging in the back of Rebecca's mind. The Nightshade Brotherhood, and Leo Salvagno, tried poisoning Giulio Panza. Under what circumstances would Leo betray his pope and support the emperor's cause?

"You have my sincerest gratitude, Corrado."

Silence again as they drained glasses. Florimondo refilled each.

Amerigo continued, "The Ghibellines gather in Arezzo and Florence. One does not know which brother, neighbor, or city official is for the emperor or the pope these days. Fortunately, we have stouthearted young captains like the fellow I brought tonight."

"Ah, yes," Corrado said. "Dante Alighieri? He seemed the most convincing of tongues. Wooed many swords to the cause?"

"Indeed, he has rallied the masses."

A silken voice interjected. "Has losing your eye hindered your efforts, condottiere?"

Amerigo's laugh sounded like wind through a marshland. Rebecca sensed danger behind the mirth.

"A badge of honor, Maurizio. A small sacrifice to purge the city-state of papist fools."

The door opened. A gentle thud of metal against wood paused the banter. A scent of roast fowl, fruity and fatty, met Rebecca's nose. Clinks of cutlery against plates began in vigor. The mashing of meat, cartilage, and skin nauseated her. Never had the sound of chewing pleased Rebecca.

"The duck is outstanding," a new voice said.

Corrado interjected. "Dear Maurizio gifted my home with the finest mallards and hens from Venice."

"And they have been prepared to perfection by Corrado's excellent cooks," Maurizio responded.

Would Atropa Belladonna be effective in food, Rebecca wondered?

"A fine gift," Corrado said. "You honored my guests."

Grunts murmured their approval. Maurizio pitched the conversation elsewhere. "Our weavers are experimenting with duck down. The applications are numerous, although they aren't certain of its merit in comparison to wool's durability in clothing, for instance."

"As long as the florins keep flowing north from the Arte della Lana," Florimondo said. "Experiment with the fowls all you wish!"

The son's laughter at his own remark was met with silence. Rebecca cringed at the bald stupidity as she imagined the occupants had. A firm slap to wood stifled the guffawing.

"Is that how you address the head of the largest trade guild north of Rome? Maurizio, my dear friend, please accept my apologies for my son's rot for brains."

Maurizio cleared his throat. "No offense taken, Signore della Torre. He is young and not yet acquainted with our business."

"And he may never be," Corrado said.

"Father," Florimondo said, clearing his throat. "Signore Maurizio, please, I'm sorry."

Before Maurizio could accept, the door opened again.

"Signore?"

"Ah," Corrado said. "My Austrian bodyguard. Come in! Florimondo, go fetch more wine and return with better senses."

Quick footsteps padded across the rug. The leather-plated mahogany door groaned as it emitted the fool of a son and admitted the Austrian bodyguard. Rebecca never heard the Nightshade Brother's voice, so she had no clue whether it was the escaped assailant who killed Father Lorenzo or not. Either way, doubt crept into her spirit. The room was full of a member of the Nightshade Brotherhood, a seasoned mercenary captain, and three men. Rebecca snuck inside with ease. Killing Corrado and escaping with her life would be the challenge.

"There's no issue, Adam," Corrado said.

Adam grunted. Rebecca keened her ear to the shifting voices and tension in the study. She opened and closed her mouth, nearly exhaling at the realization she was holding her breath.

"The boy has a point," Amerigo said. "I gather you've invited us here for more than celebrating my promotion, Corrado. Let's not be shy."

Maurizio said, "Si, my thoughts as well. What do you propose dear Corrado?"

Corrado clapped his hands. "Indeed! Antonio, would you do the honors? It was your plan after all."

19

— · —

THE ESTATE OF CORRADO DELLA TORRE

"**I** was appointed as Chief Judicial Magistrate in Milan," Antonio said. "Matteo Visconti has no clue I prefer the old guard to the new governor."

Corrado paced around the chairs, the fatted grease of duck and rich notes of berries lingering as he passed Rebecca. The della Torre patriarch, one of the wealthiest men north of Rome, a shrewd descendant of noble blood, did not detect the assassin against the wall. He continued to pace as Marti addressed the study.

"I propose an expanded trade alliance. Signore della Torre will invest a *significant* sum of pfennigs and groschen into the Arte della Lana. Signore Maurizio, this insurance from the emperor gives you less risk to increase textile production. The expanded profits in Milan, Florence, and Pisa will then be reinvested into the magistrate's discretionary fund."

A round of whistles and grunting laughs murmured. Corrado jumped back into the proposal. Rebecca imagined Corrado's smug face at his subversive cleverness.

"By removing those ridiculous Ambrogino d'Oro coins from circulation—"

"—Which our contact in Genoa has orchestrated—"

"We will destabilize Visconti's power through simple economics."

Amerigo said, "By reinvesting in the Magistrate's judges, you'll bring the entire republic to heel."

Rebecca made a mental note to alert Father Lorenzo of the "contact in Genoa" —whoever that may be—but a pang of melancholy reared its head. Her report would go to the Fixer. She squashed the loss that left a tear in her heart. Surviving this contract required her full faculties.

"Control the judges," Corrado said. "Control Milan."

A small group of wealthy, scheming men controlled Milan from the closed-door studies, feasting on ducks and their own hubris. No wonder Visconti and the Lombard League hired the Sons of Saint George to clear these pieces from the board. Albeit, the Viscontis did the same from their residences. The push-and-pull of wine-laden nobles from the safety of the mountains would affect the people of the republic in unimaginable ways. Rebecca's fellow common folk were clueless to their inability to determine their own fates.

"Won't the emperor lose a taxation stream from the Arte della Lana guild?" Amerigo asked. "If profits are rerouted to Milan?"

The merchant answered. "There's so much construction happening across the republic right now, including the new canal, that the magistrates can hire sympathizers as laborers and import materials from Austria. The emperor will receive a cut from the new basilica fund, which won't be approved until the pope loosens sanctions against Rudolf."

"Matteo is the runt of the Visconti family," Corrado said. "But no fool. He won't become bullish on new construction."

Through a full mouth of vittles, Maurizio said, "Visconti inherited a flaccid rabble of soldiers from his granduncle. Any army you levy, Amerigo, could support the magistrates."

"That is precisely why we're celebrating dear Amerigo's promotion," Marti said. "As insurance."

Rebecca heard enough. Marti was either one amazing liar or he was no longer working for the Lombard League. She could not judge. Faith demanded she trust his allegiance to Visconti. Before Rebecca revealed her presence, the door opened again, followed by Florimondo's waspish dismissal of the waitstaff.

"Finally," Corrado said.

Using his arrival as a distraction, Rebecca lifted her head. The della Torre conspirators were seated or standing as she expected them to be. Corrado leaned against his desk, his guests sitting between her and the Austrian, Adam. Maurizio was the first to gasp at her revelation as he faced the wardrobe from a leather chair.

"A ghost!"

Rebecca hurled a passatore. Maurizio's dying breath gurgled among the startled men. Antonio jumped to his feet, but Rebecca kicked his legs from under him. She pressed forward as Adam drew a blade. Corrado sprinted to hide behind his Nightshade bodyguard. The fool of a son, Florimondo, fumbled with a short, ceremonial sword. Rebecca grabbed a stone paperweight from the desk and threw it at him. The stone smashed into his forehead, and he hit the rug with a clunk.

"Florimondo!" Corrado shouted.

Amerigo di Narbona—the greatest threat in the room—loomed over Rebecca. A scar pinched the skin from forehead to mid-cheek in grotesque fashion, healed over a severe gouge. At some point during the controlled chaos, he drew a mace from the wall. He hefted it as if he was preparing to teach a novice soldier how to wield his first weapon. In Corrado's study, it was decorative, yet spikes protruded from the iron ball.

He kicked the low table to create space between him and Rebecca. She drew a shortsword and another passatore. The Nightshade Brother snarled at Corrado's grasping, cloying grip. He drew a blade, and the trio circled one another. Rebecca pushed the group counterclockwise, then changed direction to keep Marti behind her. She recalled Lorenzo's training. The blade in her grip was an extension of her arm and hand.

Amerigo swung. Rebecca parried. The Austrian took advantage of the soldier's advance, also lunging at Rebecca. She pulled the pommel into the air and deflected his short blade's thrust.

Adam stumbled backwards. Rebecca mock-lunged at Amerigo. She feinted towards Adam. Both men overextended themselves in a rush to parry, giving Rebecca intense relief. For all their savagery, they were frightened of a woman. The stalemate must cease if Rebecca stood a chance at surviving. Blood of Florimondo and Maurizio drained onto the refinery. Rebecca shifted right, giving Amerigo space to swing the mace. She launched herself into the air using the table and plunged her blade into the condottiere's neck. He roared like a lion but could not dislodge her assault. She ripped the blade from his neck and staggered into the desk.

In her moment's glory, she failed to protect Marti. A squelching brought her attention to the back armoire. The Nightshade Brother plunged his blade into Marti's neck and heart repeatedly, blood coating his naked hand. The Lombard League lost a member, but Rebecca could still see her contract through. Corrado crawled towards the door. She lunged.

Adam blocked her swipe. He swung again. Rebecca twisted away once, twice, three times, becoming dizzy and disoriented. The host stood at the door, his son's limp body blocking his egress. Panic painted Corrado's face, as he must have known he would not leave his study alive. In their spat, Adam settled by the window. He smirked at Rebecca, trapped by a litter of corpses and the emperor's assassin.

Unsure what gave her the idea, Rebecca hurled the shortsword at Corrado's heart, but did not wait to confirm if it landed. She sprinted full tilt at Adam and tackled him through the window.

The glass shattered against his back. Rebecca squeezed her eyes closed, praying the stunt would not cost her more than she intended to pay.

Two stories above the manicured lawn, the fall lasted an eternity. They hit the ground with a violent crunch, Adam beneath Rebecca. The fall knocked the wind clear of her lungs as she lay atop the Nightshade Brother who killed Father Lorenzo, the man who escaped her in the tunnels.

The commotion must have seeped into the party because shouts and screams burst through the shattered window above. The music trailed off, levity turned to chaos.

Lungs emptied, bruises formed on her elbows, forearms, and knees. She pressed her torso upwards. If the passatore in Adam's gut didn't kill him, the dent on the back of his cracked skull did.

His foot twitched. The adrenaline of the fight and the impact of the fall made Rebecca woozy.

She rolled onto her back to slow the spinning earth beneath her. Guests spilled onto the estate grounds, rushing to carriages and horses. Fair ladies and gentlemen would seek sanctuary in adjacent manors. A horse galloped through the hedges and across the lawn. A rider in black boots jumped from the saddle and grabbed Rebecca by the surcoat. She was too weak, too exhausted to fight the abduction.

The figure tossed her over the saddle like a rucksack, whisking her away from the estate and her consciousness.

***

Fire cackled. The smoke enveloped the larch tree stand's understory. A horse whinnied, plodding a soft ground from a recent sprinkling. Rebecca's entire body ached. The throb behind her brow protested as her eyes flew open. She bolted upright against a log, instinct telling her she wasn't alone.

Azzo sat across the fire. Although her vision swam, it was indeed her fellow trainee. Her knee throbbed as she kicked backwards to take a seat.

"How's your head?" He offered a hand.

"What do you think?" Rebecca allowed him to pinch her chin and rotate her head side to side. The slight motion turned her stomach. "I fell from the second story."

"And onto a Nightshade Brother, I'm assuming?"

She winced the memory into clarity. Rebecca recounted her escapades in the estate. Azzo's mouth hung open at all the right twists and turns. She couldn't help but smile at the victory. She dispatched the della Torres and the Nightshade Brother who killed Lorenzo. Azzo clapped his gloved hands at the news. His enthusiasm for her success and their shared mourning for the priest endeared him to Rebecca.

"His name was Adam. Oh! Have you ever heard of Condottiere Amerigo di Narbona?"

"I have not."

Rebecca accepted a crust of bread and waterskin. Pins and needles shot through her left arm. She cradled it across her chest, flexing her fist to shake the fall that left her tender.

"A mercenary," she said. "He was gathering troops in Florence for the emperor." Pine and sodden earth, horse and ember filled Rebecca's nostrils as she drew a deep inhale. Rebecca spared no detail as Azzo listened rapt. He asked her to repeat several exchanges between the conspirators, and she focused, conceding a great effort to recall details they discussed. "You realize this will satisfy my debt to Rustichello?"

He nodded. Rebecca didn't believe joy lay beneath his smile. To break the uncomfortable moment, Azzo tossed her a notebook. She recognized it as Father Lorenzo's.

"He gave it to me," Azzo said. "After—"

Rebecca thumbed through the pages, blood splatter decorated the spine. Her eyes roved each page, glossing over the text in her desire to absorb all his innermost thoughts. She would require more time to investigate his journal, especially the entries regarding his struggle with over-consumption and her humors. Azzo jabbed his index finger on the page he wished her to inspect.

A sparse entry. Two drawings and a question. A crude sketch of a hand and foot were replete with slice marks. Lorenzo circled the blade's entry wounds. His question read, *Did George's devil wound Franco?*

Rebecca angled the journal towards the light. Near the vertical stab lines on both the foot and ankle were two round marks. Lorenzo's intended focus. She shook her head at Azzo.

"George's devil?

"Something's wrong, Rebecca. What did Lorenzo know? What are those marks?"

Rebecca leapt to her feet, knees roaring in pain burning like the embers beneath the logs. Azzo mirrored her, concerned at the jolt.

She held the journal and asked, "May I keep this? Until we search the crypt?"

Azzo agreed. "You want to inspect Lorenzo's corpse?"

Rebecca pocketed the journal and grabbed the horse's reins. "Franco's limbs are hidden in the marble chest."

* * *

As Azzo didn't press Rebecca about her former relationship—and failed pregnancy—with Leonardo, she didn't press him on Boccanegra. One inquiry was enough to reveal the sexual nature between the captain of the people and Azzo, encouraged by the Fixer. She was grateful it allowed them to pass through the palace and into the crypt without alerting the Sons. Rebecca approached the topic from another angle as they reached the crypt by torchlight.

"What does Tommaso think of your tryst with Alessandro?"

Azzo paused. His black silhouette slumped ahead of her. He turned and whispered, "Tommaso is a more generous and understanding man than I've ever encountered. I don't deserve his affection."

Rebecca gripped his forearm. They reached their destination and stared at their fallen mentor. Father Lorenzo was laid on the table, a sheet covering his body, foot to neck. The stench of death became all too familiar to Rebecca. She handed Azzo the torch and turned her back on Lorenzo's body. They returned to the palazzo for a reason and needed answers.

"Here."

She pushed the lid and took a deep breath before plunging her hand into the dark. She squirmed. Azzo squeezed her elbow, but she wished he hadn't. Her bruises were still too fresh.

Rebecca withdrew Franco's hand and his severed foot, cut below the calf. Azzo held the torch close as she inspected them on the wooden table. Rotating the hand, Rebecca found the two puncture wounds along the blade wound. The same two punctures lined the stab on the ankle.

"What the fuck is that?"

"Lorenzo suspected Franco was stabbed to conceal these wounds," Rebecca said. "They were the cause of death."

"Didn't he say something about the devil when you found him?"

"George's devil." Her mind raced. What killed Franco?

Footsteps approached. Volta emerged from the shadows.

"Azzo, Rebecca, follow me," his booming voice rattled the skeletons and coffin lids. "Time to be initiated."

20

INITIATION

The behemoth guard made no mention of the severed limbs on the table. He led them through the tunnel to Saint George's tomb, a place Rebecca wished to never visit again. The air was thick with smoke. Candles littered the floors and atop stands of various heights, giving an appearance they floated in the warren. Wooden braziers roared on either side of the altar.

The Fixer welcomed them with arms outstretched, the triptych shimmering with life behind him. Black-cloaked Sons lined the walls. Rebecca recognized *The Corsican* crew members. Each held an inverted crucifix. The heads of their wooden staffs were sharpened into spearpoints with a carved claw gripping the blade tip. She grabbed Azzo by the back of his tunic to prevent him from stepping into the grave. Two men, hog-tied and black-bagged, lay prone in the dirt.

"I sent you both into the wild," the Fixer said. "To achieve victory in battle." He wore chain mail, greaves, and shin guards. A white tunic with the scarlet Cross of Genoa painted his chest, while a longsword sat on his hip. "Were you victorious, Azzo?"

The tomb hummed with a pulsing energy Rebecca could not explain. Her vision twitched, her injuries vibrated. The orange light gave the illusion of movement on the portraits behind Rustichello. The dragon slithered, Faunus danced, and Saint George's eyes judged. She blinked the tears from the corners of her eyes.

Azzo bowed. "I believe I was."

"You believe?" the Fixer said, laughing. The Sons and Volta mock laughed in unison. "Did faith secure Boccanegra's allegiance or did the flesh?" He strode around the altar and drew his blade. "Come forward."

Rebecca grabbed his arm, but Azzo sauntered to face Rustichello. She gulped, mouth dry, and startled at a Son who tossed a bundle of grasses onto the brazier. The air was rank with hemp buds.

"Boccanegra agreed to grant *The Corsican* safe passage," Azzo said. "The galley will suffer no harm while he wages war on Pisa."

Rustichello took Azzo's wrist. He tugged him over the burial mound and positioned it over the basin. With a flash, the Fixer nicked his skin. He held his arm still as blood dripped into the basin.

"You have honored Saint George. Volta."

Volta shoved Azzo by the shoulder. He offered him a dagger. Behemoth yanked one of the bound men from the grave and positioned him on his knees in front of Azzo.

The Fixer took a chalice from the altar and poured some of the liquid into the basin. "Azzo of Naples, do you swear to uphold the tradition of Saint George? To protect the innocent, to combat the devil?"

Rebecca stood transfixed. She sensed what was coming, but the mention of George's devil sent goose pimples across her skin. Her eyes stung in the smoke. She glanced around the room to spot Tommaso or Captain Marchetto, but neither were among the sentries.

"I do," Azzo said.

Rustichello joined Azzo. "Then kill this Nightshade Brother, a pagan who stole into our holy palazzo like a thief in the night. Bring him to justice." Azzo glanced at Rebecca. A slight weight lifted from her conscience—she killed two Brothers in the past week. Another could safeguard their fraternity.

Azzo slashed at the black-bagged man's throat. His gurgle beneath the cloth indicated he was gagged. Rustichello brought the chalice under the wound and collected blood. He kicked the flailing, dying man back into the grave and turned the chalice over into the basin.

Rebecca bit a chunk of skin from her inside cheek. The blood in the basin, between her teeth, the stench in the air, gripped her stomach. Her breathing became shallow. Volta moved Azzo to the wall and gave him a sacrilegious spear. The Fixer returned to the altar and bent out of sight. He pointed the longsword at Rebecca.

"Rebecca, daughter of Milan," he said, tossing her a blade. "I sent you into the wild to achieve victory in battle. Were you successful?"

She examined the tool. It was beautiful. Gold inlays, black steel. The pommel fit in her palm. She would guess it would fit perfectly in her custom sheath.

"Corrado della Torre and his son are dead."

The Fixer whispered in her ear. "I'm proud of you, daughter." He cut her wrist and gathered her blood for the basin. The Fixer snapped at Volta. Behemoth grabbed the second Nightshade Brother and knelt him before her. Rebecca grasped the blade. The woozy feeling in her forehead and gut required tempering. She recalled the nerve before killing patrons, the power over men's lives. A facsimile of the undeserved power the patriarchy dispenses to men at birth.

"Bring this man to just—"

Rebecca slit the Nightshade Brother's throat. Rustichello gathered what blood he could from beneath the black bag and kicked the twitching corpse back into the grave. Rebecca accepted the spear from Volta and watched as the Fixer lit their commingled blood on fire.

"Lord, have mercy on us."

The Sons responded in prayerful unison. *Lord, have mercy.*

"Ye holy man of God, George, have mercy on us."

George, have mercy.

"Faunus, benevolent savior of Saint George, have mercy on us."

Praise Faunus, god of wood, field, and fire.

"George, defend us in your righteous battle."

Defend us in battle!

"Pray for us."
Pray for us.
Amen.
Amen.

Rebecca's skull felt like it was about to fly off into the ceiling. She struggled to form spittle and thought the painting of Faunus caressed George's cheek on the golden portrait. Another flash of color caught her attention from the grave. Unsure if anyone was paying attention to her or if they were all in a shared state of euphoria, she jumped into the dirt coffin. The man she killed wore a surcoat. It had been sullied, but the unceremonious jostling loosened some from the inner lining.

A crimson fabric.

She grabbed the black chiffon mask and tugged it free. Doctor Leonardo Salvagno. He died with the knowledge his demise was by Rebecca's hand.

The Fixer watched from the ledge. "He needed to die. Don't you understand, my daughter? Panza as well. They were investigating you. I couldn't allow them to take you away."

Rebecca lifted the cloth on the other man's head to reveal Giulio Panza, the vintner from Marti's manor. The man she failed to interrogate for his trade routes. Azzo peered in at the victims.

"Panza was Nightshade Brotherhood, too?"

Rebecca scrambled from the grave. Her fellow initiate pulled her to her feet. Volta and the Sons took a step inward to tighten the circle.

"They were not Sons of Saint George." Rustichello smirked. "They were not family." He returned to the altar and placed his hands upon the white and red drapery. "You are now family, Rebecca. You are my son, Azzo." The flames burning the blood in the mound's peak flickered in his eyes. He stared, unblinking, at their dance. "Your debt is forgiven, daughter."

Rebecca inched towards Azzo. He held both of their clawed spears. She sheathed her new dagger, Leo's blood stained its metal.

"The Sons of Saint George must throw off the yoke of a petty squabble," the Fixer continued. "Della Torre. Visconti. Secular pawns obsessed with self-interest and familial preservation. They are thinking too small for me—for us—for this holy fraternity."

Rebecca stepped forward in feigned interest to inch closer to Azzo.

"Papists and imperialists," the Fixer said. "The Sons were founded on bigger ideals than land grabs and earthly titles. Valor. Might. Slaying the devil in the shadows. The Sons are strong! Through our faith in Faunus, our tribute to George, and each other, we'll thrive for another hundred years!"

The Sons pounded their spears and grunted. Rebecca flinched. At some point during Rustichello's declaration, they closed ranks. Her brain was catching up to her ears. She shed no tears over discarding Leonardo's love, but she killed him to satisfy the Fixer's endeavor for power.

"Do you not fear reprisal from Matteo Visconti or the della Torres?" Azzo said. He glanced at Rebecca.

"Ha! The della Torres are gone!" the Fixer said. "Their lineage severed by Rebecca. Matteo and the Lombard League have no cause for our services. The Sons may operate as we desire."

"As *you* desire," Rebecca said. "Are we to understand a grander plan, Fixer?"

"No, Rebecca. 'Father.'"

Azzo placed a hand on her forearm. They were surrounded and outnumbered. The hashisha smoke burned her nostrils, weakened her grip, and slowed her reflexes. The Fixer wanted compliance and he got it.

"Do we need the Lombard League, *father*?"

"Did you not slay the della Torre swine, Rebecca Guarna? You are an instrument of the Sons now."

"My contract with Captain Marchetto—"

"Null and void!" He became serious. "Look around, my girl—his men are mine. You serve my desires. And together, we shall become the most feared order of holy knights."

No argument could be made—he forgave her debt and enslaved her. Rebecca snatched the spear from Azzo. She brandished it in Rustichello's face. He laughed in her face, a ripple of mirth filled the room. The arrogant sycophants chuckled in unison.

"Should you wish to leave my service," Rustichello said. "I won't kill you. No. I'll turn you over to the Lombard League's Magistrates. Imagine how much the governor would pay for the Blade of Milan—the *woman*—who slaughtered his citizens? It does not matter. I told you once and will tell you again—I own you."

Azzo lowered Rebecca's spear. She complied. To fight the man who saved her from the Primaluna estate felt petty.

"Yes, father," Azzo said, kneeling. He dragged Rebecca by the forearm. In her current state, she dropped to her knees without much resistance. Following his lead, she bowed her head.

"Praise Faunus," he continued.

Praise Faunus.

"Praise Saint George."

Praise Saint George.

"Long live his Sons under your most glorious reign."

Long live Rustichello.

The Fixer dipped his fingers into the basin. He made the sign of the cross in blood and hot oil on their foreheads. The Sons beat their spears into the dirt three times.

Rebecca killed Corrado della Torre, Amerigo di Narbona, and the Nightshade Brother responsible for murdering Father Lorenzo in spectacular fashion. Her talent, her skill—not a courtesan from the stews nor a man born to privilege—survived training. Did she not earn a place among the Sons?

"Amen," Rebecca said, in unison with her new family.

21

A Ship with No Sails

Rustichello granted Rebecca passage to *The Corsican*, a liberty given without constraint now that she was initiated. Permission to row to the galley alone should have been a thrill except for its purpose—to rescind her agreement with the captain. The scroll in her tunic pocket stated nothing regarding penalties for breaching their terms, but she had not yet begun her service. The Fixer doubted any cause for concern. Marchetto would see reason. He must.

The sea had not yet restored Rebecca's favor after swallowing her prized dagger. She closed her affections for the churning golem into a tight corner of her mind. The Fixer's gift, the gold-trimmed replacement, sat on her hip. Now that she was initiated, the tool would be part of her full regalia. She wore the same black tunic, surcoat, and wide-brimmed hat the night she dumped the Fixer's hashisha into the sea. A transgression yet to be discovered due to the quantity of buds in his possession. A child's prank.

A wind blew in from the west, whipping spray into her face. She docked beside the galley to secure purchase against a torrent. The sailor on lookout duty waved her permission to climb aboard. Rebecca cast furtive glances at the sailors to spot a familiar jawline or hooked nose from the initiation ceremony. She knew there were eleven Sons of Saint George aboard among a sparse crew of thirty-five.

It was difficult to believe naught but five days passed since the ceremony. Rebecca woke the following morn from a restless sleep. She choked back tears for Leonardo during the silent light of a delicate dawn. She never intended for him to die, let alone by her hand. Her cell offered refuge from the glistening triptych in George's tomb and the humming mound that sent vibrations rattling beneath her skin. The new blade confirmed the evening occurred. She spent the next few days burying her former lover while avoiding the Fixer. Until she couldn't. His first order to the sole daughter of Saint George was to pay Captain Marchetto a visit, to inform him her services belonged ashore.

The crewman admitted her to the captain's quarters. Rebecca closed her eyes and filled her lungs with salt air. She entered. A quill scratched on parchment. Marchetto sat at his desk peering through a round piece of glass. It was positioned above the page, and he shifted it left and right to magnify the ink on paper.

"Rebecca Renucci," he said, the gravel in his throat grating unharmonious over the quill. He spotted her blade. "Or should I say, daughter of Saint George?"

She bowed. Rebecca pulled the chair out, but he waved his index finger. "I did not invite you to my quarters, nor did I allow you to sit. On what business do you disturb my reflections?"

Rebecca withdrew the scroll. "I was sent . . . ordered . . . by the Fixer to nullify our agreement." She held it aloft. Rustichello advised her to rip it, burn it, or shred the contract in Marchetto's face, but she could not bring herself to shame the captain so. He studied her eyes, unblinking. Rebecca held his gaze.

"And do you wish to do so?"

Rebecca opened her mouth. Closed it. Opened.

"Come on girl," he said, dropping the quill. "You must have your own opinion. Do you wish to rescind our agreement? To break your vow to serve on a single expedition beneath my command?"

Rebecca sat. "Can you petition Rustichello for me, captain?" Marchetto crossed his arms. The captain's beard hid the fold of jowls pressed by his creeping tunic collar. "He'd listen to you."

He studied her in silence, the seconds turned to minutes, and he uttered a nondescript cry. Rebecca didn't know how to interpret his outburst. They had not spent much time together, and their last encounter ended with swordplay.

"Even if I wished to needle that self-satisfied prick, what good would my intervention do? You trained with a secret fraternity, have been initiated, and now you don't want to do what they tell you? Am I to understand you were so naive to believe he'd allow you to walk away?"

Rebecca clenched her jaw. Marchetto's jab stung. She owed him and now she needed to retract the pledge. Any retort felt impotent at the loss of her word's integrity.

"Before you respond," Marchetto said, shifting the glass and candle away from the ledger. Rebecca stole a glance at the page. A manifest detailed quantities of cargo including pfennigs, groschen, and wine. Rebecca dragged her eyes away at the captain clearing his throat. "Tell me—did Benito Renucci teach you to flee when life gets hard?"

She stood. Rebecca drew her blade and stabbed the ledger. Marchetto didn't flinch. He folded his hands in prayer.

"Remove your blade from my ledger."

Rustichello controlled a dozen Sons aboard the galley, but Marchetto's loyal crewmen doubled in number. She hadn't intended to pick a fight with the captain, especially one in which she'd lose. Rebecca sheathed her blade.

"Fight your own battles, Rebecca." He unfurled the contract scroll. "No one is coming to save you." The captain set it on fire.

Rebecca wished to slap the contract from the flames, but it was consumed. Although her father was gone, an expedition to Corsica breathed life into a vague idea of what she could pursue after the stewhouse. After her debts were repaid.

"I am the sole daughter of Saint George. The only woman in the history of the order. I've been initiated."

"And you are so impressive," Marchetto said, tone dripping with contempt. "*The Corsican* has orders to depart by week's end, sole daughter of Saint George. My crew will remain in Corsica on extended leave. I wish you luck in your endeavors."

A storm brewed in Rebecca's chest. She scowled at Tommaso as he waved from the aft. The row back to the drainage tunnel chapped her knuckles. Her fingers chilled, cold claws like the new spear that rested against the wall in her cell. A reminder winter had not yet fully departed in the northwest.

What did an initiated Son, or daughter, of Saint George do when not ordered to execute a contract? How best to while away her hours? The halls beneath the palazzo sat bereft of spirit in Father Lorenzo's absence, void of conscience with the lingering stain of Rustichello's ultimatum. Rebecca's feet dragged her into the crypt. Someone, presumably Volta, entombed the priest among the others. A fitting resting place for Lorenzo di Costa.

Azzo let her keep his journal, which she thumbed through beneath the light of a single torch. Her pulse quickened at an entry about her.

She displays the proper temperament. An ideal candidate to stomach the rigors of the Sons. The heated humors, the disdain for authority. Rustichello sees promise in her potential as I see a young Rustichello in the girl. Although I wouldn't utter those words to Rebecca.

Lorenzo's analysis chafed her already sour mood. She scoffed and read another entry to purge the reflection from her palette.

I've become his prisoner. The lurking investigations to uncover faithful Sons, oppressive. I fear this might be the undoing of a hundred years of tradition. Would she provide the proper motivation? Pride in serving a dozen popes, His holy mandate chuffed aside for what? To be tested by love lost? Surely his honor would not be shaken by such a frivolous sentiment. If I could send word to Parma without my missive being intercepted, I could confirm it. Could she be trusted?

Lorenzo was whose prisoner—Rustichello's? The Fixer didn't have time to disclose her love affair with Leonardo to the priest before he died, but here he reflected on her love affair with the doctor. Or was this dated prior to Rebecca's time in Genoa? Either way, Lorenzo was wrong. She didn't love Leo, and Lorenzo would not have needed to send a missive to determine her heart's allegiance. Then who was *she*, the jilted lover, he wrote about? Rebecca pocketed the journal.

No one is coming to save you.

Captain Marchetto's words might as well have been a slap. What did she expect? Her father, alive and waiting for her to join him in Corsica? Father Lorenzo to shield her from Rustichello's fraternity? Leonardo abandoned her to siphon coin from patrons, content to have his way with her until he wasn't. Had he desired her freedom, her unfettered love, shunting her away to the convent in Salerno was not in their best interests. Rebecca could not hide behind others, relying on their patronizing or plotting. As she once swore to never sleep with Leo again, she decided, on bended knee at Lorenzo's coffin, to be the woman she desired. The person neither Martina nor Benito or any Son of Saint George or lover could be.

Rebecca withdrew the journal again. She opened to the page with Lorenzo's sketches of Franco's wounds. The priest's declaration beneath the severed limbs chilled her spirits.

The devil.

She extinguished the torch and waited in silence until her eyes adjusted to the pitch. Rebecca's faith was marred by bitter memories of judgment by hypocritical believers. Father Lorenzo proved faith could feel different, more personal—a drive to pacify her inner torrents—apart from the earthly church. Not all devils resided in the depths of hell.

Rebecca crept back to the main tunnel. She held her breath as she hugged the wall all the way back to the Fixer's study. Hiding in the shadow of the campanile staircase, she prayed the storeroom door was unlocked. Checking her resolve, Rebecca strode across the tunnel and unlatched the handle with care. With a small creak, it opened.

She slid inside and exhaled. Rebecca reached into the black for the wooden hashisha crate. She dumped so much into the sea, yet the Fixer didn't notice any missing. How stupid, how infantile of an assault. As suspected, his stockpile was sizable, restocked and then some. Rustichello couldn't smoke what she burned. She realized there were no lamps or torches in the storeroom, so she snuck back into the hall and pressed an ear to the Fixer's study.

Quiet.

Once inside, Rebecca held her breath. Once she confirmed it was empty, she exhaled. She strode to his table and gathered a lit candle. In the roving light, she paused to examine a scroll on his desk—the contract to eliminate Corrado della Torre signed by "C.P." Rebecca lifted the parchment. Below that letter was another signed by "C.P." and a third.

Rebecca thumbed through Lorenzo's journal. The letter reminded her of the entry she read earlier in the crypt. *Parma.* She began at the beginning of the journal. Rebecca skimmed each page, line by line. She couldn't stop. Without noticing, she was in the Fixer's chair, hunched below the candlelight. Lorenzo's slanted scrawl revealed many inner thoughts and beautiful, original prayers she'd revisit later. And then she found "C.P."

"Coraline di Parma."

Realizing the Fixer could return any moment, Rebecca pocketed the journal and adjusted his chair. She stole the candle and returned to the storeroom. Uncovering the mystery of Coraline di Parma couldn't dissuade Rebecca from burning the hashisha. Not everyone can have what they want.

What she noticed in the light though could not be burned. Adjacent to the crate sat a chest filled with Ambrogino d'Oro. Gold shined in the firelight. The other crates required prying with her dagger. She popped open one lid after the other, a dozen filled with the gold coin. The currency minted by Governor Matteo Visconti I. The tool to cement his power among the republic and beyond. Rebecca closed the lids.

Regret washed over her for proceeding with the initiation. The alternative seemed obvious, at least to Azzo at the time. Voices crescendoed from the tunnel. She leaned against the door.

"How is he still alive?"

Volta grumbled.

"The final shipment arrives this week, Volta. Load the chests on *The Corsican* before that bastard sets sail."

Rebecca gripped her blade. What other crates could Rustichello mean besides the governor's gold?

"Leave della Torre to me."

The study door closed, muffling the Fixer's rant. She pocketed a handful of buds and waited for Volta's lumbering to fade. If Corrado della Torre lived, what did it mean for her debt? Could she be uninitiated?

22

— • —

PARMA

Rebecca crouched in the shadows. Azzo returned from his spying duties as her knees began to protest. He tossed his surcoat in the corner and fiddled with the laces of his tunic. She squinted at his form, tensing in the pale moonlight of his cell. With a flourish, Azzo spun and threw a passatore into the corner. Had Rebecca not been squatting, the blade would have pierced her torso.

"Azzo." She stepped into the light, unarmed.

He relaxed his grip on a second passatore and accepted his discarded knife with a look of consternation.

"I could have killed you."

"If only your aim was as true as mine."

He sheathed the blades. "Trust me, no need to remind me." He tapped his shoulder. The flesh wound would have left a scar. Behind his somber mask, Azzo's face looked refreshed. The rings beneath his eyes, gone, the creases on his forehead less severe. The curtain of greasy hair was less greasy and combed and tied back into a loose bundle.

"Is this what you expected?"

Azzo smoothed his tunic front to barter for time. He took his seat and untied the twine in his hair.

"Serving in Boccanegra's guard?"

Rebecca nodded. He shrugged. "Joining the Sons was Tommaso's idea. If this keeps me close to him, I can bear that duty."

"Marchetto departs for Corsica in a week," Rebecca said, taking a seat across from him. "He told me so himself."

Azzo's expression told Rebecca he didn't know, but he recovered quickly. "Listen, Rebecca, about the initiation—"

She leaned back and crossed her arms. "Did you know? Who was under those black bags?"

Azzo raised his palms in supplication. "Salvagno and Panza were guests in Boccanegra's court. The Fixer is hell-bent on secrecy."

She studied his face, scanning each and every feature. Azzo didn't blink. Had he not encouraged her to obey, she had no doubt the Fixer would have her slaughtered and dropped in Panza and Salvagno's shared grave. Azzo realized it a heartbeat before she did the other night, and for that, she resented him.

"I'm sorry, Rebecca."

"I don't need an apology."

Azzo fussed with his surcoat and withdrew a coin purse. He handed it to her. "Here. Take it. Run. You've paid your debt. Go."

Rebecca inspected the offering. Azzo earned coin while she dug out from behind. Her victory in Primaluna, now a distant memory. Had she not wanted to escape, to go north or board *The Corsican*? Men bought and sold her allegiance still.

"Why?"

"Because," Azzo said, "we're friends."

"I told you I don't need a friend."

Azzo dropped his hand. "You're a stubborn bitch."

"And you're not listening." Rebecca wanted to hug him but resisted. Instead, she handed him Lorenzo's journal. "Do you know Coraline di Parma?"

Azzo accepted it, inspecting the page with the mystery initials earmarked.

"C.P.?" he said. "You figured it out. She signed the contract on della Torre, right?"

Rebecca nodded. She knelt beside Azzo and whispered her recent discoveries. Franco's strange puncture wounds, Lorenzo's admission he was a prisoner, the chests full of Ambrogino d'Oro gold.

"And now Rustichello wants to kill Corrado himself?"

Rebecca braced for Azzo to laugh. She needed to trust someone with her hypothesis to justify remaining in Genoa.

"What if Rustichello is the 'devil' in Lorenzo's journal? Franco said 'Saint George's devil' killed him."

"No man is the devil. That doesn't explain the wounds or why the Fixer imprisoned Lorenzo."

Rebecca paced, too energized to remain still. The answer was near, but they couldn't see it. "I killed Leonardo. I can't just run now, Azzo."

He leveled his gaze, understanding dawning behind his eyes.

"You wish to live as an assassin? The sole daughter of Saint George?"

"You doubt my ability? Why? Because I'm a woman?"

He laughed. "If I said yes, you'd throw another passatore into my shoulder, wouldn't you?"

"I'm considering it."

Azzo gripped her forearm to stop her from pacing. "Boccanegra prepares to lead the navy to Pisa in three days' time. Rustichello is the Sons of Saint George, as the fraternity is his will. If there is a seed of doubt to his integrity, remaining in his employ seems foolish."

"The Nightshade Brothers killed Lorenzo," she said. "For some reason. It means something, but I must learn how it's connected."

They stood in silent contemplation. Rebecca's head pounded behind her eyes like it did in George's tomb the night of their initiation. In hindsight, she could not have been more relieved at sharing the experience with someone else. It confirmed her sanity.

"I need to see this through a while longer," Rebecca continued. "To whatever end."

"To whatever end?" Azzo said.

***

The Fixer and Rebecca crossed the Parma stream by horseback. The spring rains had not yet turned the trickle into a deluge. Rebecca didn't consider her actions when the Fixer saddled his horse in Genoa—she simply followed suit and declared she was joining him. Rustichello laughed through his joint, the sweet haze of bud competing with the manure. Rebecca deflected awkward questions about how she knew what he rode to do with an offering—stroking the Fixer's ego.

"My training shouldn't cease just because I'm initiated. I can still learn from the best."

Rustichello didn't argue. A jolt of danger rang through her bones when he shared their destination—Parma, a small town residing in the heart of the Reggio commune. Her plan to stick close with the Fixer led her closer to the mystery woman, but would it solve why the Fixer did not excommunicate her for failing to kill Corrado?

As dusk fell, night watchmen populated bridges and town squares. They bore northeast and walked their horses. Citizens finished their evening stroll. A few passersby nodded at the Fixer and eyed Rebecca, donned in such masculine garb, with scorn or confusion. She felt a sense of ease here unlike in Milan or Genoa, though, the space between homes more spacious, the sunset on the horizon on full display beyond the stream. They lashed the horses on a post near the entrance to a field with cypress dotting rows of marble mausoleums.

"Why have we come to Parma?"

The Fixer drew his black chiffon mask and unbuttoned his surcoat. He wore a sheath filled with passatore, their matching blades at his hip. Turning his head to appraise Rebecca turned her stomach to ice. She braced for a dubious response, but he told the truth.

"We're here to end the della Torre bloodline."

Rebecca tied her hair atop her head so it would sit comfortable beneath her mask and hat. They carried on by foot, weaving south through the town. She waited for an abandoned alley to press the matter.

"Did the bloodline not end," she whispered at the Fixer's heel, "in Primaluna?"

The Fixer checked their route. "He'll be in the residential quarters of the Studium." He waved her to follow.

They sprinted across the piazza, shadows beneath the starless night's canopy. An imposing four-story stucco palace with a campanile looming over its center framed the square. From behind a pillared archway, he pointed to the building adjoining the palace.

"Founded over four hundred years ago," he said. "Scholars travel all the way from north of the Alps to study in those halls."

Rebecca half-listened to the history lesson as they weaved to the street behind the Studium. The Fixer pulled a rope from his belt. He pressed Rebecca aside so he could swing one end while he held the loops in his other hand. A clawed hook was tied on the end.

The tool wrapped around a stone ledge. Rustichello walked on the wall vertically, rope hanging between his legs. When he reached the stone end, he waved Rebecca to follow. She gripped the rope and mimicked his stunt. Navigating in silence, smoke among a pitch-dark night, was thrilling. Sweat formed beneath her chiffon mask as she reached the ledge. The Fixer jumped to the opposite roof, the hook carried him over the ledge.

"Bring the grappling hook with you before you jump!"

Rebecca wobbled to her feet. Using her full core strength, she squatted to untangle the hook. She looped the coil around her torso and took a deep breath.

"Come on, daughter," the Fixer said, beckoning her across. Rebecca set her gaze. She took a leap of faith.

Her right arm slapped the roof, but her left hand pinched the ledge. She squeezed her left muscles with all her might to hold on, knees crunched towards her chest. She couldn't breathe for fear of falling. The Fixer stood above her, staring head tilted again. Her right arm slipped, but he grabbed her by the back of her surcoat and dragged her over the ledge.

Rebecca rolled to her back and kicked to her feet as quickly as possible to take some semblance of control over her life. Rustichello snorted. He took his hook back and retied it to his belt.

With one final jump, he cleared the gap and landed on a balcony on the backside of the Studium. As if he knew exactly where he was going. Rebecca could make this. Her weight would pull her to the destination. She took a running head start and cleared the gap. Slipping on the landing, she bounced her shoulder into the wall. She was glad the Fixer slipped through the window and didn't witness her clumsiness.

Once inside, the scent of lingering candle smoke tinged with parchment and leather struck Rebecca. The Fixer was nowhere to be seen, so she drew a dagger. With a step forward, the wall across the room shifted towards the doorway. His figure emerged from silence and utter stillness to the faint light behind the door. Rebecca glided as best she could to follow without making a noise.

In the hallway, the Fixer's weapons were still sheathed. He led them past humble walls and modest window trimmings. Inspecting the first room, the Fixer found it devoid of their target. He nodded at the room across the hall for Rebecca to do the same. She crept to the door and turned the handle deliberately.

A child's bed filled with a sleeping girl sat in the corner. Her chestnut curls draped a tiny pillow, chest rising and falling in gentle harmony. Rebecca walked backwards from the room, eager to let the girl rest in peace. As she shut the door, the unmistakable rattle of a death gurgle issued from the hall. She followed her ears.

The Fixer stood over a bed, two victims with their throats slashed lay beneath their sheets. Rebecca approached as he dried his dagger on the duvet. Neither were Corrado, but an elderly man and woman. Rebecca supposed they were husband and wife, as the man's hand was still grasping the woman's. Rustichello killed them as they slept.

"Who are they?"

The Fixer held his finger to where his mouth was beneath the chiffon mask. He pointed to the next room. She kept on his tail as he leaned his head against the door. A snore broke the beating of Rebecca's heart, startling them both. A man slept in a chair at the top of the stairs. A sword in its scabbard lay in his lap. Rustichello poked her chest and pointed to him. She knew what she must do. The Fixer watched her as Rebecca crept forward. She wanted to shake him awake, tell him to run, but pinched his nose and covered his mouth with her glove. She pierced the guard's heart.

She returned to the room. A man lay in bed, hands on his chest, head wrapped in gauze. Florimondo della Torre. She recalled throwing a stone paperweight at his head. He survived the blunt force. Fear drenched Rebecca's brain. She froze, warm steel clutched in her hand. The Fixer expected Florimondo to die in that room, though her contract was for father and son. The Fixer nudged him awake. Rebecca pulled the door closed behind her.

"Who's there?" the son asked.

"'For a son dishonors his father,'" the Fixer said. "'A man's enemies are the members of his own household.'"

Florimondo scrambled to sit, his arms thrown to defend against the Fixer's slashing. Rebecca stepped forward but couldn't stop it if she wished. He brutalized the final della Torre. The Fixer tore the bandages from Florimondo's head and tossed them on the ground.

Their deed complete, Rebecca returned to the hall to find the girl standing in their way. Eyes wide, she froze at the appearance of two black-clad, faceless figures. A silent scream branded her face. Rebecca was quicker on the draw than Rustichello. He slashed at the girl, but Rebecca blocked it. She pivoted her body between them. The Fixer punched her side, but she leaned in. He swiped again. Rebecca pushed the girl against the wall. Three more swipes, three more parries. It was imperative Rebecca did not assault the Fixer. She desired not to give him a reason to kill her for protecting a defenseless babe.

"No," she said.

The Fixer tilted his head. Rebecca found the effect still chilling given the evening's ruse. The valley of deceit between them ran deeper.

"Is she a della Torre?"

Rebecca maintained her stance, one foot ahead of the other, knees bent, their matching blades pressed against the other.

"We accomplished our goal," she said. "She hasn't seen our faces."

They could not see the other's eyes, but Rebecca sensed the Fixer scrutinizing the situation. A whiff of hemp and sweat hung between them.

He lowered his blade. Rebecca waited to sheath hers until he did. Keeping her body between the man and girl, Rebecca ushered her back to her room and closed the door without another glance. Rustichello hooked his grapple to the balcony ledge and they repelled to the street. Rebecca may have signed her death warrant, but there was no scenario she'd allow him to kill an innocent. The elderly couple enjoyed long lives, though Rebecca could not commentate on the merit of their contributions to Parma or the republic. The guard died in the line of fulfilling his oath.

Rebecca held her tongue until they crossed the stream and the Fixer removed the black chiffon mask. The clouds shifted and stars illuminated their road southwest.

"Tell me, Rustichello," she said, daring to tempt fate. "Did I swear an oath to slaughter mindlessly or do the Sons of Saint George stand for something greater?"

The Fixer reined his horse in ahead of Rebecca's grinding them to a halt. "Do you hear the hypocrisy spewing from your lips, daughter? I plucked you from the stews like a putrid bundle of smudge, a worthless existence, and you raise a blade on a fellow Son?"

"She was a child!"

"Who will now grow up with a chip on her shoulder," he said. "With vengeance in her heart to inflict suffering on others as she has been hurt this night."

Rebecca's fury drained from her shoulders into her stomach and flowed from her fingertips and toes until it soaked the earth, thirsty for her invisible pain. It wouldn't take a rich imagination for the Fixer to fill in the blanks of Rebecca's childhood. Death and the Void waited for them all yet Rebecca molded a young soul tonight in her image, for better or worse.

"How did you know Florimondo would be in Parma?"

The Fixer scoffed. He tossed her reins back in her face and urged his tawny forward. Rebecca kicked her mare.

"Who is Coraline di Parma? That girl?"

Rustichello slowed his horse to a halt. He sat still gazing ahead. Rebecca wished he had drawn a blade as opposed to the interminable silence that raged from his rigid figure. Crickets chirped and the wind turned leaves over. Rebecca heard the drumming of her heart against ribs.

The Fixer whispered, "Utter that name again, Rebecca Guarna, and I'll sever your tongue. Speak, and I'll carve the eyelids from your face and make you watch as I dissect Martina Renucci. When I'm finished, you'll go to *The Corsican*, not for some brilliant expedition, but as a mute bitch to be dragged beneath the keel."

Rebecca believed each foul word. Her tears fell in a steady stream, muffled by the gallop back to Genoa by cover of night. What the future held for that little girl, she wouldn't know, but at least she was given a choice to decide for herself.

23

THE TRIUMPH DECK

"Well?" Rebecca asked. "What did he say?"

Azzo joined her and Tommaso in the drainage tunnel, worry painting his face. She hadn't expected such a swift response, but they didn't have the luxury of time. The Sons arrived tomorrow with their final shipment, and Boccanegra and his navy intended to sail the day after.

"You've got an agreement," Azzo said.

Rebecca's shout of joy echoed in the tunnel. Tommaso rolled his eyes and clapped Azzo on the forearm. The Ligurian Sea brought brine and a foul decay of rotten egg to their noses. She ignored the first mate's attitude and pressed her fellow initiate.

"He wants four chests instead of two."

Rebecca deflated. Breakage was to be inevitable, yet she hoped to deliver more for the governor—her bargaining chip depended on it.

"Do we have another choice?" Rebecca asked, knowing the truth.

Azzo shook his head.

"Prepare for a fight," Tommaso said. "The Sons would rather die than lose their precious cargo."

"No! One death," Rebecca said. "Our plan is a success if it results in a single death."

Tommaso smacked his lips. "You wish to steal twelve chests of gold from the jolly boats commanded by Sons faithful to Rustichello and not kill a single man?"

Azzo intervened. "We must try."

His support meant she could attempt her gamble. Without it, she felt like a child trying to steal figs from the counter again. "Thank you," she said.

"Friend," Tommaso said.

Azzo and Rebecca raised a brow at the first mate.

"He desires to hear it from you," Tommaso said, glaring at her.

Rebecca received encouragement from Azzo since they met on the southern road to Genoa. Even Tommaso aided her while she convalesced aboard *The Corsican* when her back was sliced open. Now, she plotted to kill the head of a hundred-year-old fraternity of assassins. She not only needed them both, but wouldn't be drawing breath without them.

"I could use a friend," she said, holding out a hand.

Azzo grasped it. "As could I."

"Then I better hide in plain sight," Tommaso said. "The captain is expecting me. I'll keep these wineskins hidden until we come ashore."

As Rebecca was not on contract, she decided to hover near the storeroom to make herself useful. The careful dance of not drawing unwanted attention required little imagination. The Fixer may bark orders at her to assist with the manual labor, although he avoided her like the pox since they returned from Parma.

"Rebecca, wait," Azzo said. "You've been summoned."

She accepted the scroll and slit open the black wax seal. The summons were scrawled by a fastidious hand addressing her by "Signorina Guarna" and signed by "Coraline di Parma."

"She found me."

Azzo nodded. "There's no obligation to meet her. She arrived at the captain's palace today. Alone. There's no word or sight of men-at-arms or even an escort. Boccanegra passed that to me—I haven't even seen her."

Rebecca read the note again. She was invited to meet Coraline in the home of her host at twilight. Could Coraline be the specter she witnessed sneaking through the tunnels all those months ago? Rebecca's suspicions extended beyond a midnight visitor. Coraline's proposal could not be disputed. She would meet her in the captain's palace that night.

"Before I forget," she said, producing two chest sheaths filled with passatore. She handed one to each of her friends. "When the time to act is upon us, use these. Slices, nothing fatal."

Azzo and Tommaso accepted their upgraded sheaths. Rebecca took them at their word to show restraint, as was her intention however difficult that may be.

***

The anticipation quickened Rebecca's breath. She arrived in the palace armed and without the black chiffon mask. Each step a labor, burdened by the weight of the Fixer's actions in Parma. Leonardo's accusation in these halls was the closest she came to atoning for her past sins. Dread turned her guts as she accepted responsibility for Rustichello's crimes of her own volition. If Coraline was who Rebecca believed her to be, the price could be steep.

Azzo assured her the halls would be near empty, the sentry stationed at the gate or the city boundary wall. With Boccanegra preparing the fleet, all able-bodied soldiers were conscripted on naval duty. She stalked through the atrium and placed her feet with care on the marble staircase. The captain of the people's court would be her first stop. In truth, it was the only room she had experience with given Leonardo's audience.

Burning incense of juniper and sage wafted into the court from an alcove. Rebecca followed her nose to a side chamber and found a table set for two beneath a high rectangular window. It faced the courtyard below, the Cathedral of Saint Lorenzo in view.

"I traveled to Genoa alone at great personal risk."

Rebecca's heart all but stopped. She whirled around, hand on her dagger pommel. The woman who summoned her emerged from the shadows and stood behind a chair. She indicated for Rebecca to take a seat.

"Who are you?"

They sat.

"You know who I am."

"Coraline di Parma—but who *are* you?"

She lit five stubs for candles with an oil lamp on the windowsill and placed them around the table. The table was set with a fine linen and a deck of paper cards sat neatly stacked in front of Coraline's place. She began to shuffle them.

"And?"

An invisible line drew Rebecca's curiosity from her depths, and a burgeoning need to know if she was right spilled from her mouth, though she sensed danger beneath the surface of Coraline's demeanor.

"You're a member of the Lombard League."

Coraline split the deck into three piles. She offered the smallest of bows and restacked the piles. "I rode once the doctor hadn't returned. He's dead."

It was a statement, a scolding jab, so Rebecca examined the cards. The backs were painted, gold foil highlighted the background. A crowned dragon consuming a man stared at them from the center. Rebecca recognized the family seal—Visconti.

"What are these cards?"

Coraline's hazel gaze pierced Rebecca's innermost being as if she read her thoughts. She didn't want to blink, but shrunk on the inside. The woman before her resembled someone Rebecca met recently.

Her host laid three cards face down in front of Rebecca, three in front of herself. "Matteo Visconti believes in . . . spiritual . . . wisdom. Mining his past, present, and future through personal examination."

Rebecca found her feet flat on the ground, hands on her knees. She sat on the edge of her seat. The sumptuous burning herbs reminded her of the stews.

"These trionfi—*triumph*—cards," Coraline continued. "Allow him to do so. I designed and painted this collection."

"Visconti is superstitious?" Rebecca clarified, unsure how these relics fit into the church's rituals. "Although he is a Christian?"

Coraline's voice held a world-weariness Rebecca thought betrayed her years. She fanned the remaining cards along the side of the table and placed both palms in front of her. Rebecca felt the tether between them again and could not look away.

"Yours," she indicated. "Mine."

Rebecca sensed a trap. She turned her head without tearing her eyes from Coraline until she could steal a furtive glance into the black of the room. A shadow hung in the air. The ill-made and ill-appearance that should not be brought into the light.

"The past." Coraline turned the card on the right in front of Rebecca over. A skeleton holding a crooked staff stared back at her. "Death. Did you kill my parents?"

Rebecca's assumption was correct. Rustichello slaughtered the elderly couple in Parma, yet these cards portended Rebecca's past.

"No."

"My brother?"

The sleeping guard? Rebecca thought. She shook her head.

Coraline drew another card from the deck. "The cards reveal the truth." She placed it atop Death—an inverted sword gilded with lilies and ivy. "The blood on your hands was wrought for revenge, not ego."

Rebecca thought of the patrons in the stews, the men who had it all. She didn't know what expectations or response to offer to this cryptic divination, which Coraline accepted as tacit agreement.

"It was you, then, who allowed my daughter to live."

Another statement, though Rebecca made the connection. Coraline resembled the little girl in Parma, or rather the daughter resembled the mother.

"As you said, the cards reveal the truth."

"The League will grant you pardon for murdering fellow members, those in the stew and men since joining the Sons of Saint George. The Signori di Notte at the Breaking Wheel," Coraline said with a grimace. "Gruesome, but the magistrates will close their eyes to it."

Rebecca flushed. "I didn't kill the night watchmen and I haven't killed any Lombard League members in Genoa."

Coraline raised her brows. She turned the middle card. Rebecca's stomach plummeted.

"The present." A queen, fair-haired and defiant, holding a scale and sword. Her vestments were gold and cerulean. "Justice. The desire for moral scruples and an upholding of the law."

"Banco and Panza," Rebecca said, "were both Lombard League members."

"And the doctor, yes."

Coraline drew another card from the pack. A page holding a cup. "A lover?" She placed it on the queen.

Rebecca blushed. "I have something the League wants."

"You have hindered our efforts. Some men rule by might, others by wit." Coraline picked Rebecca's last card. "For two hundred years, the della Torres tormented Matteo's ancestors. He required a woman to prop his confidence," she said with a bow. "But he is a severe leader. Counsel must be given with the utmost certainty of confidence." She turned the card. "The future." A wizened, bearded sage peering into a casket from the heavens heralded by two angels playing trumpets. "Judgment. One might read this as your downfall—a final sentence or a light admonishment—or your salvation." She pulled one more from the deck. A golden disc. "The pentacle." Coraline swept Rebecca's cards into a pile and stacked them on the windowsill. Her own lay before her.

"The gold the Sons have been removing from circulation. I'll return what I can along with the Fixer's heart."

Coraline considered Rebecca. "A prudent investment. You uncovered the truth. When?"

Rebecca sighed. "Podesta Antonio Marti. The Nightshade Brother killed him at Primaluna. I thought it curious, but that evening ended with me toppling from the window. Rustichello hired the Austrians to clean up loose ends."

"I did not know Marti betrayed the League," Coraline said. She turned over her first card—the past. "The Fixer will not be an easy man to kill." The card showed a couple, hands intertwined, beneath a blindfolded angel. "Lovers." Rebecca knew the bitter taste. She could smell it on Coraline's tongue.

"He's your daughter's father?"

Coraline turned the middle card over—the present. An angel trapped on a wheel, facing Rebecca. "An inverted Wheel. I could not love him when I learned what he is, nor could I allow him near our daughter. The chaos he's caused the League has turned my will to iron resolve."

Coraline turned the final card—the future. A young boy frolicking in the hills. "The fool. A new beginning, perhaps." She gathered the cards and shuffled them into the full deck. "Or a reckless venture."

The incense watered Rebecca's eyes as the candles grew dim. "How does this end, Coraline? Do you accept my offer in exchange for pardon?"

"I suspected we desired the same outcome. But can you deliver, Rebecca Guarna?"

"You may play a part yet." Rebecca gave Coraline a tinderbox. "Should you wish to avenge your family."

24

— • —

SONS AND DAUGHTERS

L aughter echoed through the drainage tunnel preceding the jolly boats. The Sons arrived unfettered by naval ships or prying sentry eyes. As the tensions mounted between Genoa and Pisa, trade rivals, Alessandro Boccanegra's fleet could apply the appropriate pressure along the coast. Rebecca marveled at the ingenuity of Rustichello's plan and timing. Siphoning resources from Milan, sabotaging food deliveries to Genoa, removing the middleman between him and the Nightshade Brotherhood. And now, he'd send his final shipment of gold to Corsica while the Lombard League was none the wiser and the fleet could not inspect merchant ships. Rebecca prayed for Father Lorenzo to watch over them.

She waited on the dock with Volta to moor the boats. The chests sat behind them. Tommaso rowed a boat with four Sons while the other boat held three. Several men remained aboard *The Corsican* to receive the shipment. The first mate searched the dock. No Azzo.

Rebecca tied off the lines. She spotted the wineskins littering Tommaso's boat. They made quick eye contact, but she didn't linger. The other boat unloaded a crate gingerly. Volta accepted it with a grip as delicate as if his ham-hock hands might crush a flower.

He lumbered back inside while the Sons loaded the chests. Rebecca stood to the side inspecting each man. They smelled like wine, bullshitting with one another and grunting as they lugged the heavy wooden chests into the boats.

"Lend a hand, will you?" Tommaso said.

Rebecca grabbed the other end of a chest so their heads could bend low. She was pleased to be active to hide her nerves.

"Did they all drink?"

"Most. Where's Azzo?"

Rebecca shook her head. Doubt in her plan and her friend's absence raised her heart rate. A Son stumbled while lifting a chest.

"Oi! Steady on."

Another fell sideways. Confusion set in among the group. With their hands either full with the chests or tending to the fallen crewmates, Rebecca turned and gathered her spear from its hiding place. She coated its blade with the same belladonna mixture Lorenzo used to poison her and Azzo during their stealth training. The right tool would keep her enemies at a distance while not tempting her to kill anyone with the passatore. She trusted Tommaso to exercise more control.

Rebecca sliced the thigh of a man checking the fallen Son. He shrieked. She slashed the abdomen of another Son as the undrugged sailors realized they were under attack. Two men in the jolly boat drew swords. Tommaso sliced their backs one, two, three times before they made the dock. Their roars turned to groans as one collapsed after another.

A grizzled Son of Saint George, Rebecca recognized as Father Lorenzo's drinking friend, drew a longsword. He slashed at her. Rebecca parried. She twirled the spear upwards and the butt rammed his stomach. Not to be deterred, he drove her backwards with a lunge. The blade connected with the top of her shoulder beneath her left ear. Steel drew blood and Rebecca dropped the spear. She drew her blade.

Tommaso dropped the final Son near the boat. Rebecca rolled to avoid the hammering blows of the grizzled sailor. From her back, she threw a passatore into his sword arm. He shouted in pain. She launched to her feet and shouldered him backwards. The man swayed.

"Rebecca, hurry!" Tommaso said, pushing a Son out of his boat.

She tugged the throwing knife from the grizzled sailor's upper arm as he fell to the ground. Gathering her spear, the pair tossed the Sons' weapons into the water. She took pride in filling the wineskins with the correct amount of belladonna and of her accuracy in slicing away from vital organs. By her estimation, they had four to six hours before the Sons reawakened, though Volta wouldn't be far behind.

The first mate had the same thought, as he jumped from the boat and began towards the tunnel. Rebecca gripped his upper arm. "You go, Tommaso," she said. "Get that boat to Boccanegra's galley and I'll find Azzo."

He inspected the scene—seven unconscious sailors, the boats filled with gold. Rebecca conveyed her resolve on her face. She maintained his gaze and nodded. He jumped in the boat and she untied it, giving the jolly boat a shove to ease his departure.

The other boat sat filled with five chests of gold, enough coin to start a new life anywhere she desired. Tommaso rowed to Boccanegra's galley, leaving three Sons aboard *The Corsican*. She could disarm—or kill—three men. How could Captain Marchetto turn away a pair of willing and able hands along with a portion of this treasure? The governor wouldn't miss the already stolen gold.

Azzo.

Rebecca sprinted into the tunnel. She clung to the shadows. Without knowing Volta, Azzo, or the Fixer's location, she needed to tread carefully. Rebecca decided on the distraction while she prepared the wineskins. A final fuck-you to the Fixer. In the case she didn't survive this plan, at least she hindered his comfort.

She grabbed a torch from the bracket and ducked into the much less full storeroom. She threw open the hashisha crate and tossed in the torch. Not waiting to feel the effects of the smoke, she slammed the door and tore down the hallway.

A hiss issued from the tunnel on her right. Rebecca froze. She felt stress wash her brain, a chill emanating from her core. Did she imagine an echo escaping Saint George's tomb, or had Faunus awoken? Rebecca squared her hips towards the tunnel, squinting into the black. She gripped her blade and spear, unable to break her gaze.

Volta's lumbering steps broke her concentration. She hid in the shadows of the tunnel. Smoke and light emanated from the storeroom, and Behemoth passed with a quickening pace to investigate. Distracted, she sprinted after him and drove the metal pommel into the back of his skull. She kicked the back of his knee. Volta dropped to both knees, the crack echoing in the tunnel with his deafening howl. She cracked him in the head again and again until his face planted on the flagstone.

Breathing hard, Rebecca untied the rope she hid in her surcoat and bound his wrists to his ankles with much effort. There would be no way to lift him, and she couldn't waste the time. Rebecca cut his tunic and breeches from neck to ankle. She ripped every scrap of clothing from his body. Behemoth moaned. She stuffed his mouth full with a wad of tunic until she finished pulling his clothing free. When she was finished, he lay nude in the fetal position. Folds of fat rolled over his waist, his thighs thick as tree trunks. She noted the massive pectoral muscles and forearms beneath a coat of hair.

Rebecca slapped him until his eyes opened. Volta twitched against the bonds, snarling through the cotton. She held a finger to her mouth.

"I'll let you go if you answer my question."

He jerked like a wriggling fish out of water.

"Be a good boy. Where is Azzo?"

A stream of obscenities couldn't escape his muffled lips. Rebecca pressed her blade against his scrotum. Volta calmed with haste.

"I'll ask you once more before making you an eunuch—where is Azzo?" She raised her brows.

His shoulders slumped and he nodded. Rebecca pressed the flat of the blade into his testicles as she ungagged him.

"He's not fucking that pervert, Tommaso?"

Rebecca shoved the cotton back in his mouth. She pressed the tip of her blade into the tip of his penis. He whimpered, sweat beading his every pore. Volta held as still as stone, terror in his eyes. The limp dick hung perpendicular in the air.

"Shhhh, shhh, shh. Just tell me where he is."

He nodded again. She removed the cloth.

"In the campanile! The prison cells."

Rebecca removed the blade from his flaccid member. His body slunk in relief. She flicked the blood from the steel and stood over Behemoth. His brutality during the water torture tested her pact with herself not to kill unless it was the Fixer, or absolutely necessary. Instead, she kicked him in the face twice to knock him unconscious—with pleasure. He could remain nude and humiliated until she found her friend.

There had been no prisoners during Rebecca's tenure in the palazzo. Had she been successful in kidnapping Banco, Rustichello may have left him in the tower. Rebecca steadied her breath as she took one stair at a time. Sprinting the stone with Azzo during training forged hard muscle. She mustered the gumption necessary for one final contract. This kill would be done with a singular purpose—not rage, not resentment, and not on the behest of a man—but licensed by her own making.

Rebecca gripped the inverted crucifix spear, the claw carved in wood gripped the point. The first four cells were empty. She pressed on. Braziers burned. A furnace was lit. Along the back wall of a cell sat a table with dozens of metal tubes and a shelf with three tiers. Weaved wicker baskets sat on each plank. Across the way sat Azzo. He sat on his ass, hands bound behind his back.

"Rebecca!"

She leaned the spear against the cell door and rushed inside. Rebecca cut the rope and helped him to his feet. Azzo had a black eye.

"What happened? How were you captured?"

"We must go. Now." Azzo grabbed her by the wrist, but the Fixer appeared in the door. He wore full chain mail and his white tunic with red cross, greaves, and longsword at his hip. An unlit joint pinched between his teeth.

"Have you come to join Azzo, daughter?" He barred their exit with her spear. "Or me?"

"Rustichello, I know about Coraline. About who was in the Lombard League. You betrayed the Viscontis. The pope's mandate."

He laughed. The Fixer lit the joint. "Rebecca, you of all people should appreciate the hypocrisy of the church. The emperor's quest at territory is a vainglorious attempt to extend his legacy. I alone can be impartial. I am the Sons of Saint George! I control the Nightshade Brotherhood."

"You sent me to die in Primaluna, didn't you?"

The Fixer took a deep drag. He squinted at them as he coughed. Rebecca thought he was bargaining for time.

"Yes, I had intended for you to die at Lake Como," he said, lighting another joint. "My original plan was to present you to Matteo Visconti as the assassin responsible for Banco, Panza, and Salvagno, but I felt you could do so much more damage by my side. As my daughter."

"You wished to kill your own flesh and blood daughter," Rebecca said, drawing her dagger. "You acted as a coward from the shadows."

Rustichello lunged. He smacked her fingers with the spear's back end, forcing the dagger from her hands. He spun the weapon around and dropped the blade to chop into her torso. Azzo shoved her out of the way and raised an arm in a defensive block. The Fixer cleaved his left hand clean from his wrist.

"Azzo!"

A gut-wrenching scream filled Rebecca's skull. Azzo writhed on the floor, gripping his bloody stump. She cradled him as the Fixer sauntered across to the other cell. Removing her surcoat, Rebecca wrapped the arm in the fabric to stymie the bleeding. She snatched her blade.

"Rustichello, your Sons are disabled. The gold is in my possession."

The Fixer coughed. He hacked and cleared his throat. "The Sons of Saint George will emerge from the shadows. Manipulating economies, disrupting trade routes, operating from prosperity. Do not fear, Rebecca—our numbers will swell with the inclusion of the emperor's Brothers—and under my leadership, our methods have become refined."

He took a metal tube from the table. The glass barrel was a thin cylinder with a pointed tip and bronze plunger. It held a yellowish green liquid.

"Emperors, popes, nobility," he said. "Our new order will invoke the proper fear of Saint George's dragon."

Hissing emerged from the baskets. Chills rippled along Rebecca's skin. Red eyes reflected the burning brazier, peering through the weaves. She stepped backwards instinctually. The Fixer pressed towards her, his eyes distant, glowing in the flickering firelight.

"You ordered Adam to kill Father Lorenzo," Rebecca said. "Because he knew of your treachery."

"As Faunus administered the demon's blood to George in the wilderness," the Fixer continued, "I will cleanse my enemies with the venom of Ashkelon!"

Rebecca drew a passatore and took another step backwards. She prayed Azzo didn't bleed out like Father Lorenzo.

"How did Franco die, Rustichello?"

He circled Rebecca. With her back to the shelves, Rebecca launched a passatore. The Fixer swiped it aside. She drew another. The hissing persisted.

"I sent my Sons to Silene, and in those unholy lands, they found Saint George's dragon. The savage Libyans worshipped the beast. But I, Rustichello da Pisa, conquered evil."

Rebecca bumped into the table filled with syringes. The metallic tips were razor sharp with a small hole in the end for the liquid to eject. The Fixer's ragged cough refocused her attention. He blocked the exit.

"Azzo!" Tommaso's voice called from the staircase. "Rebecca!"

The Fixer hid behind the wall. Rebecca would attack when Tommaso appeared. The one good outcome from their visit to Parma was learning about Rustichello's hook. Rebecca stole hemp rope from the armory and tied an end through the eyelet of a passatore. She drew the blade and swung it in a circle to build momentum. The Fixer's eyes came into focus at the contraption. She let the steel rip towards his face.

The blade forced him into the corner. Rebecca flinched as she yanked the blade backwards. The steel was coated in belladonna essence. She regathered the rope and swung it wide. Rustichello blocked with the spear, but the rope wrapped around the clawed end. Tommaso appeared in the doorway, sword drawn.

Rebecca tugged. The spear slipped and clattered to the floor.

"Rebecca."

One step into the room and the Fixer lunged.

"Tommaso," Rebecca said. "Behind you!

She launched the blade. It connected with Rustichello's chain mail, but didn't pierce it. The Fixer plunged the syringe into Tommaso's neck.

"Behold!" the Fixer said. "The ancient serpent's toxin."

Tommaso twitched and seized. He clutched his throat, purple veins bursting on his neck. He spluttered to the floor, dead within seconds.

Rebecca launched a passatore at the Fixer. This time, her aim was true. It thudded into a weak spot in his armor. She swung the sling blade and forced him against the syringe table. Rebecca jumped over her poor friend's body and lobbed the rope once more. It wrapped around the shelves.

"You have no safe harbor, Rebecca. Your crimes in Milan, you killed Lombard League members, you slaughtered the della Torre patriarch," the Fixer said, through a dry, rattling cough. "Join me!"

"Rot in hell, you piece of shit."

She heaved the rope, the shelves crashed to the floor. The baskets tumbled, several landing on the Fixer. Naja—cobras—five feet long, onyx and furious, flew spitting from their wicker balls. Rebecca sprinted to the adjacent cell and gathered Azzo. Pale as the moon, he cradled his severed limb as she tugged him along the cells. They bounded two stairs at a time, the hissing and shrieks and smashing of shelves above echoing throughout the campanile. In her attempt not to kill, Rebecca estimated the wrong amount of belladonna to dilute in the wine, for she heard the Sons' voices grumbling from the drainage tunnel.

"Azzo," Rebecca said. "Help me put out these torches."

He mumbled assent and tossed the surcoat over the torch on the left. Rebecca doused another in earth and sand. They pressed on, putting each out until they were left with only the scent of their sweat, fear, and tang of torched cloth. The Sons, groggy from the belladonna, padded into the main tunnel, unaware of what lay ahead.

Rebecca braced for the Deceivers to slither into the tunnel from above, Franco's "devil of Saint George."

25

DECEIVERS

I n the dark, the crushing dark, Rebecca's breath pounded against her chest, her throat, her lips. She chewed the inside of her lip, swallowing an exhale. Azzo leaned against her, still as a statue. Rebecca didn't know which tunnel delta they hid inside. The cobras slithered past, searching with their tongues, undulating across the flagstones. A hooded neck flared. A head reared. Hiss. Strike. Grown men shrieked in the crushing dark.

The saliva preceding vomit lined Rebecca's mouth. She wished to float above the pitch-black ground, away from the pitch-black snakes, wriggling in a bundled mass of muscular scales. When her throat filled with tinny warmth and thuds of sailors convulsing against walls ceased, Rebecca urged Azzo forward. A tentative step. Halt. His stumped arm bumped into her back; he moaned. She sensed the devil coil, erect. Rebecca pressed against the wall, pinching tears into her eye sockets. With a final prayer into the Void, she bolted into the main tunnel.

Following her nose to salt air, Rebecca stumbled over the legs of a dying sailor. She broke his pitiful grip. Their feet found purchase on the slick stairs, a cool breeze met their face. Coraline waited on the dock, a Siren guiding them to refuge and the sea, the sea, the Ligurian Sea.

26

FATHER

"**G**et in the boat!"

Rebecca shoved Azzo over the dock's lip. He slammed into the chests. She grabbed Coraline's arm, but the lady did not budge. Her gaze was set on Rustichello da Pisa. Blood trickled from his temple, purple veins blossomed on his neck. In one hand, he held a cobra by the neck, the tail coiled around his forearm, and in the other, a syringe.

"A compound of belladonna and Ashkelon's venom," he said, a cough puncturing his declaration. "My masterpiece! A weapon to bond the Sons of Saint George and Nightshade Brotherhood." His head bobbed.

"Did Franchesca and I mean so little to you, Rustichello?" Coraline asked.

He leveled his gaze on his former lover as if seeing her for the first time. "Here to kill me, Coraline?" He now stood on the dock. Rebecca drew her dagger and stepped between the jilted lovers.

Rustichello coughed and hacked. "I castrated Visconti. I severed the head of the della Torre family once and for all! We choked Boccanegra into compliance by sabotaging his trade partners, Rebecca."

"We did nothing together," she said. "You used me."

The Fixer wheezed. His eyes drooped. "The pope, emperor, the League," he said, phlegm catching in his throat. "You'll suffer at their hands without me. The order will outlast you."

"Then that is my fate," Rebecca said. "And I will accept it."

He threw the cobra at them. Rebecca flinched, but Coraline slugged the serpent into the watery tunnel using the torch. The last act of cowardice brought Rustichello to his knees.

"You've been smoking all day, haven't you?" Rebecca asked, relieved at the Fixer's addiction. Father Lorenzo's words reverberated in her mind—the body was a temple and cleanliness was holiness.

Coraline handed Rebecca the tinderbox filled with hemp bud joints. "Your daughter laced the bud with belladonna and I swapped them this morning." She held the fire to his face. Terror gripped bloodshot eyes. His throat seized. The Fixer's head thudded into the dock. "Goodbye, Rustichello."

"You'll have to row us to Boccanegra's galley," Azzo said. His face was drained of color. Tears streaked his cheeks. "Or the deal's off, Rebecca."

Azzo kept his word. A man unlike others in Rebecca's life. Her heart ached at Tommaso's death. Glad her friend did not see the fear in Tommaso's face. Rebecca helped Coraline over the ledge into the jolly boat.

"Rebecca!" Azzo shouted, pointing behind her.

The Fixer roared to life. In a burst of primal energy, he brandished a dagger and lunged. Rebecca lunged quicker. She leaned her full weight against the pommel of her dagger, his initiation gift. The steel sunk into his neck all the way to the handguard. She eased him to the dock and kicked his corpse into a watery grave.

Rebecca rowed them out to sea. The chests added significant resistance, sweat beading on her back, before exiting the tunnel. Coraline offered to take turns, but Rebecca refused. She needed to see this through, to deliver her payment to the captain of the people's galley, to store in good faith for the Governor Matteo Visconti I. Rebecca held Azzo's gaze. He nodded approval.

"To whatever end."

After unloading the chests, Coraline offered Rebecca a white chiffon hankie to tamp her face dry. Rebecca leaned against her friend while the lady rowed them back to another dock, avoiding the cobras still occupying the tunnels beneath the palazzo. Rustichello's deceit left an indelible mark on Azzo, his son, and Rebecca, his daughter.

27

THE BLADE OF MILAN

The Lombard League sat in council at the governor's manor. Rustichello's deception wrought a palpable tension among the republic's wealthiest patrons. A half dozen members were slaughtered under the ruse of Emperor Rudolf's orders. Not used to being targets, these patricians required someone to blame. With the Fixer dead, the one person with the deepest connection to the Pisano they could lambast stood among their numbers. Had eight chests of gold not arrived with the Lady Coraline di Parma, she would have been broken at the Wheel.

"As a gesture for my penance," Coraline said, addressing the governor directly. "For entrusting Rustichello—"

"Your former lover," a beaded-eye Genoese said. He drummed his fingers on the blondish larchwood table.

"My former lover," she continued. "I owe this League an apology. Our dear friends may still be seated among us had I known the extent of Rustichello's depravity."

Matteo Visconti tried to interrupt, but she held a hand to silence the leader of the Lombard League. He held his tongue in deference.

"Our tryst was in error. I must reiterate my commitment to our shared vision."

The interrupting member helped himself to wine from the side table. He made a show of fiddling with the decanter, huffing and scoffing as he gulped the governor's excellent vintage.

"How do we trust your judgment, Coraline? The pope's plans require a safeguard. We are his last line of defense against the emperor."

The governor kneaded his forehead with fingertips. "Settle your nerves, my friend."

A knock dissipated the repartee. Coraline ordered the pikemen to open the door. A black-clad figure with black chiffon mask filled the frame.

"Signori e Signora," he said with a courteous bow.

Coraline gestured to a seat at the table. He unbuttoned his surcoat to reveal a six-dagger sheath. Before accepting the offer, he walked to the window and unlatched it. Matteo's pikeman awaited their governor's instruction, but the Visconti heir waved them at ease. Azzo breathed in the first notes of summer. He returned and placed his hat in front of his seat. His mask remained in place over his head.

"For Christ's sake," the combative League member said.

"Please," Matteo said, indicating for Azzo to be seated.

"On behalf of the Sons of Saint George," Azzo said, "thank you for our invitation."

"Our?" Matteo asked.

Azzo raised a finger at a pattering of footsteps running across the roof. The League stared at the ceiling in confusion, the pikemen gripping their weapons. The steps subsided. A second black-clad figure swung into the room through the open window. They somersaulted between the sentries to mitigate the impact of the landing and sprung to their feet amid shouts of shock. The pikemen launched forward. All League members save Matteo and Coraline were on their feet. The "our" to Azzo's company parried a lance with two blades, disarming another without causing injury. Once the spears lay on the ground, she strode shoulder to shoulder with Azzo.

The pikeman sprinted to the weapons, but a fist slamming the table calmed the room. Matteo stood.

"Hold."

Beneath the wide-brimmed hat, a white mask hugged the contours of the head, fully obscuring the newcomer's identity. They bowed.

"I must enhance my guard," Matteo continued. "Are we finished with the theatrics?"

Azzo nodded. Rebecca scanned the room as the members retook their seats. The most influential benefactors of the Papal States gathered to meet with them—Azzo, a waif from Naples, and Rebecca, a courtesan orphan from Milan.

Coraline assured them they would have the ear of the governor after defeating Rustichello, so she did not fear reprisals for her "theatrics." If she were to craft a fearsome reputation as an independent assassin, she'd need to evoke mystery and competence in the minds of her allies.

Matteo Visconti, the former soldier turned governor, near forty, retained his stature from the army. Broad shoulders sat below a bold jawline. His interlocked fingers on a taut stomach appeared to be hewn from stone. To Rebecca, he possessed one sign of a diminishing vigor in an otherwise handsome figure—a receding hairline.

"Let us begin with introductions," the governor said.

The room stared at the newcomers. Rebecca placed a hand on Azzo's chair back. To maintain anonymity and carry on Saint George's purge demanded more of her, of them. Rebecca's newfound purpose required a new name.

"I am the Blade of Milan."

Azzo added, as they discussed, "And I am the Blade of Milan."

Murmurs shivered around the room. Matteo Visconti smirked.

"Are you both not Sons of Saint George?" He pointed at them but addressed Coraline. "When did that dog Rustichello begin recruiting women? Did you know about this?"

Coraline sought to assuage her male counterparts. Rebecca admired the unflinching rigor in her spine.

"Governor," Coraline said. "Rustichello recruited a woman to impress me. While the Blade standing before you is worthy of the tradition of Saint George, the Fixer's efforts to woo me into his good graces were misplaced, especially given the carnage he wreaked on our League."

Matteo pressed his palms together. "Matters of the heart are indelicate, my lady. You do not owe this council further explanation."

Coraline bowed. She retook her seat, ignoring the silent exchange between her fellow League members.

"Thank you for your kind endorsement, Lady Coraline," Rebecca said.

"The League has our assurances there will be no dealings with the Nightshade Brotherhood nor remaining Sons of Saint George."

"The emperor does not cower from a fight," the clergyman to Coraline's left said. "There will be consequences to Rustichello's failure."

"Father Jacopo," Matteo said. "Poised to be anointed bishop of Milan later this summer."

The priest resembled the larchwood table—ramrod straight back and rail-thin. He sat erect. He appraised Rebecca and Azzo through callous black eyes.

The governor continued his introductions. "Emilio Paoli of Genoa." He indicated to the fidgeting wine drinker. "A shipbuilder. He outfitted Boccanegra's fleet with over one hundred eighty galleys." Emilio's chest swelled.

A pompous man with immeasurable power, Rebecca thought.

"To his left is Philippe Legrande of Burgundy, Giulio Panza's trading partner from the northwest. Pope Honorius prefers their vintage to the Tuscan varietals."

The dashing mustachioed Burgundian with thin gray hair nodded. Emilio raised an empty glass to him.

"And of course, you both know Lady Coraline di Parma, heiress to her family's charming estate."

The entire League shifted its attention to Coraline. Now that the governor forgave her past relationship with Rustichello, the lady held their utmost command. With so few members remaining,

Rebecca sensed the League could use a firm yet nurturing hand to replenish its former strength. A matter for the elite to sweat.

"Father Jacopo is correct," Matteo Visconti said. "The emperor's collusion with the Fixer will not go unchallenged. The Nightshade Brotherhood are decimated. Boccanegra sailed for Pisa, but our losses were substantial. Can you"—Matteo looked to both Rebecca and Azzo—"assure us no remaining Son will seek retribution on the League? In Rustichello's memory?"

Azzo leaned forward. He kept his mutilated arm in his lap but held himself with dignity. "We are committed to rooting out the final traitorous Sons, but will need time to learn how deep Rustichello's influence spanned."

"Up to the challenge?" Emilio asked, sneering at Azzo's arm.

Rebecca drew and released a passatore, the throwing knife thudded into the table between Emilio's fingers.

"The blade that killed Corrado della Torre," Matteo said with a laugh. He admired the accuracy. Plucking the blade from the table, he offered it to Rebecca.

"Did Corrado suffer at the end?"

Rebecca sheathed the passatore. On this side of her initiation with the Sons of Saint George and uncovering Rustichello's deceit, Rebecca held a new appreciation for life and death. While she had no regrets, Father Lorenzo's guilt offered a potent message.

"He responded as all men do when faced with their demise."

The governor squinted. Whatever gruesome detail he wished to hear didn't come. He snapped at a pikeman. Matteo handed him a key. The guard strode to a portrait of Ottone Visconti, Matteo's granduncle and predecessor. The frame hinged open to reveal a safe. After relocking the vault, the pikeman set a chest in front of Azzo.

"Now that the della Torre estate is razed to the ground, we could work together again in the future. Rally a few good men, or women."

Azzo opened it to reveal Ambrogino d'Oro, silver grossi, and even florins. He craned his neck at Rebecca.

"As the governor said, stay near," Coraline interjected. "We could use your services in the future."

Azzo stood, and they both bowed to Matteo.

"Should you need us," Azzo said, "send word through the Lady."

Rebecca gathered the chest. She felt it time to exit before they changed their minds and either rescinded the reward or had the pikemen spear them to death.

"Two hundred years," Matteo said. "My family battled the della Torre swine. I am the Lombard League and you have my gratitude."

"Signore Visconti." Azzo and Rebecca bowed.

"Now please leave my manor the normal way."

***

Pine and sodden earth, horse and leather filled Rebecca's nostrils as they departed Milan. The Ticino river shimmered beneath a bridge on the southwestern road. Ahead stood a cluster of sycamores, the spot Azzo convinced her to continue the journey to Genoa. She studied the lines scrunched in the corner of his eyes, the sun reflecting stray gray hairs among his greasy curtain.

"What?"

"Are you okay?"

She knew he understood her meaning. Even with the chest slung to his saddlebag and the Fixer's conniving subterfuge behind them, there would be no consolation for losing Tommaso. Rebecca wanted to feel guilty, to own the kind-hearted first mate's death, but every which way she squared it, she could not accept responsibility. Had Tommaso and Azzo been trapped in the campanile with the Fixer, she'd have rushed to their rescue as well. The fiend responsible lay at the bottom of the drainage canal. The Ligurian Sea may have claimed him even.

"I will be."

"More Sons of Saint George might return to the palazzo."

"They'll receive quite the message," Azzo said. "Seeing as we didn't exorcise Saint George's devil—or devils—I guess."

Rebecca imagined the cobras lying in wait for unsuspecting assassins. How long must they wait before the deceivers died off naturally in the belly of the palace?

The pair laughed. Rebecca intended to return to the palazzo, but not yet. The glimmer of their payment swam behind Rebecca's eyes. The coin meant validation, but nothing in and of itself. It proved Rebecca could be more than an abandoned daughter. More than an abused courtesan. Greater than a trained dagger. Or anyone she desired.

Rebecca and Azzo arrived in Genoa. A breeze carried a hint of sea on its breath. She missed her expedition with Marchetto, but she didn't need an agreement, or permission, to go as she pleased. Not as the Blade of Milan.

"Shall we hire a ship?" Rebecca asked. "I'd like to visit Corsica."

From the World of The Blade of Milan

Figs

Rebecca danced on her tippy-toes, tongue between her teeth. Her fingers slapped the rough-hewn wooden table, searching for the out of sight bowl. A sunbeam caught her eye, turning all to white. No matter. She could not see above the tabletop, anyway. She was eight. *Why would Papa hide the figs? Where is he today?*

She discovered Papa's letter upon waking, placed on the floor next to their shared bundle of rags for a bed. She admired his penmanship, even recognizing her favorite word.

Mama didn't bother reading the rest to her because she didn't know how to. Papa read and knew how to draw. He was teaching Rebecca her letters, although she'd rather kiss his bearded cheek or chase him with the straw broom. Mama never laughed at Papa's games, and she never wanted to play.

Her feet returned flat to the ground, and Rebecca inhaled. She went onto her toes, brow furrowed, and arched her arm over her ear. Rebecca's fingers drummed the earthenware bowl's lip. It wobbled, and the fruit jostled in their clay prison. She knew the figs smelled like fresh, spring grass; their skins were as fibrous as the parchment of Papa's note.

Rebecca's mouth watered. She prepared for a final attempt. As her hand crawled towards the bowl, a splinter pierced her third finger. Rebecca gasped at the table's betrayal, tears welling in her eyes. The prick caused a terrible pinch, but instead of retreating, her resolve grew. She stretched through the pain and freed the gems from their hideaway. Rebecca squealed, stamping around the rags and angular chairs of the modest second-story room.

Ignoring the wound as it drew a red pinhead, she chomped into the first teardrop-shaped piece. The nectar coated her lips and seeped onto her fingertips and palm. She crunched seeds between the jammy innards. In her next bite, a tinny, warm salt joined the sweet pulp of her bounty.

Rebecca skipped to the window, where she ejected the blood-tainted remnants of her first prize onto the streets of Milan. *There was no need to foul my treat.* Deciding to savor the second, she peeled the fig apart and fed herself one half at a time to replace the iron taste.

"Those were the last figs your father will ever pick you," Mama said, her voice sultry and bitter.

Rebecca froze. She hadn't heard Mama return from the market. Wiping her hands on the tattered dress, no more than their bed rags, she thought, *Would Mama scold me for eating the figs or dancing?* She turned to find Mama examining the clay bowl. She placed half a round of bread, dotted with green spots, on the table and scowled at her mini-reflection as if she were scouring the letter neither of them could read.

Martina's House

Whump. The Ambrogino d'Oro coin engulfed Rebecca's entire palm. She admired the *M* on the gold payment's face. "Do you know who that is?" the patron said, flipping the coin to its obverse side.

Rebecca flinched. "I'm sorry. Thank you, sir. I'm sorry." She curtsied. "And welcome . . . I'm sorry." She tried to pocket the admission fee—Mama's secret to running the most profitable brothel in Milan—to avoid further impropriety in lingering on the man's wealth. He grasped her hand. Rings adorned several of his fingers under the crimson velvet surcoat draped over his forearm. The patron lifted her chin and said, "There was no offense."

Rebecca sighed.

He opened her palm, so the coin perched expectantly. She examined the etching. A man with a staff and pointed hat stared back, unseeing. "I *shall* take offense if you withhold your answer any longer, though."

Rebecca's eyes filled with tears. His smile relieved her of the burden of twice offending a guest. She stuck her tongue between her teeth and willed the answer to grow like fruit on a vine. Rebecca remembered the holy men who blessed the rooms sometimes.

"A priest?"

"Indeed." He caressed her shoulder. "Saint Ambrose was the bishop of Milan. Can you guess when?"

She scrunched her nose. "Umm . . . five years ago?"

"A *thousand* years ago."

Rebecca flushed. Her guess sounded childish, even ignorant, in comparison to the rich man's knowledge of the faith. Although the gold warmed in her hand, it felt further out of reach.

"How about this?" he said, kneeling. "Should I teach you about Scripture? I could share a few passages with you each time I visit your mother's stewhouse. Would that please you?"

Rebecca nodded. *Have I noticed this patron before?* A new thought bullied its way forward—Mama would never play such a game. She mustered her best manners to shake Dread's arrival. "Yes, sir, I'd very much appreciate that." She curtsied again.

He deposited another coin into her hand. "For you." He held his index finger to her mouth to stymie any protests. Satisfied, he passed his surcoat to Rebecca, whose teenage frame all but collapsed under its weight. He showed himself through the antechamber to select a companion for the evening.

Mama appeared in his absence. Never had Rebecca been more pleased to stow a garment, giving her newfound wealth folds of fabric to hide behind. As she hung the surcoat, a tug dragged her by the hair into the cupboard. Her scalp screamed.

Mama barked in hush tones. "The bedchambers won't scrub themselves!" With each word, she swatted Rebecca's backside. Rebecca tugged again as Mama let go. The momentum of their scuffle launched Rebecca into the closed door. The wood buckled against her force, but its hinges did not give.

Without waiting to nurse her bruises, she dropped the payment at Mama's feet and scurried from the cupboard. Rebecca grabbed a brush and bucket, disappearing into the first unoccupied bedroom.

She scrubbed the floor until her knuckles were raw. Moans crept through the wall, the grinding rhythm falling in time with her chore. She cringed at the pervasive cooing, worse than the sound of Mama's voice. She sidled into the next two rooms to stack chamber pots, head bowed to ignore the nocturnal activities. The urine glimmered in the torchlight from the back alley, reminding Rebecca of her newfound possession. Back inside, Rebecca dabbed the sweat from her brow as she drew a bath for Paula, Zita, or Maria.

It was Paula's generous bosom, abundant hips, and unshorn bush Rebecca shielded her gaze from. She kneeled next to the prostitute, washing her back in the tepid water. *Papa left me with Mama five years ago*, she thought. *Now I found a way to leave* her.

Rebecca sneaked to the bar for water to slake her thirst. She overheard Mama and the learned patron in the antechamber. "What does she have to be so glum about?" he said. "She works in the greatest brothel in the republic of Milan." Mama twittered in feigned mirth. Rebecca could not discern another word.

"One day soon," Mama said, showing their esteemed patron out. Rebecca gripped the coin in her pocket, imagining it swelling to a heap of her own, and agreed.

One day soon, I'll have enough.

Rebecca's Payment

Laughter filled the brothel. Rebecca heard it from a bedchamber. They piled in like sheep in the wool houses, preparing for shearing. A new girl mopped the rain dripping from their guests, her flustered grumblings muted by the plucking of lutes.

Rebecca weaved between the usual crowd, caressing stubbled cheeks and patting shoulders, to retrieve a new flagon of red. She dropped a few coins onto the bar and smirked at Maria.

Mama's voice pierced through the jovial evening at Rebecca's back. "How is the signore tonight?" Rebecca's jaw clenched. "Every extra minute you dwell in his company *after* his poke costs me money," Mama continued, inaudible to all but Rebecca over the patrons' drunken guffaws. "Don't you want my brothel to succeed?"

Rebecca hooked a flyaway curl behind her ear. Maria placed the flagon on the counter. Grateful for the excuse to ignore Mama, Rebecca snatched it. The madam thrust her hand into her daughter's pocket. Rebecca remained still, unable to prevent the assault with the bottle in hand. Mama grasped at nothing. "If you're hiding coin from me, Rebecca, I'll . . ."

"You'll what?" Rebecca said. "Turn out your best *courtesan?*"

Fuming, the daughter jerked out of Mama's clutch. She was relieved at her foresight to safeguard her savings under the floorboard below her bed. Each coin earned through degradation and grit represented an investment in her future, a vision unbounded by the shackles of her past. Although, she made one luxury purchase. A black-handled stiletto. The fixed-blade, adorned with a brass pommel and guard, rested in its leather sheath against her thigh when she wasn't *working*. She longed for the solitude of the silent hours after twilight to caress the steel and flip the blade in practice. But until she could escape from Mama, her budding knife talent would lie dormant.

"Your father left you," Mama said. "Not me."

Rebecca steadied her breath. Mama's words bruised more than the slaps and punches she endured throughout the years. She smirked in Mama's face, the madam's visage a cruel and faded reflection of her own.

Back in her entertaining room, Rebecca found the learned guest propped on the bed in naught but his breeches. "I was beginning to wonder if another patron took your fancy," he said.

Rebecca refilled his glass. "Unlikely."

He shifted positions to make room for her on the bed. Draining her wine, Rebecca sidled against his bare chest. "Are you sure you're not a noble *lady*?" she said. "Because you drink like one." Smiling, he tossed his glass back. Rebecca encouraged him to consume the rest of the flagon. His hand slithered past the nape of her neck, over her bosom, and discovered tender thighs to get in between. She adjusted her hips to comply.

"You are upright and just," he said. "Like Job."

Rebecca stared into his unfocused eyes. Her stomach turned as she struggled to maintain the saccharine veneer. With a peck on her forehead, he said, "I'll be off."

Swaying as he got to his feet, he buttoned his woolen under-shirt. Rebecca guided the black singlet over his head and clinched the belt around his waist. He patted the pockets of his surcoat. "I seem to have forgotten my coin purse."

Rebecca's chest constricted. *Maybe I am to suffer as Job did*, she thought. "You forgot your pouch?"

"I shall return with full payment," he said, donning the crimson surcoat. "And then some."

Rebecca saw him through the barroom revelry and into the rain. Lost in a blind rage, she tore back to her shared quarters to find Mama waiting, blade in hand, near her bed. Rebecca held her breath.

"You may keep it," Mama said, tossing the blade at her feet. "For a price." She left.

Rebecca threw herself to her knees to search under the dislodged slat. The space beneath the floor lay barren.

ACKNOWLEDGMENTS

This book would not be possible without the love and encouragement from my parents or the enthusiasm and badassery of my
sisters.

I owe a debt of gratitude to my dear friend Cassie Gafford whose
keen insights shaped my storytelling skills. Thank you for being
there at the beginning.

To the Philly Writers Group and my literary friends, thank you
for your constructive feedback on craft. To Robert Jones Jr. and
Jake Chase, thank you both for your willingness to Beta read my
early draft and poke all the holes in my logic! You strengthened
my narrative.

Thank you, Matthew Schildkamp, for teaching me structure,
giving me space to tease ideas, and the endless encouragement.
Having you as a thought partner and friend has injected joy
throughout my writing journey.

To Cindy Marsch for polishing my flash fiction pieces. This was
essential to bring Rebecca to life. To my Developmental & Copy
Editor, James Abbate at Kensington Independent Press, thank
you for your efforts. I'm grateful for Jonathan Sainsbury's most
excellent cover and map designs.

And to Julie, many an hour in our lives were traded for me to
write, edit, anguish, disassociate, and doubt. Your patience and
refusal to allow me to quit has meant more to me than you know.
Thank you for being a living example of fortitude.

About the Author

Warren R. Basla holds a Master of Science degree in Global & International Education and Bachelor of Arts degree in Cultural Anthropology from Drexel University. He works as a Director of Development at an education non-profit in Philadelphia where he also lives with his wife and their rescue greyhound. He serves on the Blue Stoop Advisory Board and is a member of Philly Scribes. He can be found online at warrenrbasla.com. This is his first novel.

AFTERWORD

Dear reader,

Thank you for reading my debut novel! I hope you found the setting, characters, and history as immersive and thrilling as I did while writing the story.

I'd ask you to consider writing me a positive Google review, or on whichever outlet that you purchased this book. Feel free to share your recommendation with your networks, friends, or book club peers.

With your help, I intend to continue writing novels for you, for myself, and for those who have not yet been initiated into the Sons of Saint George.

W.R.B.

www.ingramcontent.com/pod-product-compliance
Lightning Source LLC
Chambersburg PA
CBHW050315110726
47899CB00007B/2249